Kelly Creighton facilitat
community groups and
include the DI Harriet S
(DI Sloane book 1) and *Problems with Girls* (DI Sloane book 2); novel *The Bones of It*; story collections *Bank Holiday Hurricane* and *Everybody's Happy*, and poetry collection *Three Primes*. She co-edited *Underneath the Tree*: an anthology of Twelve Christmas Stories from writers in Northern Ireland. Kelly founded The Incubator literary journal, showcasing the contemporary Irish short story. Recipient of a 2017/18 ACES Award from the Arts Council of Northern Ireland, she lives with her family in Newtownards, County Down.

kellycreighton.com

@KellyCreighto16

THE TOWN RED

DI Harriet Sloane Book 3

Kelly Creighton

FRIDAY
PRESS

First published in 2021
by Friday Press
Belfast

ISBN: 9798596320886

www.fridaypressbooks.com
@friday_press

For Ryan

Prologue

In the dead of night, it's his eyes I see. Hazel, they were. Not that I ever see them in real life anymore. Now when I see Jason Lucie, he has no eyes at all. Just two hollows. Deep and black. Because my dreams have no colour or every colour all at once.

Two tunnels run right through his head. I see them when I try to get my bearings, let my feet ease to the floor, try to find my slippers. They are not by my bed where I usually leave them. When I go to bed sober, that is.

This is not my carpeted bedroom floor but a well-worn, threadbare rug. Yet I know it here. It's my very childhood. I was born from this floral wallpaper, I'm sure. They pulled me screeching from an ovule in one of these trippy bronze flowers.

I run my tongue across my lips and taste sour water. My head goes to fall off when I move it. I crave ice and bleach. Want to scrub the skin of this place, peel away this shedding paper.

I force my eyes open and look for my phone. It is after midnight. A new day; 3.24 a.m.. First of June and my birthday. I'm officially forty.

Using the flashlight on my phone, I find the bathroom. Trying not to wake Charly and Coral, I pee in the dark, allow no buzz from the overhead lights. But I forget about quiet as I flush. The acoustics from the old cistern is a jazz band in my brain as I stagger into the kitchen.

'Fallen asleep in your clothes again,' I mutter, drying my hands on my jeans. Through one squinted eye, I look around the chalet then I fetch myself a glass of water. Outside, Lough Erne laps like a parched kitten at a wet bowl. My sisters snore palely in their rooms. Charly moves in her bed, and the springs groan.

I take my drink outside and stand by the water. It is cool out, refreshing. I close my eyes, remembering how I ended up here, blindfolded in Coral's car. Our older sister had driven us here yesterday as a 'surprise' after Charly's birthday dinner last night.

Charlotte and I are twins; I was born on the wrong side of midnight. We were born on different days and in different months. Coral brought us to our old family chalet in County Fermanagh, which was no surprise. What else is there out this direction? She thought it would be sweet. I suppose she wasn't to know. *No one* knows that the last time I was here, I had just run away from home and him, my then-husband. Four days at gunpoint at Jason Lucie's mercy.

It was in this chalet that I took time – and far too little of it – to get myself together. I was a shell, fractured completely. The sore on my head oozed and wept. My teeth tingled in my gums. My life had changed completely.

When Coral brought me here yesterday with that bloody leopard print Ann Summers thing over my eyes, she wasn't to know any of this or how much it would bring me back to that time. But I can't blame this place for the dreams. They started again a short while ago, came totally out of the blue.

2

Last night we drank and talked and toasted us, the babies of the Sloane family, being in the land of forty now too; where we join Coral and our two big brothers Addam and Brooks. Coral pressed Charly to make a birthday wish. She wished for Louboutin heels.

Last night I almost told my sisters about Jason. Ultimately I didn't. I just needed to forget him, move on. Think about shoes.

I look out at the granulose dark-blue lough. It is like a tray sliding back and forth. *Have it. Don't have it.* I imagine Jason out there. He is everywhere. He is every shadow, every tree. He is watching me with those deep black eyes, just like he used to, for years, only now in real high-definition technicolour; he is waiting to tear into my life again.

There is a surge in my guts, hands reaching in and pulling everything out. Like some surprising visceral birth, I vomit right on the grass. I stumble back into the kitchen and swig some wine straight from the bottle. My throat is raw. I don't raise a glass but the whole bottle. I toast the future silently, alone.

'My birthday wish … to stop seeing Jason Lucie every time I close my fucken eyes.'

I take a swig and go back to sleep, waking five hours later with the bottle still in my hand. Merlot spilt all over the bed.

—

Chapter 1

What a difference a day makes. But two days? Twice the difference? It felt like a different world when I woke at home in my own bed with Paul beside me. Our alarm went off before we were woken by the boys. I threw the covers back, stepped into my slippers and shuffled into their room. It felt sinful to wake them, fast asleep and smelling like baby lotion and ammonia, their nappies fat, Mohawk-like black hair sticking up from their sweaty foreheads.

They smiled as they were being tickled awake. Red lips curling around their dummies. Creasing up and chortling. Paul appearing by my side and joining in. A wholesome moment to start my day. The day could only get worse. Soon the boys were getting washed and crying about something or other, then Paul left for the hospital, and it was up to me to get the boys to their nursery. He'd done enough all the weekend while I was away on the girls' trip. Paul had given me a gift voucher for my *big one*, loads of moolah on it. The kind of voucher that could be spent in any big chain store in the UK, the kind you see in the garage right by the till. When the voucher fell out of the birthday card he gave me, I was relieved. It would stay hidden in my purse. I was determined to spend it on the rashest thing I could.

*

It was cloudy and warm as I deposited the brothers Sloane to the nursery. On my father's advice, I had stopped using the Day Nursery beside Strandtown Police Station and found a place in Malone where they were at a safe distance.

I ran to the car to dodge them as they cried out for me. Rowan – the softer of the two – started first and Jared must have thought, *that looks like fun, I'll cry too.*

I made my way to East Belfast through rush hour traffic on the Outer Ring. Chief Greg Dunne was on my mind. Two days before – on my birthday – Dunne had spent the morning playing golf, and when he returned to his car, he found a viable bomb strapped underneath. I'd considered contacting him, seeing he is my boys' biological father, but our relationship was never such that I could call Greg Dunne, and now even less so.

Regardless, I had thought about his near-miss a lot. They concluded that the device had been fixed outside his home the night before he discovered it. Dunne's niece, my colleague Superintendent Fleur Hewitt, had told me what the media was not privy to just yet.

It reminded me of Father checking under his car back when he was the Chief Constable of the RUC. Naively, perhaps, checking is something I often forget to do.

It reminded me that the old days hadn't really gone. My stomach knotted with remembrance. It scared me that Greg could have been killed. Much as I can't stand the man, the news bit me like a let-go-of tape measure.

I made it to the briefing a little late. 9.10 a.m. Monday 3 June 2019. The day finally had come, and I'd been waiting a year for it. Karen Ward's sister Janet had been waiting longer than I had. Forty years longer.

'Like I was saying,' said Chief Dunne eyeing me as I pulled up a chair, spilling my overflowing coffee. 'This case has been worked a few times. Needless to say, we have a plethora of new techniques to use now, and we are going to use them,' he said with dull authority. 'We are going to treat the murder of Karen Ward as if it happened just an hour ago. Janet Ward wants justice, as I'm sure we can all understand. So, put yourself in her shoes. Treat this case like it's a member of your kin.'

I wanted to get him alone and ask how he felt, but I wouldn't bother. Even if Greg was shook, he was not likely to tell me. We would just have to pretend the bomb attempt hadn't happened.

'Sir, we have Janet waiting in the canteen at the moment, waiting to talk to us. She'll give us a great insight,' said Fleur in her thick Glaswegian patter.

'It was a long time ago,' added Dunne, 'and who knew Karen better than her sister? Use this opportunity to ask the right questions. Alright?'

Everyone made a move to stand up. 'I'm assigning it to you, Harry,' Fleur said. 'You missed that part with being late. And you'll work on it with Higgins.'

But I already knew that. Fleur and I had become good friends in the last year, painting the town red regularly together. She had made me promise to keep it zipped.

'How was your weekend?' she asked me when the room cleared out.

—

6

'Fine,' I said.

'Just fine? You don't know how to party!'

I scoffed. If anyone knew that I liked to party, it was Fleur.

'Coral surprised us; she took us away for the weekend.'

'What did you get up to?'

'Dinner,' I said, 'then we went to our folks' old chalet on the lough.'

'Get you! *Cha-lay!*' Hewitt laughed.

'Yeah, get me. It should be torn down.'

'I'd love that. Little pet project on the side.'

'You'd love to tear it down?' I pictured her in a bulldozer and wearing a hard hat.

'No, Harry. I'd do it up. Why don't you?'

'I think I have enough to do,' I said.

'Aye, whereas I've loads of time to be idle,' she said.

I did think she had more time on her hands than I did. She wasn't looking after twin toddler boys. Though work did consume Fleur. I'd once wanted her job, was dead sure it was mine, now she was welcome to it. If I had one more thing handed to me, I'd crack.

This work project, the cold case, however, bring it on. The murder of Karen Ward. I had been more than keen to get started.

In the canteen, Janet was sitting with Sarge Carl Higgins. She had flown over from London to talk about the case. Janet had short brown hair, wore red lippy and dressed in soft silver and ivory layers. She was rubbing a locket between her fingers.

'Do you remember me, Ms Ward?' I asked, 'I'm DI Harriet Sloane.'

7

'Och, of course I do,' she said, reaching out, I thought, to shake my hand in hers, but she ended up holding it between hers so I could feel the silver locket, then she began rubbing my hand like someone might rub a rabbit's paw for luck.

Janet and I had shared a flight from London a year before. She had appeased the twins during a rough flight. And she had appeased me, to some extent, being a nervous flyer.

I couldn't pinpoint when my fear of flying started but now, during take-off and landing, and through any turbulence, my chest would hurt.

During that flight, she had held my hand too. This stranger. I'd hated that Hewitt said we couldn't help Janet when she turned up at Strandtown looking for our support.

'How are those beautiful boys of yours?' Janet asked.

'Great. They turned two last month,' I said.

She smiled kindly. 'Fun and games now.'

'Superintendent Hewitt,' Fleur introduced herself. The last time she had seen Janet face-to-face, there had been tears. Now Hewitt looked justifiably proud since she had secured the money and reopened the case. Janet set the locket down on the table and shook Hewitt's hand before she scooped the locket up again.

'Tell us all we need to know about Karen,' said Hewitt, diving in.

'You probably know this, but …. '

'Doesn't matter,' Hewitt interrupted, 'tell us anyway. Pretend it's just happened.'

—

Janet gave her a double-take and shuddered. 'We lived in Clarawood House,' she said, 'the tower block, near Orangefield.'

'Know it well,' said Carl Higgins clicking his pen on and off with his thumb.

'We lived there since we were born,' said Janet. 'I'm a year older than Karen. We lived with our mother, who died of cancer in early '79. Not long after Karen did.'

This was before any of us were born, I thought.

I did a quick calculation and determined that my mother would have been two months pregnant with Charly and me at the time of Karen's death.

'Karen cared for Mum, and so did I,' Janet said, then she looked at the ceiling. 'What else, what else … Karen was a smart girl, but she wasn't pushed at school as much as she should have been. The teachers saw her as a carer. They would have got her to get their personal shopping during class. I left school in 1976 to get a job in the Silver Sea.'

'The Silver Sea?' asked Hewitt.

'A Chinese restaurant on the Cregagh Road,' said Janet. 'I was a waitress, then they opened a takeaway part, and I would also make deliveries.'

'Karen got a job there, too?' I asked. I had already read the notes, but we still needed Janet to tell us.

'She did,' Janet said. 'Karen passed her driving test as soon as she could and then she was out delivering on the nights when I couldn't. It was only a bit here, a bit there.'

Higgins jotted down some notes.

—

'Takeaways weren't as popular as they are nowadays,' said Janet.

'Karen was last seen on 6th November at six-forty in the evening,' I said.

'Right,' Janet confirmed. 'She was working, dropping a delivery off to East Belfast. That was her last call.'

Hewitt looked at her file. 'Then,' she said, 'the next day, 7th November, Karen's body was found in a patch of woods. Found murdered, and she was naked.'

Janet lightly exhaled.

'Karen's clothes,' continued Hewitt, 'were found in the bin near the entrance. She had been suffocated, they said at the time, with a pillow.' She looked up from her notes.

'I'm sorry I have to ask this,' I prewarned Janet. 'But Karen had not been sexually assaulted, isn't that right?'

'That's what I believe,' said Janet. 'Her locket was removed. It matched this one.' She held out the locket she was holding; it had a heart engraved on it in a curving, twisting style.

'You must have been over this so many times, hen,' said Hewitt, 'but please do tell us a little bit about that day.'

'I heard that the van had pulled up outside the flats, and there were eyewitnesses who saw Karen pull up.'

'Who were they?'

'Neighbours,' said Janet gritting her teeth. 'They saw Karen with a man. But no one saw the crime. If they had, maybe we wouldn't still be on this roundabout. But we have always known who did it.'

I sat forward in my seat.

___

'Who do you believe killed Karen?' I asked Janet.

'A neighbour of ours; a witness. Wayne Simpson.'

'He was never convicted,' said Hewitt.

'And for all these years, he has thought he's gotten away with it,' said Janet.

I sensed she thought it would be easy: that we were better equipped now; that we would go to this neighbour's place and find hard evidence, and that would be that. Case closed.

If it had been going on this long – and it had – a nice quick solution was likely not going to be the case.

'What would you want us to know about Karen?' I asked Janet.

Janet smiled and looked me in the eye.

'Karen had a sense of humour,' she told me, 'and a really dirty laugh. If it was me who had been killed, I know she would have not stopped until there was justice, and not for any other reason other than Karen had to be right. She was stubborn like that. We might have been sisters, but I'm not made of the same stuff she was. I get tired. I give up.' Janet's eyes glazed over. I couldn't tell if she was close to tears. 'So I want to do this for Karen because she would do it for me. And it should have been me, see. I was supposed to be working that night.'

Chapter 2

By lunchtime, I paid a visit to Kate Stile, Forensic Scientist, who was at her desk reading Karen Ward's autopsy report.

'She died from suffocation. It was not manual asphyxiation, not with bare hands,' said Stile holding her hands up.

'It was a pillow, possibly; a smothering,' I said.

There was a pillow mentioned in the old case files. It had blood on it. Probably Karen Ward's.

'There were no pressure marks, so probably a thick pillow,' agreed Kate. 'No bruises were found on the victim's neck, but she did have asphyxial signs: pinpoint haemorrhages in her pupils, her eyes were bloodshot, and her gums were bruised and bleeding.'

'Why would a pillow be outdoors?' I asked.

'Weren't people, in general, more inclined to just dump their rubbish back then?'

'I can't believe Janet never got an answer,' I mused, stealing a look at the report.

'The technical side wasn't as advanced as it is now. Hate to state the obvious, Harry.' Stile closed the report and looked up at me, no hint of faith on her face.

'But there was DNA that we can trace now?'

'Forensic samples were taken at the time. Says so in the old reports I've been reading. Unfortunately, Harry, I can't trace where the samples are now.'

'Where in the hell have they gone?'

———

I spun the autopsy report around to face me and began flicking through it.

'I've spoken to a retired tech who was working here back in the eighties,' said Kate.

'Eighties was *after* Karen's murder.'

'I know, but he said that in cases like that, where physical evidence is missing, it will have been lost or destroyed. There's little we can do about it now.'

'That's not what I wanted to hear, Kate,' I said.

I went to my desk and immersed myself in all the paperwork I *could* find. With the force going digital and files being misplaced, there was nothing much about Karen Ward's murder that I could trace other than the slim volume we already had.

I read her mother's statement first: Pearl Ward stated she was in bed all day. Pearl was terminally ill. She did not see her youngest daughter come home. Pearl said she was alone; Janet was out that night with friends. She'd encouraged Janet to 'shower her head' from work and her role as a carer; therefore, little sister Karen had taken her shift at the Silver Sea. The next morning, Janet was home, getting ready for the day. Pearl was in bed. Neither had realised that Karen had not come home.

Before they had the chance to discover her bed had not been slept in, a mother walking her children to school via the park at the back of their tower block found Karen's body. Attached to Pearl's statement was some further information. A few weeks after the sad discovery, Pearl was admitted to the hospice, where she received end-of-life care.

She was only forty-one years old when she died of breast cancer at the start of '79, leaving Janet wholly alone.

*

'Janet mentioned witnesses,' I said to Higgins as I finished the working lunch he had collected for us from Wee Buns bakery at the end of the road.

'There were three eyewitnesses at the time,' Higgins said. He stood and pinned up two different artist's impressions given by people who had seen Karen speaking with a man the night she died.

'Who is the first eyewitness?' I asked, throwing my pasta bowl in the bin from my seat.

'That one on your left was from Michelle Brown,' said Higgins. 'Michelle lived to the side of the block in Clara Way. The apartments.'

I could picture where he meant. When you approached the tower block, to the left and then behind you, were four-storey maisonettes.

'Now,' he said, 'Michelle Brown saw Karen talking to a man as she stood outside her work van. Michelle thought little of it at the time.'

How many times had I heard that! There was often a distinction between what you thought you were seeing and what was really happening. It is only afterwards when the weighty nature of small encounters seize you. Higgins held a page closer to his face, making me think he needed reading glasses but was too vain to wear them, being the fashion victim that he is.

'Says here,' he said, 'Michelle Brown had been watching out for her son to come home for his tea … because she needed the car. They shared a car,' he broke from reading to explain to me.

'I gathered that,' I told him.

'She gave a good, clear and detailed description, and of what the man was wearing. Brown bell-bottoms, a jacket, possibly denim. This is retro, hey?'

'Right up your street, you mod,' I said.

Higgins laughed sarcastically.

'That first one is the sketch artist's impression based on that statement.' Higgins pointed at the board.

I looked at the sketched face, the small eyes, the long hair, a bulbous nose. Higgins took the opportunity to finish his sandwich crusts.

'Okay, it's a start,' I said. Standing to label it as being Michelle Brown's impression.

'We're probably lucky to have that,' said Higgins taking a napkin from the bakery bag and wiping his mouth. 'It would have been getting dark at that time of year, around seven-ish. Or slightly earlier.'

'Early November, it would have been already dark,' I said. 'There were lampposts in the area, but not over the spot where Karen parked the van.'

Higgins began shuffling his next set of papers. 'Then we have eyewitness two.' I looked at the sketch on the right. 'There's no sketch from number two,' said Higgins.

'Who was that?'

'A little boy called Kenneth Hall. He phoned the police from a payphone.'

'What age was Kenneth?'

'Nine, at the time.'

'Young!' I said.

'Very. He started to say that he had been looking out at the park when he saw someone dragging Karen away, then the line went dead. I'm kind of surprised the operator even took that seriously.'

'I'm glad they at least kept the report,' I said.

'The boy gave his address, maybe that's why.'

'Did he live in the flats too?'

'No,' said Higgins. 'This young Kenneth lived in Sandhill Park, off Sandown Road. But he knew Karen well, it seems. Kid stated that Karen was his babysitter.'

'That's good, and his house could have backed on to where Karen was found. Though it depends on which house. Do we have a house number?'

'We don't.'

'Okay, what else, Carl? Did the police ever speak to Kenneth?'

'Yes. When they spoke with him, he said nothing. Could have been a hoax.'

I tapped my fingers on the desk. 'Could have been an overactive imagination,' I said. 'Imagine being a kid and hearing that your babysitter got killed not far from your house. Your imagination would go there.'

'Certainly would.'

'So, the third eyewitness?' I looked at the sketch on the right of the board. 'Is *that* Wayne Simpson's?'

I knew the name Wayne Simpson very well. I had been itching to get at this case.

It had been all I could do to stick to my regular workload of paramilitaries and drugs before Karen Ward's case reopened. I already knew that Wayne Simpson had been the prime suspect. He was always hanging around during any press coverage at the time. He had even been charged, but like Fleur Hewitt had mentioned, not convicted. Simpson was the man who many locals, Janet included, had always thought killed Karen, and yes, I conceded, it could have been him. But I wanted to come into this case open-minded; cast the net wider than anyone had before. It seemed like a wasted opportunity not to.

I also did not want to discount him as a witness, even if he was just copying what he had heard elsewhere.

'So, Wayne Simpson,' said Higgins. 'This oil painting on the right was the result of the description Simpson gave of the man he saw talking to Karen.'

Higgins pointed at the other impression. Like Michelle Brown's one, it was of a man with a large nose, small eyes and long hair. I labelled this one too.

'Is it just me,' asked Higgins, 'or did every man with a middle parting back then have a look of Bobby Sands about them?'

'Didn't take you for political, Carl,' I said, taking photos on my phone of both sketches.

'I'm not apolitical,' he said. 'But mostly when it comes to men with middle partings.'

I burst out laughing. His vanity and my lack of it had found themselves in an easy middle ground. Carl Higgins had finally sheared his hair and now gone were the days of the Liam Gallagher shag-mullet.

Carl looked cuter without all that hair flicking about his face, indeed more professional.

'Is your girlfriend a fan of the new hairstyle?' I asked him.

'Her idea,' he said, 'don't tell me you don't like it, Harry.'

'Okay, I won't tell you,' I said.

'I wouldn't take advice from you.'

'No, I wouldn't either.'

Higgins squinted at me. I turned my seat to face him, waiting for the incoming critique.

'You've got good hair, Harry,' he said, 'but you don't style it very nicely.'

'And I style it with you in mind, too!' I said with false disappointment. 'We're police, not on a catwalk.'

'But weren't you a model?'

'Me? No!' I scoffed.

'As a kid.'

'Oh, for ten minutes,' I said.

I almost blushed, but I couldn't. Having a laugh and a joke to disperse the depressing nature of the job was one thing. Carl wasn't allowed to mortify me. He remembered that Charly and I were on a TV ad for gravy granules as kids and that much later, our young faces were on a billboard right outside Strandtown.

'Chin-length would be nice on you,' he said, reaching out to touch my hair.

I brushed him off with a tut but a little flirt now and then felt fine. Carl had wound me up for ages about our kiss at the Christmas party eighteen months before.

But as drunk as I might have been, I remembered that it was not the one-sided fumble he joshed it was.

'Getting back to the reason we're here,' I said, growing tired of thinking about the ways I humiliate myself with drink on me. 'All any of this tells us is that Karen got out of the work van, talked to a man, and a couple of people saw her do it.'

'It could have been the perp,' said Higgins.

'Also, it could have been deflection. I suppose only time will tell us.'

'Or not,' he said moodily.

Chapter 3

Clarawood House was the only tower block on the estate. Despite its height, all fifteen storeys, it always astounded me when I drove into the grounds. Clarawood House was grimy cream and grey, and held fifty-seven dwellings. Enter the area, and you were directly confronted with the reception area. Union Jacks waved from the top of the tower block. At the side, a massive electric box was covered in blocked out graffiti. A few football flags shivered over windows. A pair of wall signs celebrated loyalist paramilitary organisations.

A remnant of the fifties, the place had been home to Karen and Janet Ward all their young lives. From their births in the early sixties till Karen's much-too-premature death in the late seventies. Janet had left for London soon after, initially starting a new life in another tower block. Janet had told me the day before how she had lived with an aunt at first and now lived in Hatfield, in a lovely home, I assumed, judging by her stylish labels, perfectly coiffed hair and soft Northern Irish accent which had not discoloured much. But she had slowed it down, enunciated clearly, perhaps to be understood in her work as a teacher, from which she had recently retired. Now, to my eye, this girl from Clarawood House dragged up as a lovely middle-class lady. *Lady*: the perfect description of her. She had studied in London, had a commendable career, then raised a daughter.

Soon Janet was about to become this glamorous grandmother.

I stood looking at the stern tower block that Tuesday morning as Sarge Fergus Simon set up a mobile unit at the narrow entrance of Clarawood. All day, it rained on and off. Between showers, people stood drinking tea outside. During one faintly longer dry spell, a little girl dressed in pink cycled by us on a pink bicycle. She had wilting brown hair and giant brown eyes that stared back at me. She did not smile second when I smiled first.

I could not picture Janet there, now. And nor had she wanted to return when I asked her to meet us. Janet was happy to advise, to have her memory jogged. But she politely declined my request that she would visit at the mobile, or the estate, to see if there were any familiar faces around. It was an ask, but I had hoped that her presence would spur someone into talking.

Graciously Janet remained adamant that she didn't want to return, so I didn't push. She had already told us that the night of her murder, Karen made her last delivery to a woman on Ladas Drive, then she returned home. When Karen arrived home, she got talking to a man; that was all Janet knew. But even that was second-hand information told to her by police, who had been told that by Karen and Janet's previous employer, Kwong Li. Li had given a statement. We had no copy of it, but we knew he had died in the nineties.

Though it was early days – just the second day of the investigation – there was no rush to get the perpetrator, should they commit another crime.

It was way too late for that. If they were inclined to recommit, the damage was already done. That did not mean that I did not feel some urgency. I did. If we did not find the killer, and relatively soon, Karen's case would be closed again, the money and resources pissed away. Janet Ward would be back at square one.

We walked away from the tower block, turned and looked at the maisonettes. They almost boxed the whole area off, leaving a small car parking space in the middle. In one of these four storeys, Michelle Brown – Eyewitness number one – had lived and maybe still did. I'd found nothing of her online the day before. I wondered if she'd moved out, but I had seen that a Vernon Brown remained in the house. He was on the local committee, going by Google.

Vernon lived in the furthest apartment on the right, which had a clear view to where Karen's van would have been parked that night. There was a Spanish lizard attached to his wall.

'Vernon Brown, he's a person we should speak to,' I'd said to Higgins before we went walkabouts.

'Okay,' he said, gathering leaflets from the back of the service car for our newbies to hand out to people in the area, which they unhappily did. Clean out of training, the fresh intake at Strandtown – local boy Dylan West and Latvian national Gido Kalnina – wanted something meatier.

I understood no one enjoyed their traineeship, but West and Kalnina took their paper bundles all the same and strode around the area, including Orangefield and Cyprus Avenue.

Every so often, our paths would cross, and they would make a show of looking busy, make out like they were about to speak to someone who would expertly dodge them, pull an umbrella down or a hood up, conduct a dubious new conversation on their mobile phone and strut on.

Sarge Simon stayed in the mobile all day, should anyone come in with information about Karen Ward from forty-one years ago that they hadn't wanted to tell at the time.

'Circumstances and loyalties change over the years. It's not too late to do the right thing,' Supt. Fleur Hewitt had said on the morning news, though everyone around Clarawood looked at us as though we were not to be trusted, completely mad and much too late.

*

By mid-afternoon, Higgins and I returned with a search team. Once the schools were out, kids hung around in the muted peach communal area of Clarawood House itself, keeping out of the rain.

That foyer was the first place I was ever attacked on the job, smacked in the face by a drunk woman. It was a shock to the system when I'd never been struck in my life before that. Discounting the many fights I'd had with my twin sister.

Higgins and I walked back to where Karen had parked her work van that November evening in 1978, just by the side of the flats, facing the Browns' place. They were still not home.

Behind the block, towards Greenville Park, Karen was found dead the next morning. Her clothes were uncovered at the other end of the park, shoved into a council bin. A bloody pillow was found stuffed into a hedge. Possibly it was her blood. Possibly it was the murder weapon.

'Perhaps he left through this way,' said Higgins when we located the spot where the bin used to be. Then we walked back to the area where Karen was found, down a bank, partially hidden by what was now long grass and vast verdant trees.

'This is exactly where she was,' said Higgins, looking at the old photos on the iPad. 'Tucked in against that same tree. Facing away from the tower block.'

Her location would have been hard enough to see from the flats, but back then, the area was more open, and it also backed on to a row of semi-detached houses. Now there was a green wire fence between the homes and park. 'That's Sandhill Park,' I said, 'the street where the boy eyewitness possibly lived. We need to try to locate his exact address.'

'It was missing from any files we had,' said Higgins.

'This is hardly the middle of nowhere, Carl. If between the car park and here Karen had shouted, people would have heard. I don't think she called for help.'

More than that, I hoped she hadn't. I hoped she hadn't shouted and been ignored.

'Which probably,' I said, 'made the initial team believe that whoever murdered Karen was someone she knew.

And trusted. She had just got her driver's licence. Seventeen years old, fucken hell! She should have had some independence, instead of this.'

I tapped her photo on the iPad, forgetting that it would zoom in on her. I was hit by a sudden wave of sadness at how young she was, how new was her freedom. So nearly home too, and safely, though most women who are murdered are murdered in their homes. I, myself, could have been one of those stats. In that minute, I did what I usually do in these cases: I stared at the photo of Karen Ward's young, naked, dead body and silently promised her I'd catch this man.

Whether I could keep my promise was another matter entirely.

Chapter 4

In the ground floor flat, the one closest to where Karen had parked up, lived Wayne Simpson, the third eyewitness. Simpson had lived next door to Karen, Janet and their mother, Pearl. He was the first suspect and the only person arrested at the time. Or since.

We went to call on Wayne Simpson and found an old man in his place. Despite being skinny, he had a bun-round face framed by tight grey curls. Wayne was watching a game show on the TV, which he turned off to give us most of his attention. The rest he gave to the electronic cigarette he puffed constantly on.

'We're reopening a historical murder case regarding a neighbour of yours,' I said.

'Who is that?' he asked.

I doubted Wayne hadn't heard. Hewitt had been on the TV; a leaflet delivered by the newbies sat on Simpson's hall table; plus, the PSNI mobile was shacked up outside.

'The murder of Karen Ward,' I said. 'I believe you were an eyewitness at the time.'

'I just saw someone talk to her that night. I was making my tea and looked out of the window.'

'Can you show us?' asked Higgins.

'What?'

'The window you were looking out of.'

'Of course, I can. That's what I'm here for,' Wayne Simpson said.

He ambled into his kitchenette and looked out of the window. An ornament of Laurel and Hardy was perched on the sill.

'What was Karen doing when you saw her?'

'Talking to someone,' Wayne Simpson said. 'I only glanced, mind you, and kept on making the dinner. The wife was out working nights. The kids were at the Girls' Brigade. Mashed spuds and mince I was making for them coming home.'

'You were alone?' I asked.

'Aye,' said Wayne.

'Could you describe the person Karen was talking to?' asked Higgins.

Wayne puffed on his e-cig, then he said, 'I could. Do you want me to?'

'I do,' I replied.

'He was *yay* high.' Wayne held his hand up to about a couple of inches taller than him; he was about five foot seven.

'Average height?' I asked.

'Not calling me a short-arse, are you?' Wayne laughed.

'Any more description?' I asked.

'Let me see … long hair. Dark. They all had their hair like that back then. I'd have needed to iron mine.'

'And what colour was his hair?' asked Higgins.

'Dark, like I say. Wore brown or black getup; bell-bottoms or flares, and a jacket. I don't know the colour or I'd love to be able to tell you. I just remember they were taller than Karen. She was petite.'

'You seem to remember it well,' I said.

'I don't really.' Wayne examined his e-cig. 'It's just that I've told the story so much that that's what it is now.'

'Are you in any doubt?' asked Higgins.

'I could easily say yes, but no. I'm in no doubt. That was my first story, and I'm sticking with it.'

Higgins gave him a sedate frown.

'You don't sound one hundred per cent sure, Mr Simpson,' I said.

'I'm not one hundred per cent about what I just ate for my tea, Detective, but I know what I ate that night, thirty years back – '

'Forty-one,' I corrected him.

'Forty-one? Flip me!' said Wayne. 'I'm not a man who lies, that's how I have faith in my original story, and I've no reason to lie.'

'You don't?' I asked.

'Och, let's not pretend.' He smiled. 'I know they blamed me.'

'Who blamed you?'

'They saw me arrested, the neighbours. Not convicted though, and they concluded … But check my record, it's …. ' Wayne looked around for the rest of his sentence. 'Well, you could eat your stew of it. That's what I had for my tea tonight. It all comes back to me eventually,' he said smiling, his manner remaining calm and pleasant throughout the visit. Which meant nothing; the worst people I have ever dealt with were also the nicest to speak to.

'I hope Pearl never believed what they were saying. I hope she knew me better than that,' said Wayne.

'You were friends with Pearl?' I asked.

'Sorta way, aye. Until we weren't. For a while, I nearly wanted Pearl to come to my door and ask me if I hurt her wee girl. She never did. She was too sick by then and heartsick probably.'

'What relationship did you have with Karen, if any at all?' I asked.

'Business, you could say. I mean, she was babysitting for us once, then some money kinda way went missing. I mean, a ten-pound note. Nothing much, but not nothing. A lot back then, and a lot to us. That wasn't long before she was killed.'

'How long before?' asked Higgins.

'Two days.'

'What happened about the money?'

'I was going out, the missus was working nights, and I asked Karen to babysit, so she did. Said yes. The next day, money was gone. My kids were only young, five and six. Just started school … of course, you were spot on there; it *was* forty years ago, you'd be right, for the girls are in their mid-forties now. They couldn't reach the cupboard where the money was. So, I went to say to Pearl, you know, not blaming anybody, but I mentioned some money had disappeared from that cupboard.' Simpson walked over and gave the cupboard door a knock. 'At the time, Pearl said I couldn't be right. "Karen wouldn't do that, Wayne". We all defend our children. It's only natural. She didn't talk to me next time I saw her, which was the day Karen died. Or was found. The next day, wasn't it? She died in the evening and was found the next morning.'

'That's correct,' said Higgins.

'I saw Pearl outside. She saw me and turned her back. So I put a sympathy card through her door instead. From my family. A wee message that anything she needed, anything at all, all she needed was to ask. I didn't go to their door again. I should have. I should have told her I was wrong.'

'Wrong about?'

'I looked in the wrong cupboard, didn't I?' His eyes searched mine. 'The day we knew the girl was dead, I made the kids something to eat after school. Sandwiches with fish paste.' He pointed a finger, marking the memory. 'Now, how do I remember that? I don't know. I only know I do. And there … wasn't the tenner poking out of the jug in the tin cupboard!'

Wayne opened the cupboard beside the one he had knocked on and peered inside thoughtfully.

'You didn't tell Pearl you'd made a mistake?' Higgins asked him.

'No. Look, I only wanted to be nearby and to help, but I felt like an eejit. And after, I think my mistake was asking too many questions. I had little girls myself, raised them by myself, by and large, and raised them well. And I'm no murderer, I can assure you of that. But my mistake was that I should have been braver and went and told Pearl I was wrong. Karen died thinking I thought her a thief; her mother died in the hospice thinking I was her wee girl's killer.'

There was nothing left to say for now. Wayne seemed like a good egg, but how could you tell? He had had a lifetime to perfect his story, to make it sound small and understandable.

30

'Let's keep him as a witness for now so as not to muddy the waters,' I said to Higgins when we grabbed a break in the service car. I didn't want to leave the area again that day. Higgins agreed, though he didn't have a choice, and the waters were nothing but mud.

Chapter 5

Just before seven p.m., the rain began to lash. We made for the mobile where Sarge Simon was sitting reading a leaflet. '*Anyone with information should call detectives on 101 or contact Crimestoppers anonymously*,' he said. 'Want to know how many times I've read that?'

'How many?' Higgins asked him.

'Lost count.'

'You've been busy, then?' I said.

'Not one sinner. And the weather doesn't help.'

Wet weather never does. We hadn't seen rain like it in months. Though there was another reason for the absence, a more uncomfortable one. Openly helping the PSNI isn't viewed favourably. Even in this case, that was not some gangland crime where there were loyalties and repercussions for speaking up. Though I could be wrong about that. If Karen's death *was* related to the Troubles, then we were the wrong team for it. It would be handed over to the Historical Investigations Unit, which deals with legacy work.

Still, people did not want to walk into the mobile and be seen doing it. Instead, they discussed the case in passing. Like the woman we had seen half an hour before. 'I remember that,' she'd said as I walked out of Clarawood House. She'd been wearing floral capri pants and a purple top. Dressing for the weather is impossible during rainy Belfast summers. She was speaking to another woman. Both looked to be in their early sixties.

I stopped walking and waited. The woman continued telling her companion, 'I heard she was involved with somebody she shouldn't have been.'

'Excuse me,' I said. 'I wonder if you could spare a minute?' But she turned and walked off.

'On my way out the door,' she said, going out into the rain. Higgins grimaced at me.

The other woman spoke to us: 'I never heard any of that, about involvement with somebody …. ' she said, 'but I know it was the start of a chain of events around here. Whether they're linked or not, I really couldn't say.'

'What happened after Karen was killed?' I asked her.

'Was there another murder?' asked Higgins.

'Another woman living around here *was* murdered not long after Karen Ward,' the woman told us.

'Do you have a name you could give us?' I asked her.

'It was Vernon Brown's wife.'

'Michelle Brown?' asked Higgins, too quickly for my liking. I've always found his timing clunky.

'Yes,' she said.

'Can you tell us what happened to her?' I asked.

'She was strangled in her car by someone in the back seat.'

'And this was thought to be related to the death of Karen Ward?'

'Opinions were divided over that,' the woman said, looking around her, getting ready to walk away. 'But two women living so close to each other and both getting strangled …. ' She took a sip of air.

'Can we have your name and address in case we need to speak to you again?' I asked her.

'Sincerely, I'd rather not.'

'It would be a big help to Karen's sister Janet to get closure after all this time.'

'I remember wee Janet. Lovely girl. And if I knew anything else, but like I've told you …. '

A young man in a bright orange synthetic T-shirt came down into the foyer then. Outside I noticed Simon standing at the door of the mobile, stretching his legs and putting his hand out to catch the rain. When I looked around again, the woman was walking toward the young man.

'So, I mean,' she called back to me, 'I would love to help you, but I don't know anything. Hi, love, have you had your tea yet?' she asked the young man, and together they left.

This stranger had a point; the murders would have been related at the time. Strangulation. It was not entirely dissimilar. And it meant that we had lost our eyewitness. The witness we had waited all day to speak with.

'Same perp? Or a possible copycat?' asked Higgins quietly.

'Let's go to Vernon Brown's house and find out,' I said.

So we went, only again there was no answer.

A little later, Simon shut up shop for the day, and we saw him off. An old red Corsa entered the car park, and a man got out. He ran into the maisonette with the Spanish lizard on the wall. Vernon. It had to be.

Moments later, the passenger door of the car swung open, and a pink umbrella mushroomed out of it. Underneath was a woman with freshly blown-out hair she was trying to protect. She ran to the front door, went to close it when she saw me standing behind her and jumped.

'Vern!' she shouted, and he reappeared, popping his head around the corner. He was holding a wet paper bag from the chippy.

'Come in, come in,' he sang, setting the food in the kitchen then putting the lights on in the living room. An elderly Miniature Schnauzer with a buster collar slept in its fluffy doughnut bed.

'We're from Strandtown. DI Sloane and Sergeant Higgins.' I nodded at Higgins. 'We are reinvestigating the murder of Karen Ward,' I told Vernon.

'So I heard,' he said.

The woman went into the kitchen and shut the door.

'I understand that your wife, Michelle, was an eyewitness.'

'She died forty years ago,' said Vernon rubbing at raindrops that sat on the white hairs on his forearms.

'We just heard,' said Higgins. 'We were coming to speak to her and had no idea.'

'We heard that your wife died in violent circumstances too,' I ventured.

'You didn't hear wrong,' said Vernon, wiping the steam from his eyeglasses onto his shirt.

'I know it's bad timing, you have your dinner ready, but we've been calling all day, so can we talk now?'

'I can microwave my fish supper, don't you worry.'

Vernon sat down on a beige fabric seat. Higgins and I took the sofa facing.

'Do you mind telling us what happened to Michelle?'

'She got into the car. It was parked out there.' He pointed aimlessly at the front door. 'Twenty minutes later – I believed she was at her mother's and all – turned out she hadn't got further than our front door. A commotion gathered out in the car park; everyone was all around the car. And then sirens and a knock on the door. The peelers. I knew. You have a distinctive knock. While only cold callers and children rap the letterbox,' Vernon said with a smile. '*What the fuck is our Tucker up till now?* that's what I thought.'

That was a familiar name. 'Tucker?' I said.

'Our son,' Vernon said as if I should already know. Tucker Brown. It had to be. The one and only.

I tried to not react, yet Vernon had this air about him like I would know Tucker, and know *him* for being Tucker's father. But until that moment, I hadn't.

'And it *was* the police … at your door?' asked Higgins.

'You know what?' Vernon said. 'It was a neighbour coming to tell me the RUC was there. Coming to tell me about Michelle, more's to the point.'

'Someone in the back seat strangled Michelle as she sat in the driver seat. Is that what happened?' Higgins asked Vernon.

'Not strangled with hands,' he replied.

—

36

Vernon was holding his hands up just like Kate Stile had when she confirmed to me that Karen had not been manually asphyxiated.

'What was Michelle strangled with?' I asked.

'Wire,' Vernon said, his eyes becoming hard. 'Almost decapitated her.'

My jaw dropped slightly. Why hadn't this been on the system? I was cross that I had to find out like this.

'Obviously, this was before our time, Mr Brown,' I said.

'Yes, I see that.'

'And we're here to investigate Karen's murder, but I do want to find out more about Michelle's if that's alright? I'd like to ask you a few more questions.'

Vernon shifted.

'I know it's extremely tough,' I added, 'especially after all this time.'

'I understand,' said Vernon. 'They were spaced close together. But Michelle's killing was not related to Pearl's wee girl's murder, dear.'

'Was anyone ever convicted for Michelle's murder?'

'Was anyone ever, then?' he had a contemptuous tone. 'Not for things like that. Sure they protect each other.'

'Who are *they*?'

'The boys,' said Vernon.

'Do you think Michelle's murder was a paramilitary attack, Mr Brown?'

'When that happens, you know you're beat. You accept you're not going to get anything like justice. Karen's was a different story now.'

He'd distanced himself, and it had been a lifetime ago, but I could still see the pain in Vernon Brown, the hopelessness he didn't want to feel, but he felt it. Vernon was embarrassed to feel it. I had to be delicate with this one.

'Mr Brown,' I said, 'do you mind telling me what your ideas are on who killed Michelle?'

'Our Tucker.' He sighed. 'He would have fought with his shadow when he was younger. You'd bring him to the sweet shop when he was wee and he'd come back with two ounces of cola cubes, and a new enemy. *Sensitive*, Michelle called it. I don't bloody know. We were at a loss at how to manage him when he got up some,' said Vernon, 'and Michelle – sure she was soft – she always said, "Vernon, don't kick him out, give him more, more love, more stuff."' Vernon shook his head, and a drop of rain ran down his forehead then nose which he didn't wipe away.

'Wasn't he a spoilt wee shite!' he said. 'She loaned him her car, but turned out he thought the motor was his. He never brought it back for his mother when she needed it. One night, she wants to go for a spin to her own mother's, bring her a new lamp that Michelle got for her in town in the new year sales, and there is … someone in the back seat.' Vernon stopped and became glassy-eyed.

'This must be hard.'

'Ah, life's for the living, eh?' Vernon said. He bit his thumbnail. 'Wouldn't wish that hurt and that hatred on my worst enemy, but you have to let go. It's so long ago now. I'm with Agnes twice as long as with Chelley.'

Higgins' eyes darted at me, then back to Vernon.

'You think Tucker killed his mother?' Higgins asked.

'Jeez, no. Wasn't I clear? No, no. Somebody who was after Tucker.'

'You don't think it had anything to do with Michelle seeing who Karen was speaking to before her death?' I asked, and Vernon looked straight through me.

'I don't know if you are aware – if it was ever mentioned to you – that Michelle gave an eyewitness account to the RUC,' Higgins said. 'We have a sketch.'

'But that was some deviant,' said Vernon, surprised that Higgins had paired the two. 'That poor girl's clothes were removed. This was someone trying to get Tucker back for something, whether mistaken identity at first, or that Chelley saw the bastard sitting behind her and they got her before she could scream, or they were trying to get at Tucker by killing his mother, I've no idea. And I'm probably better never knowing. It won't make it better to hear why someone did that.'

'You seem quite convinced they are not related,' I said.

'It'll be through hatred or through stupidity, Chelley's killing. Neither is good enough reason for me.' Vernon had a cool blue feeling that came from him. I got the sense he was capable of great anger.

'Can I ask you about your son?' I asked to lift the bad atmosphere.

'Tucker?'

'Yes.'

'I'm sure you're already acquainted.' He smiled dimly.
I bit the inside of my cheek.
'It's drugs now with him, so I hear.'

'What was he doing before?' I asked.

'Back when his mother was killed?'

'Yes.'

'He was a bad pig back then, too. Up to his oxters in paramilitary involvement.'

'And after?'

'He did a bunk. You know, I'll tell you something, one time I was in the bar, I was rightly – now, don't take me for a drinker, it was a one-off – someone approached me, he bought me a beer, chatted a bit about nothing, the weather, sports, then he said he had a message for me. He turned around and told me the person who killed our Michelle wanted me to know he was *sorry*.'

'Who was this person who told you that?' asked Higgins squinting hard.

'Never seen him before. If I've ever seen him since I'm not aware I have.'

'And what did you do?' said Higgins.

'I shouted at him, didn't I?' I said, "Person? Fucken monster that killed my Chelley, you mean, not *person*".'

'And you'd never seen this … individual before,' I asked.

'I was rightly,' said Vernon, losing patience. 'It was probably *him*, the monster, cleaning his conscience. Either way, she's gone. She can't help you now; not about Karen, dear.'

Suddenly the room fell silent.

'It's all change,' Vernon piped up again, 'these days …. Except Tucker, the headcase. Heard on the wireless, he's facing time.'

'Tucker Brown?' I asked pointedly.

40

'Tucker Brown: His mother's blue eye,' said Vernon.

'He's under investigation at the minute,' Higgins jumped in. More clunky timing. I wasn't happy he said it, but it wasn't a lie. A few months before, we had brought in a load of the East Belfast brigade on drugs charges. It took no time at all when they had started to implicate each other. They knew they were caught, and so, to get lighter terms, the stories started flying.

Tucker Brown was the principal offender; he was going to go down for ten plus years. That was a cert. I couldn't believe that Drew Taylor had not been charged, and neither could he.

I knew Drew from around, had earned his trust when I found the person – no, *monster* – who killed his kid cousin Chloe Taylor in the PACT political office on the Upper Newtownards Road the year before.

Drew's wife, Roxanne, left him once he was brought in for questioning. He had since been released, yet Roxy wanted nothing to do with him. Any time he mentioned her, he looked dejected.

We had kept in touch since Chloe's killer was put behind bars. He finally respected me because I'd gone beyond the line of duty. Caught a bullet for the arrest.

I was out having a drink with Fleur one night in the Merchant when I got talking to Chloe's father, Jackie. He sent a round of drinks to our table. By the end of the night, defences down, we all chatted. Then Jackie left, then Fleur went, and I ended up in the company of Drew. We got talking, became acquaintances. It might not have been ideal, but it wasn't bad to have the respect of an *inside* man.

Now I'd met Vernon, I vowed to squeeze Drew for more intel on the infamous Tucker Brown.

Nonetheless, Karen Ward was my priority, and on the one hand, I hoped her killer had already had his comeuppance, been punished in some shape or form.

He merged into a monster not unlike Frankenstein's, with parts of every bastard out there going about their contented lives. Though it was little comfort, I liked to think of them keeping watch over their shoulder. Scot-free bastards like them got to me most. Kept me on the job, kept me awake at night. Infiltrated my dreams, like Jason Lucie was again.

'Do you have anything you can remember about the time Karen was killed?' I asked Vernon, bringing it back to the primary investigation, despite how alluring Michelle Brown's case looked to me, sitting there in her old living room.

'I knew Michelle wanted to go to the police. I asked her if that was wise, in case it was one of the boys. I don't mean my boys!'

'But, Mr Brown,' I said, 'I thought you believed it wasn't a paramilitary who killed Karen.'

'I knew it wouldn't have been *ordered*, but,' said Vernon, 'I thought maybe someone *slipped up*, and then they all covered up for him. But if that was the case, you hear names, and I never heard any names regarding Karen. Honestly.'

'Unlike the man in the bar with you?' asked Higgins.

'It was just some headcase that killed Pearl Ward's youngest.' Vernon stopped. He showed us to the door. 'No traffic in your mobile today?' he asked.

'Not much.'

'No, that's what I thought.'

'It was a long time ago. Maybe it's a long shot,' I said, letting my pessimistic mood slip out. Vernon's resignation about bad shit happening to innocent women was catching.

'And people don't want to speak,' said Higgins.

'I'd speak,' said Vernon. 'I'm proud that Michelle did. You see, you have to stand up to these people.'

Unless they are part of the fabric, I thought. But of course, one-on-one is a different game.

'If I knew anything,' said Vernon, 'believe me when I say I'd tell you everything.'

'He was forthcoming,' I said once we got out of the street.

'He called his son a headcase,' said Higgins.

'Without a cause, maybe they're all *headcases*. Maybe it applies to all of us, not just *the boys*.'

'And they say the Troubles are over.' Higgins tutted.

I thought back to the morning of Good Friday, which was the 21st anniversary of the peace agreement. For over two years now, we'd had no government sitting in Stormont. The big parties kept butting heads over marriage equality and an Irish language act. Meanwhile, paramilitaries were taking over our streets.

Since the break of the new year, Republican thugs were stealing ATMs. Next came rioting in Derry after a police raid. Then gunfire was released on the streets of Derry. Then a bullet hit a talented young journalist and killed her.

Afterwards, the group involved issued an apology, claiming they had aimed at 'enemy forces', i.e., the police.

'Ceasefire babies,' Lyra McKee had called her generation in one of her articles. She wrote: 'Your children, they told our parents, will be safe now.'

It was another senseless death that many thought should have shamed the Assembly into restarting talks. But still, it was now June. And there was nothing. We were still ungoverned and unravelling.

Chapter 6

The rain continued to lash all night, right into the next afternoon. At least it seemed to clear the air. At least it was cooler. People seemed more upbeat. I was more optimistic. Even Fleur Hewitt had a great big smile on her chops when she pulled up an old file on her screen.

'You won't believe this,' she said. 'In 1980, a girl was killed in Carnfunnock Country Park, her clothes were binned.'

'That's reason to smile?' I asked.

'It is for us.'

'That's not far,' I mused.

'Twenty-eight miles away from where Karen Ward was found.'

'Name?'

'Rhonda Orr,' Hewitt noted, reading the case notes. 'Rhonda was sexually assaulted. One of her earrings was never found. A little diamond stud.'

'It could have come out in the struggle,' I said.

'Probably.'

'Or the earring could have been taken as a token.'

'This could be the same perp, hen,' said Hewitt, her grin grew stronger. 'No conviction.'

'Fuck! These cases just get lost over time,' I said.

'Don't they just.'

After researching the Orr case that afternoon, I called Janet on her mobile. She told me she was in the dome in Victoria Square, overlooking all the city.

'You could be anywhere in this shopping centre,' she said. 'Bristol, London, Manchester.'

'Yes, it's a nice place,' I said, though I didn't know if that was what she meant or if she meant that all big cities have developed this generic aspect. 'Did you hear about this case in Carnfunnock at the time?' I asked.

'No,' she said quietly.

I told Janet some of what I'd read that afternoon – on top of what Fleur Hewitt had told me – I paused when I mentioned the earring. I wondered if she was thinking about Karen's locket and the matching one Janet had shown us two days prior.

'Maybe Karen's death,' Janet said after a long pause, 'wasn't a one-off.'

'Potentially,' I said.

'Well, that's frightening. What was this girl called?'

'Rhonda Orr.'

Janet gave it a moment's thought, then she said, 'Karen never took that locket off. She slept and showered in it. We both got one for Christmas from our mum a couple of years before. Karen loved it. She would never have removed it, not for anything.'

Chapter 7

My relationship was not back on track with Father. I phoned him every day, just to make sure he was alright. We were getting used to life without Mother. She'd had Huntington's for the longest time and died a year before, with a bit of help from Father.

It hadn't been well-received, the whole assisted dying thing. There were hundreds of people protesting outside the court. They reminded me of the anti-abortion crew; good with their views, good with their judgement, poor at supporting real people in dire straits.

That January, Father had been acquitted; the judge showed him sympathy. She said Father's actions were 'entirely compassionate and not at all malevolent'. I was glad to see that at least she had some common sense. Aren't we kinder to ailing pets than we are to suffering humans?

What was weirdest was my family being the hot topic of radio call-ins: *Did Charles Sloane get away with murder because he is the ex-Chief Constable of the RUC?* My mother had once been a judge herself, though. The press hated that we had been raised comfortably. Apparently, we deserved nothing other than contempt. They characterised us Sloanes as if we were all exorbitantly 'privileged' and 'entitled'; all those trendy buzz words came into play.

Social media blew up too.

I'm not into it, but I felt for my eldest nieces and nephews who use various platforms. Charly's eldest kids – the girls – were younger teenagers, while Coral's son Gus was seventeen. Then there were Brooks' kids in London, Roni and Ethan, who I hadn't seen since they were little. I wondered if they knew their grandfather had bilked anaesthetic from my partner Paul to put an end to their grandmother's suffering.

Addam, my second brother, a minister who is now living with Huntington's himself, had been giving us all the silent treatment, avoiding our calls and texts, since Father's arrest at Mother's funeral. Had it been another family, I don't doubt Addam would have been among the demonstrators outside the court. I wondered where he stood on the subject of euthanasia now he was living with a neurodegenerative disease himself. Then I tried not to wonder. I tried to focus on work, on my twins, on repairing my relationship with Father, and so I made an effort with him, invited him to join us for dinner a couple of nights a week. Though sometimes I had to work late and Paul would be left with him. But maybe that would do them no harm. Their relationship could do with being patched up, too.

Since the acquittal, Father seemed better. Still grumpy and impatient, but lighter. He may not have had public approval, but that never bothered him. I would go as far as to say that he thrived on collective disapproval.

Though not everyone had turned against him. He'd garnered a lot of support too. A few people told me they felt he had been backed into the corner where he felt that assisted dying was the only choice for Mother.

He had given us all our lives back, and now he was making the most of his freedom, and rarely was he able to take my calls. Today he called me. He was interested in my workload again like he used to be, and I told him about Karen Ward. Father remembered the case as I suspected he would.

'Didn't he take her necklace?' he asked, then he told me about the male neighbour and the young boy: two eyewitnesses. But he didn't mention Michelle Brown. Nor did Father remember Rhonda Orr's murder in Carnfunnock Country Park, but he did know who worked on the Ward case back then. Mack Napier.

Old Mack had since died, but Father knew Mack's daughter, who he had seen at a recent funeral. He had many to go to those days. At one social outing – *outing* in the truest sense – Mack's daughter told Father she had recently gone into her mother's roof space and found a vast amount of boxes of files from her father's work.

'I'll give you the address,' said Father, 'Mack Napier lived on King's Road, Ballyhackamore.'

Chapter 8

I clambered up into the loft and handed the electricity plug down to Mack's widow Anna which she connected to an extension cable, then she told me to feel for a light switch. I found the switch and turned the loft light on, saw stacks and stacks of cardboard boxes. No Christmas tree or photo albums or any of the usual bumf, but boxes and boxes of caseloads. They had dates written on the sides, from decades spanning the 1960s through to the late 80s. There were names on the boxes too.

Higgins was afraid of heights and did not offer to help me out. After twenty minutes of looking, on my knees, moving boxes about carefully while listening to Anna tell-all about her late husband Mack, I found one box that was labelled *1978, Ward*. I called Higgins to come close, so I could hand the box down to him.

'There's another one,' I said. It was soft with age. Felt like my fingers would go right through the sides. I prised it open, lifted out a file and saw the words *Karen Ward, Clarawood*. I glanced down onto the landing. Anna was holding the other box while Higgins was rummaging through it. 'This is about our case,' he confirmed.

I rifled through the notes in front of me. There were the statements we had already seen, but more than that, there were books.

'This one too,' I said, my heart thrashing.

*

'How did you get those?' asked Hewitt when Higgins and I walked into the station with the boxes.

'Her old man knew a man who knew a woman,' said Higgins.

Hewitt nodded. 'I wouldn't put anything past that old rogue Charles Sloane,' she said, which I'd take to heart coming from anyone else, but Fleur had a snarky sense of humour I was now familiar with and took with a pinch of salt. At least she recognised what had gone on, while the rest of my colleagues pretended they didn't know what happened with my family, then no doubt gossiped behind my back. Even Chief Dunne ignored what Father had done, despite him being the very man who made the arrest at my mother's funeral. Greg Dunne alongside the top brass from Musgrave's Serious Crime Suite.

I wondered if the funeral Father had met Mack's daughter at had been Mother's and if he had not wanted to say so. All sorts came out of the woodwork for the funeral, though at the time, I'd only focused on the omissions: absent friends, people I thought were friends who I'd long lost touch with.

'We have diaries from DI Mack Napier,' I said. 'Napier worked here at the time and was in charge of the Ward case. He's been dead for twenty years, but he has a whole loft full of cases that never got solved.'

'Good on Mack Napier,' said Hewitt.

'They haunted him, so his wife said earlier. Unfortunately, he died before he could see justice prevail.'

'Sounds like he was a good guy,' said Supt. Hewitt.

'Does,' I agreed.

Higgins scanned the notes, some we had seen and some we had not, then he pulled out the book I was excited about.

'What is that?' asked Hewitt. 'One of Mack's diaries?'

'No,' I said. 'This diary is Karen Ward's.'

Chapter 9

That evening Paul and I changed the boys into their PJs and tried to keep them up to see Father. He was a no-show for dinner. I'd wanted to tell him about everything I found at Napier's house. Eventually, we had to put the boys to bed, and after tea, we fell shattered into bed ourselves. That night I joined Paul again. I didn't always. I was still silently pissed off at how he'd blabbed to police about my father showing up at the hospital acting strangely, then pilfering meds. Father's absence made me think he was still in a huff. You never could tell. He was usually in a huff.

Paul didn't open his bedside read; he wanted to talk, and we'd had little time for it. I had little interest in talking to him, truly. I was still not sure how I felt about Paul. Yes, he was supportive, fuckable even – under other circumstances, like if there was a reason why we shouldn't fuck – and he was inherently good, but sometimes I'd get the ick around him.

Complicated was where I was comfortable. At least my love life was and had always been. I was never sure of what to look for in a partner, ignored the obvious red flags. I put up with shit I thought I was strong enough to withstand, and then it turned out I was not.

That's how I felt at that time. Very *unstrong*.

'What did you want to tell your dad?' Paul asked.

'Mack Napier duplicated files and held on to them.'

'Isn't that illegal?' He turned to look at me.

'Mack wanted to see the cases resolved,' I said with a shrug, lifting an autobiography of a stand-up comic. My preferred choice of reading material was always funny and irreverent.

'He literally took his work home with him.'

'It's more of a calling than a job,' I said.

Paul lifted his book, some bought-in-the-supermarket three-for-two thriller, he started to read, and I kept talking. I had wanted to discuss this with Father, and now I just wanted to discuss it. The only problem was that Paul is very straight and idealistic. He doesn't understand the drive there is to bang up the bad guys.

'I think there must be a family loyalty,' I said. 'After all this time. Loyalties in friendships wane.'

'Not all families are so loyal,' Paul said. He yawned and straightened out his book again.

This is real life, I wanted to tell him, far more interesting than that twaddle you're reading.

'What's wrong with your mum?' I asked Paul. I had no idea I was going to ask it. I had no idea I was even thinking it. Maybe it was turning forty; I had ditched the filter. I was becoming an old grump, like Father.

Paul closed his book. 'What?' he asked.

'What's wrong with her?'

'My mum?'

'Yes, your mum.'

'Explain yourself, Harry.'

'She doesn't call in … since my father's court case.'

'She didn't call much before either. I bring the boys to see her, sure. The invite for dinner isn't extended to her.'

Then I realised what was bugging me; Kaye Coulter had no interest in Jared and Rowan. They were not grandsons to her. She would not allow herself to bond with them like that. At one stage she had said to Paul: 'Let me know if you are planning to see things through with Harriet before I let myself love those little boys.'

I supposed Kaye was just protecting her heart, and I was more pissed off Paul had told me; I didn't need to know. The boys were two years old. They had no grandmother. And Greg's parents, I assumed from his age, were deceased. Plus, he was not in the kids' lives and had never even seen them. I was angry.

But I was angry about so much more: Karen Ward being killed; Rhonda Orr being killed; angry that people walked free when they shouldn't; that there were people behind bars who shouldn't be: like my eldest brother Brooks, who has a heroin addiction and was recently released from prison after a sentence for armed robbery, yet he was more inherently good than anyone.

'Kaye doesn't give a shit about the boys,' I said, knowing the anger was misplaced, but I had this feeling my boys would one day be ashamed of the surname Sloane because of Father and Brooks. Maybe they would want to be Coulters like Paul had offered, but it would have been jumping the gun. Paul didn't try to tell me I was wrong about his mother. He looked at his book, but his eyes didn't move. I turned my back to him. We both knew I was acting out. He would blame my workload. I knew the truth, that I had started to fear going to sleep and wanted to think about something else, but I couldn't read some funny anecdote.

55

It couldn't lift me from that mood, so I lay staring at the wall after Paul turned off his bedside lamp. He asked me if I would do the same, if I wasn't going to read. I closed my eyes. In the dark, there was Jason Lucie again four and a half years after the assault. He'd return any time I wasn't busy or distracted. It was driving me insane.

Chapter 10

The environment that distracted me best was work, wherever that took me. I could be professional, despite the plague that swarmed my mind. Dealing with my old trauma didn't take the same hold over me when I was trying to unpick someone else's.

That Thursday morning, work took me to Larne to talk to the family of Rhonda Orr. Life – and justice – had escaped her parents, so we went to speak with her brother Barney, who now lived a ten-minute walk away from their old house in Bryan Street. Home for Barney Orr was now a modern, mid-terrace property in The Roddens.

'Rhonda was eighteen at the time,' Barney told us in his living room. 'I was fourteen at the time of her death.'

'Was there ever any arrest?' I asked him. He said he couldn't remember one, nor there being a suspect at the time.

'I do remember my parents being downright incensed,' said Barney, 'because it looked like nothing was being done to find Rhonda's killer. I'm sure it probably was … behind the scenes, but …. '

'But they were frustrated by a lack of answers?' guessed Higgins.

'They were.'

I could only nod. Higgins had called Larne PSNI the day before to see what information they had for us.

He was told someone would call us back, but there had been no reply as yet. Higgins wanted to drop in while we were in the vicinity, but I didn't think it was a good idea. I knew none of the staff. Plus, they needed to try to unearth this old case without us adding any pressure. I doubted they had their own Mack Napier taking notes and making copies. We wouldn't get lucky like that twice.

I asked Barney what Rhonda was doing with her life at the time of her death, and he told us she was a student at Trinity College, Dublin, studying Physics. Rhonda was home after her first half-term when she went out to visit friends and catch up, and she never came home again. Barney recalled how devastated his family was at the time.

'Nobody knew how to be around us, not for years,' he said. The whites of his eyes were cloudy, like lemon juice. 'We were the family of the girl who was killed. Mum and Dad died without answers.'

This was the theme, surely. Now Barney was a grandpa himself. Little artefacts showing this were jotted about the living room: framed pictures of a son or daughter's wedding; photos of little kids; board games and puzzle boxes sat on top of one another inside the glass cabinet.

'There was a young woman,' I said, 'girl really, only seventeen years old.' I turned on the iPad and showed Barney Karen's smiling face. 'This is a photo of Karen Ward, she was killed similarly in East Belfast a year or two before Rhonda was.'

'What year was that? 1978?'

I nodded my head, and Barney shook his. 'I'd have been twelve. I wouldn't have taken that in,' he said

'To your knowledge, did anyone ever link Rhonda's death to another one?' asked Higgins.

'Not to my knowledge,' replied Barney.

'Rhonda's earring was missing, and with Karen a silver locket from around her neck. The attacks were similar in style: both girls were found in parks with their clothes removed.'

'Was Rhonda raped?' asked Barney, scratching his head. 'It's something I've wondered about since.'

'I believe she was,' I said.

'Oh. They kept the details from me. And Karen Ward, was she raped?'

'She wasn't. But they could have had more nerve the next time.'

'More confidence. Yes, they'd been flirting with violence,' said Barney. He looked emptied.

'We have reopened Karen's case.'

'Do you think that you'll reopen Rhonda's?' he said abruptly.

People were chatting in the kitchen. Women's voices.

'I can't say,' I told Barney. 'It isn't up to us.'

'If he raped my sister, there'll be DNA, and that might help these days.'

'That's true,' said Higgins.

'I don't want to give you any false expectations,' I said.

'Oh, they're not high by this stage. The culprit is probably dead by now, too,' said Barney.

When we went to leave, two women came from the kitchen. One of them was Janet Ward.

'Hello,' I said, surprised to see her.

'Hello, Detective Sloane, I'm just leaving,' she said.

'This is my wife,' Barney introduced us to the other woman. She smiled, then recited her phone number, which Janet keyed into her mobile phone.

'I'll see you all out,' said Barney, squeezing past to open the front door.

'Just wait,' I told Higgins outside. Soon Janet came outside after her separate goodbye.

'Can we go get a coffee?' she asked me, looking rather guilty. 'There's a nice wee place that direction.'

Higgins looked at me.

'Fine,' I said. 'We have ten minutes to spare.'

I wanted to ask Janet what in the hell she was doing there and to ask Barney why he hadn't said she was there, sitting in the next room to us. He let us go through telling him everything about Karen, all the while acting as if he had never even heard of her.

'I've rented a car. It's over there,' said Janet pointing at a bright orange Toyota Aygo. 'I'll meet you in a minute.'

'What is she playing at?' asked Higgins as we parked up and walked to the cafe.

'She must have done some amount of asking around to find Barney,' I said.

Janet took a little longer parking up. She ran into the coffee shop and ordered herself a latte, then sat down facing us.

'Apologies about that,' she said. 'I don't drive back home, and you need to here. I'm getting used to parking again.'

'No problem,' I said.

Janet put her phone face down on the table. 'I know that appeared strange,' she said. 'You looked really cross.' She was eyeing me.

'Shocked, more like,' I said. 'It was a surprise to see you there, that's all.'

'Once you mentioned Rhonda, I couldn't stop thinking about her, and I'm over here, *back home* where everything reminds me of Karen. I want to be reminded of her, but I'm a bit of a spare part, sitting about in the hotel, just waiting. I wanted to be proactive.'

'How did you find the Orrs?'

'I did an investigation of my own. Asked around.'

'How long had you been there, Janet?'

'A couple of hours and some change ….'

She frowned at me with care, and I realised I must have looked shocked again.

'But we had a good talk,' she said as if to reassure me.

'Barney and I, and his wife, Sharon, she's lovely too.'

'You heard us arrive?' asked Higgins.

Janet smiled. 'When you showed up at the door, Sharon rushed me through to the kitchen, and I followed her. I wasn't trying to act like I wasn't there. Maybe she thought I would be in trouble. She wanted me to keep my voice down. It is silly, really.'

I also wondered if it was slightly appealing to sit listening through the wall to what we said about her sister's case when we were not in front of her. I felt awkward then.

What *had* we said? Surely nothing we shouldn't haven't been saying, but I hated to be spied on all the same.

'Barney talked to you about Rhonda's death?' I asked. Maybe Janet had information for us. Barney had acted startled by us showing up, but he had known we would because Janet was in the other room. I *did* feel cross. I had been wittingly fooled by the two people I wanted to help the most.

'We talked about it,' said Janet, 'but we talked more about what it's like to be a sibling. We feel the same way.'

'What way is that?' asked Higgins.

'Barney and I agreed that siblings get overlooked. People think that grief is for the parents to feel. But we both went through our tough times.'

'Of course you did,' I said.

'He has very little memory of Rhonda by now, which is kind of heart-breaking, I think. Maybe her friends would be better people to talk to. He named a few ....'

Janet turned her smartphone over and went to Notes.

'Janet,' I said. 'I know you feel at a loss for something to do, but you need to let us do our job.'

'I just want to be helpful.'

'I know that, but ... just say ... someone tells you something important and then they think about it after.'

Janet stared at me intently, waiting for me to make sense.

'And we go,' I continued, 'and we talk to them, and they've changed their mind during that time. What I'm saying, Janet, is that we want to surprise people, not give them time to think of a narrative in advance of us speaking with them.'

'Oh.' She pouted softly.

'Do you see what I mean?'

'I do, and I don't,' she said.

'Just leave it to us,' said Higgins.

'Okay. Can I give you these names?'

'Of course,' I said.

'I won't go looking for people if that's what you'd prefer.'

'We would.'

'And I'd very much like to keep in touch with Barney and Sharon if that's allowed.'

'I'm sure that's allowed.' I smiled at Janet, and she smiled back.

'I'll go and pay for the coffees,' said Higgins making a beeline for the cash register.

'No, I'll get them,' said Janet.

'Let him pay,' I said.

'Oh, thank you. You are both very good.' Janet reached inside the neck of her shirt and began thumbing the locket she was now wearing.

Chapter 11

In the afternoon, we read Karen's diaries between us. I kept coming back to this, the longest passage:

I'll never be a scientist, I know that. I can't leave Mum. I am 'the wee sis'. Janet will get married and leave. I'm already replacing her in the job in the Silver Sea. I've tried to tell Mum that I want to study, she doesn't say anything about it. I told her there's a girl in my school who is applying to a university and what's more, it's in England. I didn't say how bad I want her life. I want to go away and have that choice, go and study and live somewhere else where people aren't bombing you or shooting you. Willie's cousin got kneecapped the other night. He nearly bled out and died. He was alright in the end. I hate that this is normality. I hate hearing the news. Could I even go to England? When that girl said she wanted to go to London, another girl said she'd been in London when there was a bomb scare, and she was afraid to speak. So ashamed of her accent. And there's this man who lives nearby whose legs were blown off in a car bomb. He is so dead-on, not involved in anything. It seems like potluck, and I hate that. I love Mum, hate that she's not well, but it's not my fault. I want more than this here, Clarafield and all that. I want to get a life and make her proud. Make me proud. But I'm trapped.

'I read that one earlier,' said Higgins. 'Sad, isn't it?'
'Yes,' I said dryly, trying not to show any emotion. That poor girl, she never had a chance.

64

And to see Janet, so stylish, so well put together! She had got out, she had had a family. She had told me in the canteen how she had retired just in time to become a first-time grandmother. Maybe Janet would never have left here had her mother and sister not died in quick succession. Those awful events had bought Janet the ticket to elsewhere her sister had so craved.

I looked at the list of Rhonda's friends that Janet had shared with me, I planned to pass them on to Larne when they got in touch, and in the spirit of Mack Napier, I kept them on my phone as a backup.

'Who were Karen's friends?' I asked. 'Janet mentioned Rhonda's friends, but who were Karen's?'

'Who was Willie?' asked Higgins. 'A boyfriend, d'ya think?'

'Look at this one,' I said, skipping forward through the diary, 'few of these pages are in code.'

We stared at the pages from April 1978, seven months before her death. There was a passage that particularly interested me. There were no words, just a string of random letters with clear paragraph breaks.

SEHHEWIWIQAHWGAZIAKQPSASAJPPKPDAL
EYPQNAPKAAWPQNZWUJECDPBARAN

ESKJPPAHHWJUKJA

There were a few passages like this dispersed throughout the diary. This could not be gobbledegook but things Karen wanted to say and had to keep hidden.

'Did you keep a diary?' Higgins asked me.

'Hell no, there were five of us kids, no privacy. It would have been found; I would have been ridiculed by Charly,' I said.

'I did. For a while.'

I gave him the side-eye. 'Weren't you sensitive, Carl?'

'What do you mean *weren't*?'

I had a little laugh to myself. 'We need to work this out.'

'I'm good at this kind of thing. I'll break the code,' he said. 'Leave me to it.'

'I don't know.' I was always wary of Higgins taking the *fun* procrastinating kind of jobs over any hard graft.

This code reminded me of Father and his love for crossword puzzles. Who has patience for that? Me, I would have to cheat and Google the answers.

'I know someone who is very good at breaking codes,' I said.

'I told you I'm good at it,' Higgins said.

'He'll work it out in no time.'

'First, give me an hour, tops.'

'Tops,' I said, setting an alarm.

An hour came and went, and Higgins asked for more time. I denied him and made a couple of photocopies of the diary's coded pages and put them in my bag.

Late afternoon, I went and left them with my father at Old Forge. He was standing at the door wearing a new aftershave I had never smelled on him before. He was dressed in an apple green shirt so unlike his usual style.

'You're on your way out,' I said.

'No, just out for a late lunch with a friend.'

'Oh,' I said. 'A lady friend, is it?'

Was that possible? Bloody right it was. I'd always suspected him a cheat and now he was a widower, after all. I had to get my head around that still, though I'd heard it takes two years for the reality of death to sink in. I didn't know if that was true, but I hoped I was more than halfway there. Maybe he thought he needed a woman because some people were saying men need company, they need to be looked after, that it is harder for men to be alone, that women who have been 'left behind' cope better.

Like how people say girls mature faster than boys, I've never believed that. I think they, by and large, aren't allowed to arse about as much as boys, that's all. In grammar school, we were called 'young ladies'. We were reprimanded for shouting, swearing or running anywhere that wasn't 'proper'. They were not trying to turn any of us into coppers, that was for damn sure.

I couldn't ignore the cellophane-wrapped bunch of carnations sitting on the coffee table in Father's living room. He was trying to close the door when I saw them.

'*Are* you going on a date?' I asked him straight out.

'Ah, those,' he acknowledged the flowers. 'Someone did something nice for me, and I said I would …. ' Then his face turned stern. 'Harry, don't do this.'

'Do what?' I asked as innocently as I could manage.

I thought it was sweet. I wanted to see the kind of woman who would attract my father. He was too gruff, too rough around the edges for my mother, while she was elegant and stylish.

Now, Mother *was* a lady. But there is more of my father in me, I have always been aware of that.

For a moment, I wondered if he was seeing Anna Napier, though she was even older than him. Then I wondered if he was seeing Mack and Anna's daughter, who had suddenly come into the picture with helpful titbits for Father, and for me, about the Karen Ward investigation, and Christ knows how many more.

That wouldn't be so bad, I decided. An *inside woman* could be helpful too.

'I'm a pensioner.' Father's heavily lined face darkened. 'Show some respect and stop laughing at me.'

'I'm not laughing, Daddy,' I said. I explained about Karen Ward's coded diary entries, and he told me to leave the photocopies with him. He set them on his coffee table, lifted the flowers, and followed me back out into the street.

'I don't want to keep my friend waiting,' Father said.

'No, you wouldn't want to do that,' I said to him.

I got into the service vehicle where Higgins was sitting with his copies of the pages. 'This shit is crazy addictive,' he said.

*

All afternoon we looked at the statements from Napier's loft. 'He seems to think it was the neighbour,' said Higgins.

'Which one?'

'Simpson.'

'Why?' I leaned in and looked.

'Napier mentions him every time and underlines things, goes over them again. Look at this. "He says he was home that night with his wife. She was sleeping." Napier had underlined the word *sleeping*!'

My brain was fried from reading so much; we had gone from hardly anything to too much. I decided I was no match for all that information. I felt anxious.

'I need a break,' I said to Higgins. 'I'm not staying on tonight.'

'You aren't?' he asked me.

'No. We need the code, though. I'll see you tomorrow.'

'See you,' he said. 'Maybe I'll surprise Melinda by going home early. We can work out the code together.'

'How romantic.'

I texted Paul and said I would collect the boys from the nursery. I was glad to walk out into the fresh air. My head was aching. I had hardly slept in days.

Chapter 12

I was only through the door with the boys when Paul arrived home. I told him I needed to go for a run, and Paul didn't seem to mind. I was stressed and needed the release. I tried to keep my mind upbeat, but it was sluggish. I was sluggish, mentally, physically. I got changed into my running clothes and tied the laces on my trainers, put my gun in my holster and a light jacket on over it, then I left the house in Mount Eden Road.

There were times when I ran through Malone and something slotted into place about a case, a slight detail, something someone had said. A question would form as I pounded the ground. That Thursday, it did not. Nor could I even think about Karen and Rhonda.

Having my gun on me was supposed to make me feel safer, but sometimes it had the opposite effect. I made sure to make eye contact with every person I passed. For a while, I'd even give everyone a hello or a smile: a thing women do to *appear human* to any would-be attacker. Now I hadn't the energy. I was done placating people. Plus it didn't need to be an attack. I had been catcalled more than I cared to remember. I had been chased late at night by teenagers in a car who skidded in front of me as I crossed the road, then drove off laughing, making a loop to return. Forcing me to sprint home. Men had swerved their cars pretending they were going to hit me, wound down their windows and screamed they were going to kill me.

I would get half of their licence plate. I would reach my phone too late.

When I used to run with Addam, this kind of shit never happened. No (so-called) good man would believe this shit even happens. My twin, Charly – who is never alone – would say, 'What do you think the kids in that car were going to do to you, Harry? Your mind works in dark ways!'

Anyone who was not in my line of work, anyone who had not had the marriage I'd had, would call me crazy for running with a firearm on me. But it was not me who was dark. My *gun for the run* was merely a reaction to the world we live in.

'Do you lock your house, Charly?' I'd asked her. 'Or your car?' Of course, she did.

I was not the dark one. I was working or parenting, partying or running. I was not the one killing girls in parks, holding my spouse hostage for days, raping her, threatening to kill her, exercising all my power and stripping her of her future sanity.

Life all around me was dark, even if the evening was bright and light and rose-scented. In that moment of breathing in and feeling revitalised, calm, I forgot myself, took an alleyway for a shortcut, and saw a man in a hoody at the end of the road. Right then, my heart skipped a beat. A pain ripped at my chest. I thought the man was Jason. Then I saw very quickly he wasn't.

It didn't matter; the damage was done. My body had reacted, and my headspace, and one of my favourite activities, was spoilt.

Now I saw Jason plainly again, how he was, how he used to be, standing outside, rain or shine, looking up at my old apartment at St. George's Harbour, back when I was a single woman. Before I was a mother.

This unknown man looked at me and nodded with a furtive look on his face. I had almost forgotten Jason's face. Now I remembered it. That broad smile and milky white skin. Pallid. Deathly. Except for the dreams I had of him, I hadn't properly seen him in years.

I looked over my shoulder to make sure the man wasn't following me. He wasn't. I felt for my gun and tried to regulate my breathing. I craved a drink. Ran onto the road. The temperature had dipped, or maybe that was just my blood-chilling. I was foundered when I ran into the house. Put on a warm jumper. Put my gun back in the safe. I was done with it all, I decided. Who knew that if I got startled badly enough, I wouldn't react and make a titanic misjudgement.

I couldn't explain why now the terror got me so much. Now I hated to be alone. At least when I drank, I never did it alone. I was Fleur Hewitt's wing-woman, or, not that I ever went out looking for a man, but I had one I could call. I would drink with him.

I took my glass of Merlot into the playroom. The boys were babbling their *whys*, their *agains*. Cute toddler material that is sweet in small doses. I only had them in small doses, so it was sweet.

I announced to the room that I was done running.

'Some a-hole scared the life out of me,' I gave as my reason.

'What did he do?' asked Paul.

'He scared me.'

'Join a running group,' said Paul, looking at his phone.

'No,' I said. Rowan climbed into my lap and took his bedtime bottle while Jared lay on a giant bean bag on the floor with his. Always more self-sufficient. Rowan clung to me. I kissed him on the top of his head and took a sip of my wine. This will be what they think I smell like, I thought, they will be older, in a bar or somewhere, and they will get childhood memories of me when they smell this fruity, sugary scent.

'Don't quit completely,' said Paul. 'It's good for you. You need to keep fit.'

To look right for you? I thought. Then I remembered that how I looked was nothing to him. We were like an old married couple, without the nice memories.

'Harry,' said Paul, 'are you genuinely going to give up running because of some a-hole?' I missed the times when we could have sworn in front of the boys.

The hoodied guy in the alleyway hadn't even been an a-hole. It was all down to one past a-hole, and my sudden onset vulnerability.

'Join a group, Harry. I'll happily mind the boys.'

I knew this offer; it was like when a man goes down on you because they want you to reciprocate.

'You should go out running again or training,' I said.

Paul had done all sorts of physical challenges to fill his singledom, probably to meet a woman. He had now put those interests aside.

'We're busy with the kids,' Paul said. 'They are more important at this age than my hobbies.'

'Then why do you want me to join a gym?'

'You need it more.'

'Are you saying I'm putting on weight?'

'A little bit.'

'Hey, eff you,' I said.

'It doesn't matter to me.'

'Why would it?' I asked. I could probably tell Paul I was fucking someone, and he would say, *that's okay, you need it more.* What were we to each other? Was I out on licence? Was I supposed to be his?

'Running destresses you,' he said.

'Are you saying I'm stressed?'

'I wouldn't blame you; your job is tough.'

'Yours too. You could accidently kill someone while anesthetising them.'

'Maybe I'll start the rugby training again. I've put on almost twenty pounds, haven't you noticed?'

I hadn't. I took a drink and held my little boy.

'But I'll say no matches, so I won't be away weekends.'

'Okay,' I said without a care.

'Exercise is better for destressing than alcohol.'

Patronising fucker.

I had completed the Belfast Marathon fifteen times.

'It's only a glass here and there,' I chirped.

'Our glass bank was only emptied at the beginning of last week, and it's full again. Take a look for yourself.'

He lifted Jared and gave him his bottle. Jared rubbed his eyes and smiled at Paul.

And I thought, this is not how I was raised, in a convenient, loveless relationship where someone was fucking around. Then I thought, maybe I was.

———

74

There. Now I had my excuse to repeat the past and think it was beyond my control.

Chapter 13

On Friday morning, I woke on the playroom sofa with a dry mouth and banging head. My phone was lighting up. It was Father with a text:

go back four letters in alphabet. she's left a letter out all together – no s's. a Travolta fan

*

'Go back four letters in the alphabet,' said Higgins at the door.

I showed him my phone and the text. He was disappointed he was not the only one to work it out.

'We have specialist code breakers in the PSNI, you know,' said Chief Dunne when we told him.

'I know, but there's a certain element of satisfaction you get from doing it yourself, sir.'

'As long as you wasted your own time.'

'Hours of it, sir,' said Higgins.

'Good show,' the chief said as he left us.

'So, show me what the diary segment says, Code Breaker,' I teased Carl Higgins, who looked chuffed with himself.

'Are you ready, Sloane?'

'Go on.'

'No letter s anywhere.'

'But the code starts with an s,' I stated.

'Yes, it does, but Karen has left the s's out.'

'Just show me,' I said. My head was still aching, but at least I'd finally slept.

Higgins went to each letter and back four like he and Father had said, then he wrote the passage out again.

Williamamuelaskedmeoutwewenttothepicturetoeeatur daynightfever

and under it: Iwonttellanyone

'William *amuel* asked me out, we went to the *picture* to *ee aturday* Night Fever. I won't tell anyone,' Higgins translated. 'Last line was obvious, but that missing letter s … that threw me. Amuel has to be Samuel. William Samuel, right?'

'Ah, Travolta fan!' I said, understanding Father's text now. 'How many passages were in code? Four?'

'Yeah. Four.'

'Do they get any juicer than that?'

'Not regarding William; he has to have been her boyfriend at the time. Though with regards to Arthur *amuel*, they get juicier.'

'Who is Arthur? A relative of William's?' I asked.

'That's what we need to find out. Look at this, Harry. Going forward. July, '78.'

WNPDQNWIQAHGEAZIAENWJWSWU

Higgins wrote out the letters: *arthuramuelkiedmeiranaway*
'Arthur Samuel,' I read, 'kied? I ran away!'

'Kissed me.' Higgins looked at me with a smirk on his lips.

'Have you something to say?' I asked him.

Higgins thought about it, then shook his head. 'No, ma'am.'

'The boyfriend's brother/dad/uncle tried it on with Karen …. ' I tested out a theory, saying it to see how the sentence felt. 'No one had mentioned Karen having had a boyfriend at all.'

*

I finally got a call back from Larne, from DI Posner.

'Concerning the murder of Rhonda Orr,' said Posner, 'what little I can tell you is that there were statements obtained back then from two hundred people.'

'Rhonda Orr's death seemed similar to that of Karen Ward's,' I said again, hoping this time someone would listen and take heed.

'It was a long time ago,' said DI Posner.

'Certainly was,' I said. 'We're looking for correlation to see if these two were linked.'

'Similar MO?'

'That's right, the murder of a young woman, they were both stripped. It's possible that jewellery was taken from both too.'

'Let me look into this can of worms some more, then I'll give you a summary. Can I call you?'

'Please do. We could get two birds here,' I said and gave my mobile number. Posner curtly ended the call.

Chapter 14

After lunch, I stood outside the front of Strandtown PSNI station, breathing in. The sky was azure and flawless. I shut my eyes for a moment, and could have fallen asleep on my feet until I heard Janet arrive.

'Hello, Detective,' she said with a more optimistic look on her face than she had had in Larne. 'I'm glad you called.'

I got us a meeting room and a couple of coffees, then I joined her.

'It's beautiful out, isn't it?' said Janet as she removed her thin linen jacket and draped it over her seat.

'It's colder in here,' I said, 'you might be putting that back on before long.'

'I'll take my chances,' she said.

'Well, Janet, the reason I wanted to talk to you was that I wanted to run a name by you.'

'Yes?' This time the locket was on show. I wondered if she only wore it when she knew she was going to see me, to remind me that she was alive and wearing hers. And that her sister's necklace had been removed from her lifeless body.

'Have you ever heard of William Samuel?' I asked Janet.

'Not in years!'

'We think that Karen was in a relationship with him.'

'I've never heard of her having a boyfriend, and there was only a year between us. We had no secrets.'

'I'm sorry to say that it seems there was this one.'

'Willie Samuel … ' Janet said.

'Who was he?' I asked.

'Willie lived a few streets away. In Sandown. He was this quiet boy. Quite nice, really, though his brother was trouble, he robbed a bank … or maybe he only attempted to.'

'What was his name?'

'Oh, what was it? The other Samuel brother.' Janet held her chin in thought.

'Was it Arthur?'

'Yes. It was Arthur.' She pointed at me.

'We found Karen's diary from around that time.'

'How?'

'It was being kept by the old detective who worked on the case.'

'Gosh! He must be in his nineties by now.'

'Actually, he's no longer alive.'

'Oh.' Janet clicked her tongue. 'He tried, Detective ….'

'Mack Napier,' I said.

'Yes, this is peculiar, hearing these names again. Detective Napier ….'

'Napier kept files on Karen's murder. Since it was unsolved, he held onto these files hoping to find an answer.'

'Bless him!' said Janet.

'He had Karen's diary, as I said.'

'I didn't know she had a diary.'

'We've been taking a look.'

'May I see?'

I messaged Higgins to bring it to us. When he arrived, I gestured for him to hand it straight to Janet.

'That will be all, Sergeant,' I told him.

Janet felt the diary cover and began tearing up when she opened it.

'I haven't seen her handwriting in so long.' Janet broke down, and we had to resume after a minute or two. She leafed through the pages, looking at Karen's account of her work, their mum, the odd mention of Janet. She had the book flat on the desk. She was at the page where Karen had written about feeling trapped and how Janet would go and leave her with their mother.

'I had no notion of leaving back then,' Janet explained, 'the irony is that I only left because everyone who held me here was gone. I went to England for a fresh start, I lived with family in London, and I studied because that's what Karen wanted to do. I wanted to fulfil her dream for her. I had no idea she wanted to be a scientist, but I knew she liked maths, and so I became a maths teacher. For her. To honour her.'

I remembered how Rhonda Orr had studied Physics and wondered if there was anything in that. But Rhonda studied in Dublin, Janet went to London.

'Now, look,' said Janet, 'a maths teacher wasn't even what Karen wanted to be. I'm left feeling like I didn't know my sister as well as I believed I did.'

I handed Janet a tissue to dab her wet eyes with.

'I'm sure you knew your sister very well,' I said. 'What seventeen-year-old knows for sure what they want to do with their life?' I asked, but I had known I would join the police.

81

I'd known since I was eight years old when I saw the respect my father got when he walked into a room.

'That's true,' said Janet pressing the tissue against each of her tear ducts in turn. 'I have to remember that she was young when she was writing this, that she was only venting.'

I lifted the diary away. 'If you shared a room, as I did with my sister …. '

'We did,' she said.

'Then I believe that Karen would have been prepared for you to look at any of her diaries. But here …. ' I located one of the four parts that were coded and set it under Janet's nose. 'And in three other places, she has used a code, just in case you did take a peek.'

Janet guffawed. 'That's so like her.' A smile spread over her face like warm butter. 'I love that; Karen down to a tee. A problem solver. A problem maker at times, too.'

I looked at Janet momentarily.

'I'm going to tell you this,' she said, 'because people hear that we were a year apart and sharing a room, and I know we had a lot of love for each other, no secrets between us, but at times we loathed each other's guts.'

'Listen,' I said, 'I'm from a relatively large family, *and* I have a twin …. '

'That gene is strong in your family, right?'

'Right.' I smiled back at her smile. 'Janet, what family doesn't have its problems? But you still loved each other. Don't think that we see cookie-cutter families here. I'm sure yours was better than most.'

'Mum did her best. But there was something about Karen. Since we were twelve and eleven, the dynamic between us changed and we just bickered all the time. I went to grammar school, and while Karen was expected to join me there, she didn't pass the eleven plus. So I went to Bloomfield, she went to Ashfield. That bloody test has a lot to answer for. It was like there was a wall between us. But until today, I didn't see that she actually resented me. I see that now with the diary; Karen thought I would leave and she would be a carer and do nothing more with her life. It's actually like she foresaw some things. Thank God not all things. We used to fight like cat and dog. I'm sure Karen hated me.'

'I'm sure she didn't.'

'I'm sure she did. She told me so often that I had no choice but to believe her.'

I brought Janet's attention back to the diary and the code. 'These are what she did not want you to see.'

Janet exhaled. 'Have we any idea what the code was that she used?'

'Yes, we have enlisted a couple of top code breakers,' I said, 'and these are actually passages where she talks about Willie and Arthur Samuel.'

But they weren't top code breakers, and I wondered at Napier, having the diary for decades and *not* working the code out. Perhaps it wasn't as important to him. Perhaps he did not go into his loft and look at old cases when he retired, and if he did, he just never thought to look at Karen Ward's again.

'It seemed that Karen was having a relationship with Willie Samuel.'

'Alright,' Janet said. 'I suppose he was quite a cute boy. I didn't know him, not well. I knew more of his brother, who was kind of notorious for getting into trouble. Though now I can't think why. The only specific detail I can recall is that he served time for that attempted robbery. But more might come back to me about it. No,' she said suddenly. 'I remember this too, the Chinese Karen and I worked in, got broken into. Someone got in through the roof and tried to steal the takings from the till, but they'd been banked early. That was Artie Samuel! He wasn't a successful career criminal or anything, I remember that.'

'There is one passage, Janet, where Karen talks about Arthur kissing her and her running away.'

Janet's face dropped. 'Thank God,' she said. 'I think God sent you to me, Ms Sloane. Don't I sound religious today? Believe me, I'm not. Not a bit religious.'

'That's okay. It's Harriet, by the way.'

'Harriet, I have a good feeling about this.'

'It doesn't mean Arthur, or Willie, committed any crime against Karen.'

'I don't even mean that. I mean this time around, and I mean you.'

'Me?'

'You're thinking outside of the box. It's more than was done before. When I said how great Mack Napier was, I lied.'

'Oh?'

'I'm not saying he wasn't a very nice person,' Janet got in quickly. 'And thank God he held on to this. There I go with God again! Harriet, ignore me.' Janet thumbed the diary. 'Napier had one man in mind, and for years, I had one man in mind too, and I admit I still do. But … what if?'

I waited for her to finish.

'You are looking at everything, aren't you?' she said.

'We're trying to.'

'You are going to make me look at different possibilities, and that is the way we are going to find him and close the case.'

'Thank you, Janet,' I said. 'I'll certainly try my best. But might I ask, who do you think killed Karen?'

'We all thought it was Wayne Simpson.'

I said nothing. I just didn't think he was the one.

'I'll admit though, Harriet, I'm kind of worried that Karen's name will end up tarnished.'

'What by?' I asked Janet.

'This diary. She was only a young girl. Maybe she'll have written something intimate, about a boy, perhaps, and people will judge her in public. You see these true crime magazines and documentaries; they turn real lives and deaths into intolerably sleazy entertainment.'

'I really don't think it will get to that,' I said, but that was another lie.

'She was used to being compliant,' said Janet, 'trusted her heart rather than her gut. I sometimes think Karen must have thought she was helping someone, for her to have gotten out of the van.'

'Why is that?' I asked.

85

'Because she was told to keep the doors locked. We both were. Our boss Kwong always told us to be safe. But Mum taught us to put others first. A lot of emphases was put on us helping people. Other people were the main thing. It took me a long, long time, Harriet, to learn to protect myself, to put myself first. I still have a hard time doing that now.'

What Janet was saying made sense, but also it didn't since Karen was already home. Of course, she would unlock the van door.

She was seen speaking to someone outside the van. But yes, there was the point: it could have been someone she knew, or perhaps she was being helpful, ignoring a gut feeling about someone she knew was bad news.

'No one will know about the diary, and it's all quite innocent material anyway,' I said.

'I had diaries at the time. I kept one for years, then I gave up.'

'Do you think they might tell us something? Do you think we should take a look at them?'

'I should have brought them with me,' Janet said distantly.

'Can we get them?'

'I can get my daughter Lynne to find them and post them over.'

Chapter 15

We looked at Wayne Simpson's statement again. He was right that his record was clean, and yet it seemed that Mack Napier had been convinced Simpson was guilty here. But why? I could see no reason.

I could see that Mack Napier changed rank in early 1979. A conviction wouldn't have hurt his chances of promotion. Had he wanted to solve this case or just put someone behind bars, and that someone just may as well have been Wayne Simpson? This disposable man, who Mack may have thought added nothing to society: he was an unemployed man, a homemaker, essentially.

I wondered if Napier looked down his nose at such men. Napier certainly tried to charge Simpson a few times, but there was never enough evidence to hold him for long.

Next, I read how the Simpson family was ordered to get out of the area. At one stage, bricks were put through their windows, threatening letters through their door, though Wayne didn't move and he still lived there. His wife left when their marriage broke up, but like he'd told Higgins and me, he still raised his girls there, mainly alone. And why would his ex-wife have let that happen, if she thought he had killed Karen Ward?

It was interesting to me that Janet believed Simpson was guilty, yet I was glad to see her new open-minded approach. But why the sway? Why now? Had she really felt that Napier pushed in the wrong direction?

I wondered if Father would know anything he could tell me about Mack Napier, but Napier was small stuff then and my father the main man. He paid heed more to the dead, the injured, and the bad. Napier was another cog who went unnoticed until they got their man. Or didn't. And during the brief spell that he had Simpson, Napier got his advancement.

Why was this case in the loft, I asked myself? Why was it unsolved? Was Napier covering for someone else? And why was he so set on Wayne Simpson? Had he used all of this evidence at the time, or was it hidden in his loft even way back then?

Chapter 16

DI Posner from Larne PSNI finally called back to give me some interesting information about a suspect in the murder of Rhonda Orr.

'A groundsman at Carnfunnock Country Park, one Nick Flynn, found Rhonda's body back then. Flynn was the chief suspect at the time. Flynn had a troubled past. An alcoholic, he had already been done with indecent exposure.'

Sexual offenders escalate. A first offence of indecent exposure could accelerate to rape. I couldn't deny that.

'Where is he now?' I asked.

'Flynn's dead.'

He couldn't serve time, if it was him that killed Rhonda, and possibly Karen. But at least there might be an answer for two enduring, forgotten-about siblings.

'Why no conviction?' I asked.

'There was no DNA testing then.'

'But there has been since.'

'Flynn died in 1984.'

'That was quite soon after!'

'He had spiralled by then,' said Posner. 'Drunk himself to death.'

'But he has DNA somewhere that can be tested?'

'There were forensic samples taken, swabs of the victim's vagina, anus and mouth.'

'We could do a familial DNA test if Flynn has any living relative.'

'I'll look into it.'

'Thanks. Get back to me.'

'I will,' said DI Posner.

'Promptly, please. I don't know how much longer we can keep this case open.'

'I hear you, DI Sloane,' I heard Posner promise.

At the same time, our good luck appeared. Kate Stile invited me to the lab. DNA we had once thought to be lost or destroyed had been discovered at a private laboratory, she told me.

'Hair,' she said. 'A big clump of hair was found in Karen's hand. She must have grabbed for it while she was being suffocated.'

'Can you test it against the DNA database and against Wayne Simpson?'

'We can.'

'Why is there is no mention of this hair sample anywhere?' I asked.

'There's nothing about hair in the notes you've found?' Stile scowled.

'Nope.' I'd read almost everything, some things many times, and I had read nothing about a sample of hair. 'How did you come across it?' I asked.

'The evidence, on top of not being with everything else, was not properly documented at all.'

'So it hadn't been destroyed,' I said. 'But do you think it was hidden, Kate?'

'I'd have no idea. Are you thinking that Mack Napier was bent, Harry?'

'He seemed to get a promotion off the back of arresting Simpson.'

'Good luck with that end. I'll process this as quickly as I can.'

Kate Stile paused and looked back at me, expecting me to ask her to bump it up the queue. She was forever telling me that every case was important, not just the ones I was heading up. She had been hauled over the coals for giving favours recently. Not for the ones she'd done for our chief, though. 'But, you understand, Harry, I have stuff that is more urgent,' she said.

'No rush,' I said.

'That would be a first.'

Outside I called my father to tell him the news. He answered this time. 'Do you think Mack Napier was trustworthy?' I asked him.

'I don't know,' he said. 'I didn't know him well.'

'He never progressed beyond detective?' I asked.

'Not that I'm aware of. Why?'

'I'm wondering if he hid things. We've had DNA the whole time that could have been tested years ago. Decades ago. It was in a private lab, on its own.'

'What are you saying?' Father sounded softer than usual. I always expected a bit of pushback from him.

'Maybe it was already tested,' I said, feeling unsure, 'and maybe it didn't give Napier the answer he wanted ….'

'That's an interesting hypothesis.'

'It seems like Napier needed Wayne Simpson to be the one.'

'Who is Simpson again?'

'The neighbour. An eyewitness.'

'Oh, yes.'

'Daddy? Thoughts?'

'Well, it wasn't the ultimate object, was it?' he said.

'What do you mean?'

'What year was this again?'

'1978.'

'Oh yes, *Saturday Night Fever*.'

I shrugged to myself.

'Okay, so he'd have been busy in that area,' Father said wearily, 'we were busy in every area with the Troubles going on. Right in the thick. Do you know what was happening at that time?'

'Yes,' I said. I had the utmost respect for how much harder policing was then, how much of a target they were.

'Specifically?' asked Father. 'Prison officers were bearing the brunt. Being killed on their doorsteps. Do you know what I'm saying?'

It was like a kick in the teeth.

'That's awful, of course,' I said, 'but a girl being killed *near* her doorstep, it wasn't as important because it wasn't a tribal thing? Or it wasn't as important because she was a civilian?'

'Stop putting words in my mouth, Harriet,' he said, before I had the chance to ask if it was her gender that made her death less important, or her socio-economic status.

'I am saying that policing was a different job back then. You have no bloody clue about it.'

92

I wrapped up the call with some pleasantries since nothing negative could be said about one of his boys, even one he hardly knew. Maybe his loyalty lay with a Napier woman instead. Father certainly knew them.

The call over, I felt depressed. Now I did not want his help. That time was different, alright. Yet police were still finding bombs under their cars. The old boys of the RUC were never wrong, internally investigated much less. They were also more likely than us to bend truths to fit their actions.

I had made a decision: I marched over to the car and told Higgins that we would remove every box from Napier's loft and search the rest of his house too.

Chapter 17

By Friday afternoon, I had word that a decision had not been made on the search warrant I had requested.

'Probably better you go in there all nicey-nicey anyway,' said Fleur Hewitt, standing over me in the office. 'Go in with a warrant and Napier's widow might get funny.'

'Those case files are not hers in the first place,' I said. 'All that intel should be out of there, or what if she should die – and she is ancient, Fleur – then a random person moves in and has it all?'

Chief Dunne swung his office door open.

'A word, Sloane, now,' he said.

I got up off my seat and walked to his office. Inside I looked out of the window. It was drizzling with rain. Dunne was back in his seat, glowering at me.

'What is all this about Mack Napier and warrants, Sloane?' he asked.

'I have a hunch about him, Chief.'

'Because he duplicated files?'

'Yes. That's part of it.'

'What's the rest?'

'There was no evidence that it was ever Simpson, sir. I think Napier tried to get that to fit.'

'We didn't have DNA then.'

I tried not to roll my eyes. I was fucken sick of having that explained to me like I was born the day before.

'I know that, Chief. But there was nothing, in fact.'

94

He would have been a young copper then. I remembered Greg Dunne telling me once – pillow talk – that he had always worked in Strandtown, and wanted to work there until he would retire, which he already had the option to do years prior, with a full pension. He was still holding on.

'You worked here during the Karen Ward case, initially, Chief?'

'I did, Sloane. And one thing you won't know about Napier is that he was as straight as they come.'

I inhaled. 'Sorry, sir.'

'Drop that line of thinking.'

'But don't you think we should get everything out of his roof space anyway? He had stuff there that we never would have found here, not just duplicates. It was a diary of the victim. He had originals and more. Who knows what else he hid up there.'

Dunne began to fidget with his pen.

'If my father hadn't spoken to Napier's daughter, we would never have ever been privy. There was DNA that we thought lost, sir … that Kate Stile located at a private lab, and why was it there?'

I stopped, having run out of steam. My head was pounding.

'Do you not think we have enough to do with today's workload without taking on the rest?'

'Sir, I don't mean for us to take on more. I just mean to get all that sensitive information out of Napier's house and into a proper place, so if we do reopen anything else –'

'We won't ….'

'I'm saying *if* we do, sir – because that's all Mack had, according to Anna, inconclusive cases and their info – then we know where to get them. Doesn't that make sense? Or am I missing something, Chief?' I sounded accusatory.

'It's a divergent, Sloane, when you should be working on Karen Ward's case.'

'I know, I know this, sir,' I said. 'But on the first day, you said "treat this case like it's your kin".'

He stared at me then. We never acknowledged that our relatively lengthy affair ended in a pregnancy. I often wondered, had it not been for my decision to keep the twins, if we would still be in that farce of a relationship.

Dunne got up and went to his door. I waited to be dismissed. Chief Dunne called out to everyone on the office floor: 'Where is Sarge Simon?'

Chapter 18

Fergus Simon was our resident van driver. He drove while Dunne and I sat side by side on the way to King's Road and Anna Napier's house.

'I hope his missus recognises me,' said the chief. He still hadn't mentioned the attempt on his life almost a week before. I had very nearly woken up on my fortieth birthday to the news that my sons' biological father was killed before they had ever met.

'Wait here,' he told us. He got out of the van and walked to the door. 'I was a young cop, Mack showed me the ropes,' said Greg, warmly, charmingly, in a way that made Simon give me a little look, half-shocked, half-impressed that our boss was capable of acting human for a while. But believe me, he is capable, at least to get what he wants.

Greg Dunne turned and waved at us to approach.

'Charles's girl,' she said to me. 'You are very drawn to that roof space, aren't you! Do you want tea? I'll put the kettle on.'

'No, I'm fine, thank you,' I said.

'I'll take one, Anna, please,' said the chief. 'Simon, Sloane, you can do your best removal men impression.'

'Removal *people*,' Anna Napier corrected him. 'Go on ahead, my loves.'

They sat and caught up in the living room over tea and biscuits while I climbed a ladder up into the loft. This time I was not looking for any one name in particular.

Now I noticed them all: some unfamiliar, some infamous, stuff of local legend. Fear and hope both flourished in my chest. I handed all the boxes down to Fergus Simon, one at a time. Then together, we brought them out to the van while Higgins stayed in the office making calls after much teasing about his fear of heights. At least his fear was evident and socially acceptable; he had taken our banter in good humour.

Anna and Greg were laughing. A lot. It was fascinating to me. Straight away, she had not queried him. Greg may have been a lot older than me, but he was a lot younger than Anna. He was bald with a roman face. Greg had once been the definition of tall, dark and handsome. I saw those twinkly eyes in the faces of my sons. 'We're done, sir,' I said.

In a living room with him for the first time in two and a half years, I wondered if things could ever have been different for us. If we could have been a family. If he didn't already have his own. Though they were grown and did not need him anymore, surely. How close was he to his wife Jocelyn anyway? Could I have been closer? The respect was there, and the sex had been good. I think. Though I was usually drunk during it. That's how it started, and when I thought about it, even when I secretly stayed in his family's villa in the Algarve, I could only be physical with Greg once I had a good supply of wine in me. Retrospectively, I blamed Jason Lucie's attack on me. Now, being around Greg in a domestic setting embarrassed me. It reminded me of how susceptible I had been when we started our affair. It made me shudder to recall.

*

When we got back to Strandtown, Chief Dunne summoned the two newbies, West and Kalnina, and told them to take all the boxes and put them into an empty storeroom stacked in chronological order and labelled correctly, then to give him a list of what there was. And to me, he said, 'Don't start rooting through these, don't get distracted. Just get back to the Karen Ward case.'

'Yes, Chief,' I said reluctantly. 'Thanks for doing this for me.' Dunne looked taken aback. 'I mean, for the case,' I corrected myself.

He handed the van key to Kalnina, then the newbies left to get started.

Higgins moseyed over to me with his hands in his pockets, and his sleeves rolled up. 'Arthur Samuel,' he said, 'he was Willie's brother.'

'Past tense,' I said.

'It's past tense, alright.'

'Shit,' I said, plonking myself down on my seat and taking a sip of water from my bottle that had gone warm.

Higgins pulled a seat up beside me. 'Arthur went to jail at some point for a robbery,' Higgins said, 'but it was more successful than Janet remembered. He and an accomplice managed to lift thousands from a bank in the early eighties. They then went on to intimidate a witness, who was the bank cashier.'

'A woman?' I asked.

'Does it matter?' Higgins shrugged.

'What?'

'Can I finish?'

'Was the cashier a woman?'

'Yes.'

'Okay, proceed, Higgins.' I had a flashback to how much he used to annoy the life out of my previous partner Linskey and me; Diane could not stand to be in the same room as Carl Higgins.

'The cashier didn't listen,' he said, 'she gave evidence against him, and subsequently, Samuel spent five years in prison. He also had a string of cautions, but when I looked him up, I found a death notice for Arthur.'

'Show me.'

Higgins reached for a page he had printed off already. It said that Arthur Samuel had died in 1999.

'I have the nagging feeling we've missed the boat,' I said.

Even if we could get an answer for Janet, or for Barney Orr, if the culprit was dead, then he had died a free man. And that shit hurt almost as much as if he was still walking free. Maybe more because he'll have thought he got away with it.

Chapter 19

That evening, Father was supposed to come to us for dinner, but he called and asked me to come out instead.

'What about the kids?' I asked.

'Don't you have a sitter?' he replied.

My neighbour Lola would help, but it was short notice and she was young, cherished her Friday nights. I would see her leave and hear her come in drunk in the evening. Sometimes I would see Lola out at a bar and we would end up chatting about some drunken shit. I hated to think what we had spoken about when I woke the next day and she waved coyly across the driveway.

'Okay,' I said. 'I'll ask Lola.'

'I have important news,' said Father.

'Really?'

'Charly's coming, and Coral, and Rose. You need to be there, too. You, especially.'

'Really?' I repeated. I had not heard from my sisters since we got back from the chalet on Sunday.

'I told them over the phone so as they wouldn't get shocked,' said Father.

'Told them what?' I asked.

'And they gave me their blessing.'

'For what?' I asked, impatient now.

'I'm getting married,' he said so dryly I thought it was a joke.

'Daddy!' I cried after a peal of laughter.

'I am, and I want you to be nice.'

'Aren't I always?' I had always thought myself the nicest to him, for sure.

'Just remember, Harry, I'm an adult. I'm your father.'

'What are you on about, Daddy? I'm an adult myself. A middle-aged one.'

'Middle-aged!' he scoffed. 'You're a baby. Just meet us at Malone House at eight.'

'Who are you getting married to?' I laughed again, then I stopped; I read once that women fear being murdered by men, and men fear being laughed at by women. I may as well have murdered Father just then and there.

'You'll meet her soon enough if you can drag yourself away from the scrupulous Dr Coulter.' Okay, so he was still harbouring resentment towards Paul for ratting him out.

'Can I come alone if I can't get a babysitter?' I asked him.

'I don't care. Just bring your manners, Harriet.'

I was intrigued, and it turned out that Paul was even more curious. Paul asked Lola to sit for the boys, but as I had guessed she was busy. So he enlisted the services of his mother, undoubtedly to show me that she did want to be a grandmother to my boys. *Our boys*, as I had come to know them, most of the time, until I went to work and had to look at Greg Dunne.

Even if things would not work out with Paul, I would never try to take the twins from him. I had thought about that scenario a lot. Had planned that we could take them week about. Joint custody.

It was an almost tempting arrangement. Very freeing, that split responsibility.

Weekends empty to go to the bar.

'I believe your dad has big news, Harriet,' Paul's mother said when she arrived and set her handbag on the kitchen counter.

'Yes,' I said. 'Must be a whirlwind type of thing.'

'That sounds romantic.' Kaye's face said otherwise. She narrowed her eyes and looked as mystified as I felt.

'I don't know about that,' I said, laughing again, trying to picture Charles Sloane with an ounce of romance in his soul. 'It's the first I'm hearing about a relationship, let alone a serious one.'

Kaye looked horrified at this. What else could this demented family do to horrify this careful woman?

'Where are you going?' she asked.

'Malone House,' I said.

'I love it there. Lucky you!'

The last time I was there was with Jason. His mother loved the place, too.

From one mother-in-law to another, I thought. I'm afraid I hadn't made a good impression on either. I hadn't meant to make it that way. I guess I was just not a very pliable person.

'Heard you and Mum chatting when I was getting ready. See, she does like you.' Paul smiled to himself as he drove. 'You were laughing a lot.'

'I'm not bothered what she thinks of me,' I said. 'I just want her to love the boys.'

'And she does.'

103

'They have no grandmother now.'

'They do. She is it.'

He certainly talked a good game, but you sense what you sense.

I thought of that bomb under Greg's car and how he could have been killed and never once met his sons. The night before, the New IRA claimed responsibility.

'We were unlucky this time, but we only have to be lucky once,' said the statement they sent to the Irish News.

I was angry; at the end of the day – at the start of the day – it was only a job. No one deserves to live like that. We were still doing what my father had done, checking under our cars. In some respects, it was still 1978, and we were back to feeling afraid.

I was relieved he was okay, and Greg, typical of him, was stoic and acted like he wasn't vexed, and at one point in my life, I would have been devastated by this attempt. Now, I had to move on. Move up.

*

In the restaurant, I saw Charly first. She had cut her hair up to her chin and looked so chic. Mine was neglected, longer than usual, greying at the roots. I hadn't dyed it in ages, but Charly looked great, making me remember that I had put on weight. Suddenly I felt thick in the thighs, boobier than usual, while my twin looked trim. But grim too, I have to say. Charly was biting her bottom lip, and through her concentrated stare, was trying to send me some twin telepathic wave.

She had not been fond of Father since the whole assisted death episode. But then again, she always was a mummy's girl.

Coral and her partner Rose were chatting across the table to each other. Paul took my hand in his, a thing he sometimes did in public to show everyone how together we were. I almost pulled away, but I was distracted, especially when Coral looked at me, widened her eyes and shook her head.

I reached the table and said, 'What is going on?' when I heard a woman's voice say, 'Hello Harriet, long time no see.'

I looked to the side and saw Jason's mother, Yvonne.

There was that fear I always had when I thought of her son. It was somatic, the need to run away and hide. But I couldn't; Paul was still holding my hand. He put his other one forward to introduce himself and shake her hand.

'Yvonne Lucie,' she said.

'Lucie?' Paul looked at me.

My married name. I had never taken it professionally. I had barely wanted it at all, so proud to be my father's daughter; fuck the nepotism accusations.

In front of Yvonne, I froze. Father came from the bar where he had been ordering champagne.

'Oh, you made it in the end,' he said.

'We're not late,' I said defensively.

He gave me his best don't-backchat-me look.

They both sat and it hit me; Yvonne was at Mother's funeral a year before, even though none of the Lucies had kept in touch after Jason and I split.

Which I was grateful for.

I am stupid, I thought. Of course, Father always had a bit on the side. Just like Greg.

It dawned on me that Father had not been celibate all those long years mother was ill. He was not the kind of man to make sacrifices. This was no whirlwind; he and Yvonne had been together. Who knew for how long.

Had he hurried my mother's death along so he could make it official? Could he not tell how much it would hurt me to have a Lucie in my life? But then, no one knew about what Jason had done to me, the kidnapping, keeping me hostage, the rapes, and after that, the stalking, and harassment.

I still had a scar on my head and a chipped tooth, but much worse inside me. I'd had to change numbers, email addresses and all my routines, to try to wipe him from my life as best I could. And now here they were, about to bring him in.

I recognised then that my sense of dread – all those dreams – had been a forewarning, and I'm not usually a believer in such things. I had sensed I would see Jason, he was never far from my mind, and I could not cope. Would he and his brother Alex walk in or Alex's wife Verity or their kids?

My chest closed up. I released my grip on Paul's hand and walked out, leaving him there. I jumped into a taxi outside.

'Hard?' the taxi driver asked.

'Hard?' I asked. 'Erm, yes, Hard.'

Howard, he'd been saying, as in the surname.

'Finaghy is it?' he asked.

'Change of plan, can you take me into town instead?'

He winced, then said, 'Of course I can, love.'

I called Fleur and asked her where she was. If she wanted company. I got the taxi to drop me off at the Dirty Onion.

Chapter 20

On Saturday morning, I woke in the downstairs bedroom. The night before a blank. I only knew that I had got sloshed. Then bit by bit, I remembered the outdoor fairy lights that ran from wall to wall overhead in the cathedral quarter. Fleur putting me in a taxi home. My stupid father. Yvonne Lucie, of all people!

'Are you okay?' Paul asked me. He was in the kitchen in his pyjamas, giving the boys their breakfast.

'No, not at all,' I said.

'That was a shock, huh?'

'You don't understand,' I said.

'Then make me understand.'

I made a coffee and sat at the table with it, looked at the mushed banana around Jared's hands, feeling like I was going to heave.

'I can't understand if you don't tell me.'

'I don't want Jason back in my life.'

'I understand that,' he said. 'Boy, your family!'

'What?'

'Nothing is normal with them, is it?'

'What's normal anyway?' I asked.

'I can see you're spoiling for a fight.'

'No. I'm not,' I said.

'Good.'

'Paul? Do you reckon he … you know … *finished* Mummy so he could marry Yvonne?'

'I wouldn't be surprised.'

'Nor would I.'

'That's why you left.'

I didn't answer and Paul seemed sated.

He gave me a hug. He was too understanding without understanding a thing.

*

In work, there was a delivery for me from England; three diaries of Janet Ward's. The things people keep for a long time astounds me. I'm not a hoarder by any stretch. I had already given the twins' baby clothes away to charity. I was done, maternally. Plus, now I was forty. That had always been my cut-off point. I already felt too old to be a newish mother.

I would never have held onto something from my teens, I cringed just to think about what I would have written back then. Obsessing about some boy whose name and face I could not remember by the time I was twenty-five? And for Janet to bring these chronicles to England with her – presumably from house-to-house, if she moved much over there – they must have meant something to her.

I supposed her teenage years were marred in a big way that felt worthy of documenting, whereas I was lucky that mine were cheap and unimportant.

I set the diaries out and put them in year order, 77 – 79. When Janet arrived, having received my text that we had received them, she asked if she could Sellotape certain pages together that were embarrassing.

'If you don't mind.'

I gave her some time alone with her recollections.

'All good?' I asked when I revisited her in the meeting room ten minutes later.

'Yes,' she said. 'I was worried that I wrote some cheesy content, but it's okay.'

She had made use of the Sellotape notwithstanding.

'And you are definitely happy for me to look through your diaries, Janet?'

'Yes,' she said. 'Though I don't know how helpful they'll be.'

After she left, I skimmed Janet's diary for 1978, hoping to see a mention of the Samuel brothers, but there was none. This ever-growing pile of paperwork and diaries around me felt crushing, and I was still kind of tipsy. I made another coffee and took a discrete spritz of mint breath freshener.

I skimmed 1978 again, looking for the words *sister* or *Karen* and found plenty. It didn't make for happy reading. Janet was correct when she said they had a wall between them, but Janet bitched about Karen more than Karen had bitched about her. Janet's entries were shorter and snappier than Karen's. Some days were left blank entirely, some weeks too.

This was her entry on the night her sister was killed, but not yet found:

Finally had a night off work. Karen was pissed off when Kwong asked her to work instead. She said yes to him, but if it was me asking, that wee bitch would've told me where to go.

Why would she say yes to Kwong? I thought.

Higgins was looking at the diary from the year before.

———

'Every time she mentions Karen before her death, it's negative, aggrieved,' I told him.

'You don't know what you've got till it's gone,' he replied.

After the death, there was nothing reported for a month, then in December 1978, Janet said plenty about Wayne Simpson. The first penned acknowledgement of the crime. Janet stated how hard it was to live beside him, how he showed no remorse, and how everyone thought he had something to do with 'it'. She didn't address the event itself, that her sister had been killed. She noted palpable pleasure after Simpson's first arrest, and a sense of misery after his release.

In mid-December, Janet recorded her mother going into hospice. She didn't make any note of Michelle Brown's killing.

The ensuing diary was from 1979, which began with Pearl's death. I skimmed to the start of June, egotistically pondering what was happening in Janet's life the day I was born, but the diary was blank from April onward, petering out once she moved to London that February.

Chapter 21

'Do you see anything about the Samuel brothers in the 1977 edition?' I asked Higgins.

'Not yet,' he said, fixated on the earliest diary. 'I'm reading about Janet's babysitting jobs. She'd often write about minding two kids called Kenny and Anita.'

'Kenny, Carl,' I said. 'The little boy who phoned the police – the eyewitness – he was called Kenneth.'

'I know.' Higgins nodded at the board where there was a blank space under Kenneth's name. The other two artist sketches stared at us ominously.

'Did Karen ever babysit Kenny and Anita?'

'Sometimes,' said Higgins. 'She would go to keep Janet company.'

I didn't want to talk to Janet again so soon. I made a note to contact her later and ask about these children, Anita and Kenneth. For now, the Samuel brothers were what I wanted to focus on.

'I need another coffee. Want one?' I asked Higgins.

'No thanks,' he said.

I was at the coffee machine when Constable Dylan West came and stood uneasily beside me.

'We've found something, ma'am,' said West, 'one of those boxes, it has stuff about Karen Ward inside.'

I followed him to the store where Kalnina was standing gawping at the box. He moved aside when I came through the door. They had labelled many boxes, case names and years as instructed.

This one was not labelled.

'We opened it and saw the name,' said Kalnina.

I looked inside and saw a statement from one Kwong Li. 'Good spot, officers,' I said, taking it with me. I grabbed my abandoned coffee then set the box in front of Higgins. 'Ready for more?' I asked him.

'Is that another box?'

'Certainly looks like one,' I said, tilting it. 'Kwong Li's statement,' I said, seizing it from the top, 'the owner of the Silver Sea.'

There was an attached list of food orders that Karen had delivered that evening of 6th November. Only three. The last one on Ladas Drive, like Janet had told us.

Higgins extracted a few black, bound books and records. These had not been duplicated but looked to be originals.

'Oh, you beauty,' Higgins said, opening one of the books. 'These are Napier's journals.'

'Really?' I grabbed another one.

Inside it was his thoughts on the case, diagrams of the murder scene, theories he had tried out on the page. He had never let this case go. Maybe Napier was a good guy after all.

At the bottom of the box was reams of information with the name Samuel.

'Bingo,' I said.

'If we'd only found this box first,' Higgins said with a sigh. It pissed me off.

'This box was not with the other two,' I said. 'I checked the nearby boxes over and over again. There was no way I missed this.'

'Maybe it was somewhere else.'

'Good thing I insisted on emptying that loft,' I said, dying to tell the chief what had been unearthed.

'Still feels like a waste of time,' said Higgins.

'None of this investigation is a waste,' I said, 'how can it be when it's been us painting our own picture?'

'Okay,' Higgins said, not listening. I could tell. 'Here are newspaper clippings about Arthur Samuel's arrest and sentencing.'

There were also those four oblique diary entries of Karen's; I recognised those once-baffling paragraphs. These were not in her handwriting but Mack Napier's. He had worked it out wrongly, many times, and then correctly.

No letter S! he had scrawled.

'Napier had cracked Karen's code,' I said to Higgins.

But despite my protestations, I did feel like our work was a waste; all that energy being given to the same case generation after generation, and no real headway being made. My chest began to hurt. I tried to breathe slowly, discreetly. I remembered the feeling of seeing Yvonne.

'Are you okay?' asked Higgins.

'Fine, why?'

'You seem a bit .... '

'What?'

'Like you're in pain or something.

'I'm not,' I said.

But I was in pain. My anxiety had spilt into my working day. Even though I tried to throw myself into work, I had been thinking non-stop about Jason since I woke.

I looked at our board and breathed through my nose. There was Wayne Simpson, *DNA result pending*, and Kate Stile off for the weekend. There were Willie Samuel and Arthur Samuel – persons of interest. Nick Flynn, another. *Groundsman at Carnfunnock. Deceased.* Kwong Li. *Owner of Silver Sea. Deceased.* Eyewitness: Kenneth, aged 9. I wrote the name Anita beside his name. Then I wrote *Tucker Brown*.

'You want to go there?' asked Higgins.

'I want to go there,' I said, my guts griped.

'Let's hope it doesn't come to that,' he said. 'I'm done looking at his face already.'

I rubbed the name out again. We couldn't work on this case forever; if we didn't see results soon, the case would close again. Then came a sense of horror that was so known to me by then. I was sinking. I wanted a cold, quiet room, darkness and a drink.

'Unless … ' said Higgins. 'Was it possible Tucker's mother gave this description of the person she claims was talking to Karen just to throw the light off her son? And that it caught up with her?'

'It's all possible at this stage,' I said, believing that we were looking at the person, or at least the name of a person, with all the answers.

I wrote Tucker's name up again and felt a shortness of breath. I excused myself.

'Are you going to grab lunch?' Higgins shouted after me. I couldn't speak, couldn't let him see my face. I lifted my arm to wave as nonchalantly as I could.

Then, when I'd calmed, I made a call to Martin and texted Higgins from my car that I'd be back in an hour.

Chapter 22

I drove to Upper Newtownards Road to see Dr Martin Walsh, a therapist I'd known to help people struggling with their mental health. I'd always thought it sounded like a good idea to talk about problems, but I had not followed that path. I could not, until that day. But I liked and trusted Martin, who I'd met while working a previous case when he had stayed quiet about his patients, almost to his detriment. In that regard, I thought we were alike.

'Thanks for seeing me during the weekend,' I told him when I entered his room, soggy from the showers outside. Martin was wearing his civvies, jeans and a tee.

'You sounded like you needed to talk,' he said.

'I think so,' I said, taking a seat.

Think about the last time you were here, I told myself, how you have your shit together much more. But no, I hadn't. Different shit, same lack of togetherness.

'On the phone, Harriet, you said you felt panicky and … well, you tell me.'

I was helpless, and abruptly I did not like Martin quite so much.

'I think I have PTSD,' I said casually, rummaging through my bag for nothing, just to avoid thinking about what I was saying. 'Is there something you can give me, an exercise to do or a script? Not that I'm a big fan of medication …. '

'Maybe you should have gone to your GP.'

'I rarely go to the doctor.' I zipped my bag up.

'How I work is by exploring what it is at the core, not by putting a sticking plaster on and hoping for the best. I work with the people who come to see me by talking, exploring the root cause.'

I picked at my fingernails. They were a mess to match the rest of me.

'Why do you think you have PTSD?' he asked.

'I'm just ... easily kind of ... spooked. I used to run and now I can't.'

'When was the last time you ran?'

'Very recently.'

'Then you sound like you're coping.'

'No. I've told myself that's it. I'm done.'

'Would you join a running group?'

Anger boiled inside me. 'Martin, I think I'm wasting time, yours and mine, and work's.'

'You're working today?'

'Yes, working on my day off. It's the only time I feel normal ... usually.'

'Why is that?'

'I don't have time to dwell there.'

'Dwell on what?'

'Umm.'

'Take a tissue.'

'No. I'm fine.' I sniffed.

'What is it, Harriet?'

'I had a bad situation a few years back. I was held hostage.'

Martin Walsh sat forward and looked concerned.

'I see,' he said. 'That is a lot to deal with. Can you tell me more about it? How long were you a hostage for?'

'Four days.' I looked at my hands.

Martin squinted at me, then relaxed his face. 'Can't you get counselling through work?' he said with great softness, great effort to not be hard or questioning.

'I have trust issues,' I said. 'So, impartial advice would be good. Plus, it's not work-related.'

'Where did this happen to you?'

'At home.'

'Who held you hostage?'

'My … husband. My then-husband.'

'Okay.' Martin looked perplexed. 'I thought you were here over the shooting.'

I looked at him.

'You were shot on duty last year, weren't you, by … ?'

'Yes,' I said, 'but that doesn't annoy me and it never did.'

He gripped his chin like I was fascinating to him. 'Was your marriage abusive, Harriet?'

'Not particularly,' I said. 'No … I don't think so. No.'

Martin frowned.

'He had a breakdown. It came out of nowhere. He wanted a baby and I didn't, and he realised that I was still taking precautions. It spiralled from there.'

'That's no excuse.'

'I'm not making excuses for him,' I said. 'He raped me during those days, absolutely determined to make me pregnant, and he did.'

Martin's face was now neutral.

'I had a termination, which I should probably feel bad about but I don't.'

'Harriet, there is no right or wrong way to feel. You know you were the victim here?'

'It's not a label I want.'

'Nobody wants to be hurt,' he said. 'Have you ever been advised – by a colleague, perhaps, or a friend – to press charges.'

I shook my head

'Why not?' he asked.

'Why what?'

'Haven't you pressed charges?'

'You don't get to ask me that,' I said.

I could have asked him if his wife ever found out who he was screwing. But I didn't care. I just didn't like his question. I had more reasons than Martin knew. 'I'm not going to defend myself here,' I said.

'I apologise,' Martin said. 'I would like to help you, give you space to talk about what happened. It looks to me like you have buried this trauma, but it has decided to surface now, for one reason or another.'

'Do you think it's PTSD?'

'Let's steer clear of premature diagnoses. What matters is that you have spoken about it. That's a step forward.'

'I'll feel better about it now?' I asked, sounding naïve.

'No,' he told me. 'Not right away. That was a harrowing experience. I don't have to tell you that.'

'No, you don't.'

'But you need to be kind to yourself. *Have* you ever told anyone about what happened?'

'I almost did recently,' I said, thinking of the night before. I was tempted to tell Fleur. But then I knew she'd be like, let's get the bastard, let's do him, be strong. I didn't have it in me. I just wanted the noise to simmer down and eventually disappear. At first, I just wanted to live. After that … well let's just say I knew enough about our judicial system not to trust it.

Just like doctors are the worst patients, detectives are the worst victims.

I didn't want to cry over what had happened or be precious. There was nothing worse in my mind. Besides, no one had died, after all. And what doesn't kill you makes you stronger, right? I just wanted that new strength to hurry up and kick in, do its thing. My life was too busy to give this attention.

Chapter 23

I didn't feel quite so bad after my session with Martin. Like I'd been to the chiropractor to work out some knots in my spine and was walking out a little straighter and much less tense. Higgins was excited about what he had located in the bottom of the newly-found box.

'Look,' he said, 'this is a letter Arthur Samuel sent to his brother Willie from jail. And there are lots of musings about Anita Hall.'

'Is that Kenneth's sister?'

'That's her.'

'Okay, one thing at a time,' I said, looking at the letter.

Thanks for writing to me so quick again. You know how your letters keep me sane in here. I miss you a whole lot. You keep saying you're worried about me, well, don't worry. It's not the worst in here. I put myself here, so I can't be angry with anyone. But still and all, I am angry, Willie. I'm angry about the sin. I know we spoke about it that time, but for some reason writing it down is easier than saying it out loud. What happened plays on my mind. I try to forget, like you said to. It's easier said than done! I try to stay upbeat for you, I know that's what you want to hear, that I'm doing alright. And I am, most days. Not today, but tomorrow is a new day, sure. Arthur.

'How did Napier get this?' I asked.

'A prison warden, Stanley Vincent, thought he should see it. And here.'

Higgins opened one of the black journals where he had bookmarked it. 'Mack Napier writes here that he will talk to a psychologist about what 'the sin' could be.'

'And did he?'

'He doesn't say. I can't find a written reply from one.'

'We need to speak to Beulah McGarrity,' I said.

Higgins stared vacuously.

'Beulah's an excellent forensic psychologist I've dealt with in the past. She blows my mind with what she knows. I'll pick her brain.'

I took a scan of the letter from Arthur to William and emailed it to her. Then, with that done, I read Anita's statements.

*

By five p.m. that Saturday, I had managed to track down Kenneth Hall, our then-child eyewitness. He was now living in a supported living facility off Crumlin Road. I told Higgins to finish for the day, but I was afraid to leave in case my anxiety returned.

I drove past the old gaol-turned-visitor-centre to the ordinary bungalow in an ordinary street. A social worker named Carmel let me. She had already explained on the phone that another man usually lived there with Kenneth, but that he was at *home* for the weekend.

People could be in supported living for many reasons, drug or alcohol use problems, at risk from violence, care leavers.

Carmel had told me that Kenneth lived there because he was severely disabled.

She brought me through to the living room and introduced us, then she went to check the stove where she was making a stir fry, breaking noodles up into a pot of boiling water as the extractor fan whirred and the windows steamed up. Carmel kept watch.

'Kenneth, this nice lady is here to have a chat with you,' she said.

Kenneth was a small man, fair-haired. He sat on the sofa and smiled at me. When he moved, the plastic frill of an incontinence pad that sat above his jeans rustled against the hem of his thin green jumper.

'I believe you lived in Sandhill Park when you were a little boy,' I said.

Kenneth only smiled.

'You knew a girl called Karen Ward?'

There was no response.

'Maybe something will register,' said Carmel.

There was a photo of him as a boy on top of the TV cabinet; I could not mistake that enormous smile. In the photo, he was holding a huge trout. 'Do you like fishing?' I asked him, to which there was no reply. 'I used to go fishing with my father when I was little.'

'That's was our stepdad. One of many, they say.'

This voice came from the woman who had appeared at the door.

'This is Anita,' Carmel said. She turned off the extractor fan so we could all hear each other.

'Nita!' shouted Kenny.

'Hello,' I said, standing. I was keen to speak to her too. 'I'm Detective Inspector Harriet Sloane.'

'I'm Anita Hall,' she said. I could not tell if she was taking the piss at my formal introduction.

'Oh, look, Kenny, you have a lovely surprise visitor for dinner. Siblings don't normally visit,' Carmel explained to me, 'but you have a good sister, don't you, Ken?'

'Good … sissy,' he said. Then added 'juice', like a child. *Juice* with a little rise at the end, for which he raised his shoulders to emphasise the question. When he spoke, it was in less-than-sentences.

The month prior, the twins' health visitor had sent them birthday cards, listing the things they should be able to do aged two. One of them was 'starting to put sentences together'. Which they were. Poor Kenneth, his language skills were less developed than Rowan and Jared's. How in the world could he help with our investigation?

'Come get juice, Kenny,' said Carmel.

I asked if I could speak with Anita in a different room, she said yes, but Kenneth kept calling her back. Carmel came and distracted him, asking him to help her set an extra place at the table for Anita, which he seemed delighted to do.

'You can use the staff room,' Carmel directed us.

Anita led me into a small bedroom with a baby monitor on the bedside table and a filing cabinet in the corner. Anita sat on the single bed, I sat on the chair by the desk.

'I'm here about Karen Ward,' I said.

'Oh. I remember Karen,' said Anita, blinking excitedly. 'You were friends?'

'My mum liked the men rather than to look after us, people say.'

'Do they?' I thought her reply irrelevant.

'Janet and Karen used to babysit us during the times in between. Sometimes my mum got a man and would get him to look after us while she went out looking for another man.' Anita laughed and blinked.

'Kenneth was an eyewitness at the time Karen died,' I said.

'He probably forgets now.'

'May I ask what happened to your brother?'

'He drank something from under the sink.'

'He must have drunk something bad,' I said.

'Something for the car engine ....'

'Oil?'

'No. Anti ....'

'Antifreeze?' I asked in disbelief.

'That's it,' said Anita.

'Do you think Kenneth poured the drink himself?'

Anita's eye twitched. 'I don't like to talk about this.'

'I understand, it's not pleasant,' I said. 'I'm sure Carmel told you why I'm here.' I realised she had called Anita knowing I was coming. 'I hear Karen and her sister Janet looked after you when you were younger.'

Anita didn't react.

'Who would have babysat for you the most, out of the Ward sisters?' I asked her.

'Who's the blonde one?'

I remembered Karen's photo and her light brown hair. Janet's had the same colouring now. 'I'm not sure,' I said.

'One had brown hair, one had blonde. The older one was blonde.'

'That's Janet.'

'She stopped babysitting, and then it was her wee sister.'

'Karen.'

'She was murdered,' said Anita.

'Well, yes. That's what I'm here about,' I said. 'It's been forty-one years, but we're reinvestigating.' She nodded at me earnestly. 'We want to crack the case.'

'I'm sorry I said all those things.'

'What things?'

'I can't remember now. I got in a lot of trouble.'

'Who did you get into trouble with?'

'The police said I was wasting time.'

'You had theories about what happened?'

'Theories?' Anita blinked heavily, and I realised she had a tic. Something screwing with her eyelid muscles.

'You had ideas about what happened to Karen. Or maybe you saw something?'

'I don't know. Mum lost us then.'

'Your mother lost what? Custody of you and Kenneth? Is that what you are saying, Anita?'

'Yes, there was that court stuff.'

'And was this because of what happened to Kenneth, his accident? Or was it for some other reason?'

'She was never around. That's what everyone says.'

'Anita. Do you remember Karen Ward having a boyfriend? Someone who might have come to the house to babysit with her, maybe once you kids went to bed.'

'I wasn't much younger than Karen. I didn't need a babysitter.'

'What year were you born, Anita?'

'1963.'

'And Kenneth?'

'I'm the oldest, by six years.'

'So you were fifteen, and Karen was seventeen.' It did seem strange that Anita needed a sitter or wouldn't be trusted to mind her younger brother.

'When did Kenneth have his accident?'

'He was nine or nearly nine.'

'What did he see the night Karen died?'

'A man.'

'Can you remember any more details than that?'

'No,' Anita said, and then Kenny came to the door to announce it was time for 'dins'.

Chapter 24

That evening, just before I left for home, good news dropped on my lap. DI Posner from Larne PSNI called me back.

'We've found a living nephew of Nick Flynn, the groundsman at Carnfunnock. We are going to test him for familial DNA.'

I thanked him, feeling upbeat for ten minutes until I got a text from an unknown number, which I read in the driveway at home. This is from Jason, I thought instantly, but it was not. It appeared to be his mother, Yvonne, inviting me to an 'all-family engagement party' the following night.

I think you and Jason can put your differences aside for one night, don't you? she asked and gave all the details of the party they were going to have at her favourite place, Malone House. She signed off, *Y*.

But *was* it her texting? I had an awful feeling Jason was trying to lure me there. I was being paranoid.

'What's up?' asked Paul when I walked through the door, my face like thunder.

'They are having an engagement party,' I said.

'Your dad and …. '

'Yvonne.'

'When?'

'Tomorrow.' I showed him the text. I had deleted the ones from Jason long ago, in an effort not to drive myself mad reading and re-reading them.

In the house, I poured myself a glass of wine, and Paul gave me a disapproving look. 'Want something to eat first?'

'I've eaten,' I said going into the playroom with the guard on the door.

'Are you in your little prison, boys?' I asked them, letting myself in.

'It keeps them safe,' said Paul with something of an attitude. 'Stops them going into the hall and climbing up the stairs.'

'Hi, babies,' I said, and I sat on the floor beside them. 'Did you both have a good day?' They barely acknowledged me. They were wearing blue and green versions of the same pyjamas.

'Really,' I said, 'you dressed them like twins?'

'They are twins,' said Paul.

It was my pet peeve; I remembered Charly and I being dressed the same. I hadn't bought two of anything, it made no sense, but Paul's mother had purchased these, different colours albeit because she knew I hated them to look like Tweedle Dee and Tweedle Dum, but the same outfit nevertheless.

'We had a great day,' said Paul.

I wanted to say, I'm asking the boys, only they were too young to tell me, and so he had to. But I didn't want Paul around me, making complicated things easy.

I wanted to wallow and feel pity for myself, but I could not be angry about Yvonne when I was around my boys. Eventually, they seemed to notice me. Once Rowan came over to drive a toy car over my leg, Jared decided he wanted the other leg.

Already rivalling with one another. I noticed my glass was empty and got up, went back into the kitchen.

'What did you eat?' Paul called after me.

'You're not my father,' I said.

'I'm not a father at all,' said Paul. 'Except when it suits you.'

'I allow you to make decisions,' I said when I got back to the playroom, glass in hand. 'I don't know what your problem is.' I took a sip of Merlot.

'I don't have a problem,' said Paul.

'I can't make them yours. They just are.'

Paul smiled; he seemed to enjoy that. If I said it often enough, he would stop being insecure about it. What did he want? He got with a pregnant woman. Pregnant doubly. If anyone had problems out of the two of us, it was him. He wanted *this*.

We got the boys sorted separately until Paul acted like I was already drunk and took Rowan off me, arguing that his nappy was too loose, and that last time I did that, he baptised the bed. I was tired and weary. I'd had a mammoth day emotionally.

That night I sat in the playroom and watched TV among all the toys while Paul spent his evening in the main living room. I brought my glass, a corkscrew and a new bottle with me to save me the repeat journeys, so he wouldn't be counting units, bringing it up the next day. It was Saturday night, after all. A girl has to get her kicks somehow. The drunker I got, the better I felt.

I woke on the sofa in the early hours. I'd had a dream about Jason. He was blindfolded and tied up in the chalet. Then someone held him down in the lough.

131

That someone might have been me.

I shook the sleep off, looked at my phone. The birds outside were cheeping. The sun was coming up. I noticed the light was flashing on the house phone. We had missed calls on the landline from a withheld number, and there were three silent voice messages on my mobile phone. It started to ring as I looked at it. I answered, but did not speak.

'You fucken whore,' came his voice.

The sound of it made me have to run and be ill in the downstairs loo.

Chapter 25

Later that Sunday morning, I checked my emails. Beulah McGarrity had replied. She was interested in the case and wanted to chat straight away. I messaged her asking for a visit, but she was away at a conference. Beulah asked me to scan any other letters between the two parties and attach them to the email. When I told her that was the only one we had, Beulah said she would Skype with me in an hour.

I had coffee and a shower, watched the boys and waited for her call.

'It's a sibling-to-sibling letter,' she said.

'How do you know that?'

'I can tell from the language, there is a familiarity that family members have, they can talk about things without being specific.'

'What do you think 'the sin' is?' I asked, saying nothing about jail or stealing or that it was brothers involved.

'The mention of sin is usually sexual,' said Beulah.

'Really?'

'I would wager.'

'Could it be violent? A murder, perhaps?'

'Murder, of course, is a sin, but usually, this word is related to something of a sexual nature. They both know 'the sin' and so they don't mention what it is.'

'How do we find out what it is?'

'Can't you ask them?' said Beulah.

'One is dead.'

'Then ask the other?'

*

The rain started again, only this time with more commitment. Paul said he wanted to go out for a while. I think he could just not bear to be around me. He took his gym bag and made sure to tell me that he would be back in time for the engagement party, so I had all day to think about it and decide if I would go or not go.

On the one hand, why would I want to? What if Jason was there? But then again, it was my chance to shame him. To face him and finally put the whole thing to bed. The entire day I couldn't think about anything else. And then the landline went at lunchtime, and it was him again.

'I'm warning you, you whore!' Jason spat.

I hung up and pulled out the wire from the wall. I sat shaking. He must have asked his mother for my landline and she must have found it out. It was Charly's old number; this was her old house. Yvonne must have told him where I lived. Suddenly, I remembered the tight, impatient looks she would give my father in the past when he was acting tight and impatient himself. There was no way she loved him. They were too alike. My mother was the opposite. Yvonne was none of the things Mother was. But Yvonne was not 'bad', and I had even liked her and the rest of his family a lot, at one stage.

I couldn't now. Jason might have been her son, but as another woman, she should have told him that he did not need my number, and told him to move on.

And then I knew it. She *had* told him that very thing. So he had gone and asked my father, and Father had always liked Jason hugely.

Jason was incredibly, blindingly charming.

And out of everything Jason Lucie had done, this, right now, took the biscuit. He was still trying to ruin me. That is the nature of domestic violence; there is no end to it. Those vindictive bastards can hold on to hate and bitterness like their hands are superglued to it.

I called our phone company and changed our landline number, planning to only inform the day nursery and Paul. Anyone else had my mobile number, which I continued to block him on.

I played with the boys and had a couple of glasses of wine before Paul came in. My mood was such that I did not intend to go to the party, but the minute he came home, still harbouring my crap mood, I grabbed my bag and went to Malone House.

Chapter 26

It was a lovely clear evening, and I could have walked for hours. I left that thought at the door and walked into a function room of familiar older people: RUC men and fashionable older ladies, friends of Father and Yvonne. Alex and Verity approached me. I nearly saw them double.

'Do you know what is going on, Harry?' asked Alex.

'They're getting on in years, it's about companionship at that stage,' said Verity and then she paused, considered me and said, 'Harry, I've missed you.'

She tried to hug me, but I couldn't see her without seeing Jason, so I pulled back. Verity's eyes grew with something like guilt but more like pity.

'Terribly sad about you and Jace,' said Alex and Verity shot him a look. 'I know it's water under the bridge by now, but you were family.'

'She's going to be family again,' said Verity rubbing my arm awkwardly. I looked at her hand, and she pulled it away. 'Harry, I want to apologise.'

'What for?' I asked, aware of my words slurring, and of my legs that were like jelly. But my brain felt as switched on as ever.

'We wanted to reach out to you,' said Alex.

'For years,' said Verity, 'but we didn't. We didn't know how we could since you guys split so badly. Couldn't say your name around Jason that he would sob. He was a broken man.'

I laughed at the manipulation of it all.

'But good to see you looking so well,' said Alex.

Fat, he meant. I looked him up and down.

'Haven't you aged badly?' I said.

Verity laughed, thinking I was being funny, but I wasn't. He had. Alex just stared at me.

'Seriously?' he asked.

I punched his arm playfully. 'Sure, Verity isn't fussy,' I said, and they both laughed. I excused myself.

My sisters were chatting to people. They looked sombre. There was Gus, Coral's son, and Charly's kids, wee Timothy in his wheelchair.

I waited at the bar with an eye on the door, waiting for Jason. I couldn't let him creep up behind me. Spit the word *whore* into my ear in person. I'd knock him out if he tried.

As I sat drinking, random people came up and asked me about the twins or about having been shot, some old ex-RUC officer wanted to share war stories, and I was tempted to slip my shoulder out of my top, show my scar and ask if it did it for him, but I didn't. It was a free bar. I ordered another wine and looked back at the door.

Then a woman appeared next to me. I didn't know her but she knew me. She had been friends with Yvonne for a long time, she said. She asked me about work and where I lived now.

'I don't know,' I said. 'Where do you live? What's your address?'

The woman looked at me strangely and then excused herself.

The red mist was always over my eyes back then. And I could not remember these people who came to chat, to find out who I was now, who wanted to see my scars and judge how well they had healed or not. I suppose they had watched the noteworthy parts of my life with interest, because of who my parents were. My head was spinning, and I thought, *Harry, girl, you are blocked. Father told you to bring your manners. Smile and nod.* I could do neither.

I looked back at the door. Jason still did not arrive. My nieces and nephews sat at a table, staring at their devices. I went and sat beside them. I stared at the door and out of windows, at great big, unfocused distances of my past. It was there I saw everything: Jason shaking on the floor, pulling at his hair. I saw how selfish he was. How he should have gone down solo, had his breakdown alone. Had he done that, he'd have garnered sympathy.

How could I ever hide from him in this tiny province? I would not move out of the city I loved. I would not move out of my family, though they all ignored me, and I was guilty of doing the same to them.

I looked at the kids of my sisters and remembered being afraid that Jason might kill them while trying to get to me. Which was why I had gone to the chalet after the assault and not to the family. I had kept to myself, careful and dignified.

This moment of quiet pride passed when Yvonne smiled, showing off her ring. Fuck well-mannered, her son had ruined my life.

I had once been a different person. A more trusting person. A person I had liked. Now, I hated myself. Because of Jason.

I went back to the bar, where I ordered a couple of shots of tequila from the barman, who gave me a dubious look but served me anyway. *What damage can happen at an elderly couple's engagement party?* he was thinking, no doubt.

Then I downed them both and stumbled towards Yvonne.

'Did you give him my landline number?' I asked.

'Who?' she said, acting innocent.

'Your rapist son,' I said.

That got attention. Everyone gathered around me. I felt a hand on my arm.

'Did you give your rapist, wife-beating son my landline number?'

Yvonne was gawking at me.

'Are you okay?' asked Charly. It was her hand on my arm.

'No. No, I'm not,' I said. 'Her son kept me hostage in my bed.'

I saw my nieces and nephews out of the corner of my eye, looking up from their phones, and thought, *curb it, Harry.* But I couldn't shut my mouth.

'Four days,' I said, shoving four fingers in front of Yvonne's face.

'Harriet!' Father shouted, 'Enough!'

'Why is she saying these horrible things?' asked Yvonne.

'Your son has problems,' I told her. 'He had a breakdown. He didn't have to break me too.'

People were trying to pull me away. Alex appeared in my peripheral.

'Harry,' he said. 'Come on outside for some air.'

'Your brother is a … monster,' I said. 'Look.'

I pulled my hair apart where the scar was on my head. 'He held me at gunpoint for days.' I pulled at my lip to show them my chipped tooth but there was little they could see, the damage was not anything I could show them. Chloe Taylor's killer had left more damage on me. So I tried harder.

'Tell that stalker I'll kill him if he ever comes near me again. If he ever stands outside my house or phones me.'

'My Jason has a lovely fiancée,' shouted Yvonne, 'he has no interest in you, my dear, so don't even flatter yourself. She is everything you wish you were.'

'You are one stupid bitch,' I shouted.

Next thing I knew, I was being dragged outside. My father's face was hate-filled as I was pulled away. My sisters were there, outside with me. Coral was looking at me dewy-eyed.

'Is that true, Harry?' she asked.

'You were there,' I said. 'You brought me to England for the termination.'

'What is going on?' said Charly. 'My kids are in there.'

Coral held my hands, and she cried, 'You should have told me.'

'I'm telling you,' I said.

As people left the party, they looked at me with concern or anger. Concern that I was mad, not a kind concern.

'He's phoning me again. I thought he'd stopped, and I can't fucken cope with it starting again,' I shouted. 'I can't!'

'But why not go to the police?' asked Charly.

'Don't you understand, he's been trying to keep me silent.'

'Or what, what is Jason going to do?'

'Kill me. Kill you.'

'Don't be daft.'

I made a fist and tried to throw my fingers at her. She blinked and stepped backwards. 'I'll talk to you when you're sober, Harriet,' she said.

'No, you'll never talk to me again, snide bitch,' I said.

'Don't take it out on her,' whispered Coral as she got me into her car. We watched as people left the party, and eventually Father and Yvonne, Alex and Verity beside them. I could see which side he had taken. Yvonne was on her phone, she was crying. She was phoning him probably, the bastard. I went to open the car door and Coral locked it.

'Sit it out,' she said. 'Okay, just sit it out a minute, H.'

I was shaky, still drunk, but I did feel good. Then, remembering how deranged that man was, I phoned Paul from my mobile. 'Look after my boys,' I said.

'What's wrong?' he asked.

'What's right?'

I told him I had been kicked out of the party.

'You weren't kicked out, love,' said Coral gently.

141

'Don't let anyone near my babies.'

'Of course I won't …. ' Paul faltered.

'Jason. If Jason calls, don't let him near them. He's not their dad.'

'I know that. What happened? Did he show?'

'No.'

'Let's get you home,' said Coral. I hung up on Paul.

'You have your family to get,' I told her.

'They must be indoors, still.' She sighed. 'You stay here, Harry. Okay? Don't go anywhere. H?'

I looked at her. Her eyes were heavy with emotion.

'I hear you!' I said. 'Why can't anyone just say *I hear you* to me?'

'I hear you,' she said, and tears misted her eyes.

I watched Coral go back into the building. A taxi pulled up outside, which I got into. I wasn't asked my name this time. The taxi driver just asked me where I wanted to go.

'Do you need a tissue?' she asked.

I caught sight of myself in the rear-view mirror, surprised to see I had bitten my lip and blood was trickling down my chin.

Chapter 27

In the taxi, I called him. 'The kids are with their mum. Can't you just come to mine?' he asked me.

That wasn't a good idea. Too familiar on his part.

'Meet me,' I said.

I got the taxi driver to drop me at his car, where it was parked on the outskirts of Dundonald, a suburb of Belfast where Drew lived in Tullycarnet estate. I slid into the passenger side beside him, reached across and kissed him.

'You're wasted,' he said.

'I'm not,' I said.

'Do you want to get a coffee?'

'I want you,' I said, running my hand up his leg.

He grabbed my hand and kissed me back. Hard.

'I'm sober,' I said, though I plainly wasn't. He had refused to be with me a couple of times in the past, claiming I was too bladdered. This time he didn't mind as we had sex in the back of his car like we had been doing for a few months.

Drew Taylor, a cousin of the late, young activist Chloe Taylor, was an all-around bad boy and my little secret. I was his rebound since his wife had left him. Recently she had got herself a job. Drew still loved Roxy, I could tell. They had been together since they were very young. He couldn't bring himself to mention Roxy. He said he wanted me but he did not.

We were worlds apart. He was a known drug dealer.

When the investigations opened a few months before, Roxy Taylor upped sticks. Drew had been quickly let off during the investigations, and I had not been involved in interviewing him. But I had interrogated Tucker Brown, the one who looked like he would do time.

Tucker was the only one who had not given us details about some other crime in an appeal to shorten the length of his charge. While Drew had been let off, I still shouldn't have been fucking him in his car once a week. I had always fancied him, but that wasn't reason enough. I hated myself after. But a fresh face makes you forget your own. The next day, when at work, if someone mentioned their organisation, I'd feel embarrassed about my actions. Of course, I'd be in the shit if I ever got found out. The papers would have a field day. Especially with the car sex. I just had to make sure we didn't get further enmeshed.

'You should have come to my house,' said Drew. 'I'm not a fan of this,' he said after we had finished.

'You seemed into it a minute ago,' I replied, buttoning my top up, ignoring the things he'd said during it, all his tender sentiments.

We sat quietly in the front seat. I needed another drink, or I'd start to feel things again, things not physical.

'What's wrong?' Drew cupped my face and kissed me, trying to act like he cared. I did not want him to.

'I went to the shittiest engagement party ever,' I said.

'Tell me about it.'

'Ah, sure, you don't want to hear all that.'

144

'I'd let you know. I wouldn't ask if I didn't want to hear about it.'

'Yeah, you would let me know.'

Over the years, if he was causing trouble, or if his name was attached to trouble, Drew Taylor would be defensive and rude. He is quite an adequate asshole, to be fair.

When Drew's little cousin Chloe was killed, I'm not saying I saw a different side to him, but I thought about him often. I still thought he was an asshole. Underneath that was a little boy. He was tender and caring, and then I caught myself on. This was Drew Taylor! But I did like him. My senses were always blurred with him. I ignored the fact that he had a chequered past. I'm sure he'd done some bad things, but I was also positive he was incapable of the things Jason had done. I'd seen Drew at his worst and his best. Neither was enough to allow me to tell him about Father's engagement party. I didn't say a word about my personal life. We were not friends like that.

Chapter 28

It was a week into the reopened case. My hangover from hell was setting in as Higgins drove. I asked him to stop and get us a coffee each before we went on. I'd woken that Monday morning in the spare room. Paul had kept out of my way. He did not ask about my night or about me calling him, mentioning Jason. As far as I knew, he did not know about the bombs I'd thrown at the party.

'I'm thinking of proposing,' Higgins said when we took our break, looking over Belfast lough shimmering under a bright blue sky.

'I'm taken,' I said.

'Do you think eighteen months is long enough to know someone? You weren't with the doc long before you moved in together.'

'But that was convenience,' I said. 'Kids.'

I could not believe my little baby partner Carl was thinking of marriage. Approaching thirty sends folk into all kinds of spins. For two years, I had been dreading forty. What a waste of time that was. The age itself was nothing but a number, as they say.

'They say you should be with someone for at least two years before getting married,' I said.

'Why is that?' Higgins did this sometimes, came to me for relationship advice. I liked playing the game; it was hilarious to me that anyone should think I held an answer, any answer, in the test of love.

'That way,' I said, 'you get to see them at their worst, observe how they handle the bad stuff.'

'Like what?'

'Money worries … the flu.'

'I'd say you've never had to worry about money, Sloane.'

I had been privileged in my life. I had also been with Jason for two years before we wed. In those two years pre-wedding and eight years of being married, I had not seen him at his worst until those final days.

'Do what makes you happy,' I said.

'Aye, I will.'

'What do you mean you will?'

'I'll ask Melinda to marry me.'

'Do you *want* to be married?' I asked.

'Sure it's a thing people do.'

'That's not a reason to do it.'

'Would you get married again?'

'I'd rather rot in hell.'

*

It was the first dry day in June; humid with no breeze. William Samuel was slogging away in the front garden of his red-brick semi in Cedar Grove, Holywood. He was sweating buckets, and was under pressure. Such a Northern Irish thing! No one prepares their garden for the summer when it's cooler. They waste our most beautiful days sweating and grafting, getting the garden ready, and then, summer's over.

Inside the house, William got himself a glass of iced water then joined us. 'We are reopening the case of Karen Ward,' I said for the hundredth time.

William stared with no recognition.

'She was killed in early November of 1978.'

'Oh yes, Orangefield.' He rattled his glass.

'That area,' said Higgins. 'Clarawood.'

'I remember that girl.'

I wondered about his brother's letter from jail. The fact it had been intercepted had me wondering if William ever received a copy, and what the sin was. Had they been sexually abusing Karen or someone else?

'What do you remember about Karen's death?' I asked.

'She was stabbed.' That was wrong.

'What else?'

'That she was young and it was a crying shame.'

'You were in a relationship with her at the time?'

'No! I can vaguely picture what she looked like.'

'Mr Samuel, you appear in her diary often.'

'I do?'

'Yes, you and your brother.'

'Arthur?' William sounded surprised.

'Yes, Arthur. Did the police ever talk to you at the time of Karen's death?'

'She lived in the flats, didn't she?'

'Yes, she lived in Clarawood House.'

'We didn't live too far from there, so I might have been spoken to. Like, everyone probably was.'

'You went to the pictures with Karen.'

'Did I? What did we see?'

'*Saturday Night Fever.*'

'That's a movie I still haven't seen.'

'Are you certain about that?'

'Is there a different Willie Samuel you're lookin'?'

'One with a brother called Arthur?' I asked.

'Look, I could have gone to the pictures with her back then. I was a popular boy. Good looking back then, hard to believe it now, I know.' But he left a little unfilled space in which we could protest and make his day. We didn't. 'When we got a phone put in the house, girls would always call and put my mother's head away. They would call to the door, too. Look, I'm not bumming or anything, but girls were quare and fond of me.'

I stared at him, speechless.

'Girls would say they were seeing me when they weren't, understand?'

'You think Karen made it up?' asked Higgins.

'Maybe the things she wrote were more fantasy than reality, you know.'

'In her diary, Karen Ward mentioned your cousin being kneecapped,' I told William.

'Now that *did* happen.'

'And that Arthur once kissed her.'

'Now that, I can't see being true.'

'Why is that?'

'Forty-odd years ago is too long ago to expect people to have sharp memories, you know.' He shook his glass again.

'I get that, Mr Samuel. Her sister Janet needs closure, you understand that.'

'I knew Janet. She would babysit the kids round our way. Once or twice she asked me to sit with her.'

'And did you?'

'I did. We might have had a wee kiss and a cuddle, but that's all. She was a good girl.'

He echoed the songs I heard on the radio, men singing to women, telling them they were 'a good girl'. What was a good girl? By Willie's definition, it meant not promiscuous. I tried not to sigh.

'Who was Janet babysitting at the time?' I asked.

'The Simpson kids.'

'Wayne Simpson's children?'

'Wasn't it him they thought killed Janet's sister?'

'Wayne Simpson was a person of interest,' I said. 'So, just the Simpson children … ?'

'And the wee boy who ended up with …. ' William pointed at his head.

'What is it? Finish your thought.'

'He ended up not right in the head. Wee Kenny.'

'Are you talking about Kenneth Hall?'

'He had a big sister called Anita. See how I remember the girls.' He winked. 'I remember her years later about town. Turned out mad like her mother, Maxine.'

'I thought you babysat with Janet more regularly than once or twice?'

'Maybe I did. As I say, I don't remember. Maybe four times. But I can say, hand on heart, Lord strike me down, I know there was no going to the pictures with her wee sister, Karen.'

'You don't know anything about Arthur and Karen?'

'He might have kissed her, but nothing more. He didn't have a relationship his whole life, wasn't interested in that.'

'Why not?' I asked. Surely having relationships, and having sex, is normal, but William looked stunned by the question.

'I just thought that a nice looking young man …. ' I paused; it sounded silly, as if an unattractive man would not have desires. 'I'm sure, being your brother, he had plenty of opportunities to have a relationship.'

William nodded. 'There was some carry on when he was a boy,' he divulged.

'How do you mean?' I asked.

'People talk about it easily these days, don't they? *Abuse*, they call it. He didn't, didn't call it anything, and didn't it only get him in the end?'

'Abuse?' I asked.

'He killed himself. I put it down to his past, alright?' William sounded sharp now, and I retreated slightly, put up my guard but tried to stay relaxed. Or look it.

'Who abused him?' asked Higgins.

'An older boy,' said William.

'Did he do it to you?'

'I'd like to see him try, son! He was a big lad, but our cousin Al was in an organisation and saw to him. It didn't help Arthur. He still couldn't deal with it, after, like. And I'm not naming names, for he's dead now too, the rapist. So there'd be no point dredging it up now.'

'I'm sorry,' I said, 'to hear that Arthur experienced that.'

'It fucked with his head. He never had a relationship. I do know that. No girlfriend; he closed himself off to that.'

I understood how it could fuck you up. In the early days post-rape, I contemplated suicide almost every other day.

'Which is the reason why,' said William, 'I can't believe he was trying to crack on with wee Karen or anybody. He had all that normal relationship stuff taken from him. I can identify with Janet Ward or whatever surname she goes by now. We both wish we'd seen our siblings live better lives, normal lives. Longer, at least.'

I was surviving, wasn't I? But I was attacked as a woman, and maybe that was a different shame Arthur Samuel had to live with that I don't and can't know. I was managing, kind of, to stick to the right path.

'Little Kenny,' said Higgins, head clearer than mine, not lost to any mounting recognition of what William Samuel was talking about.

'He was one cute kid,' said Willie. 'Then there was an accident. He was left brain-damaged.'

'Do you recall the accident?'

'I saw him out once; he was like a baby toting a Mickey Mouse toy. A big fella, by then. Santa was arriving at Connswater Shopping Centre, and he was there in the queue, in a wheelchair. Jeez, it was …. ' William couldn't find the right word.

'You said his sister has issues too,' I said.

'She was a lot older, but she was always a bit … you know, too.'

'Mad?' I offered.

'Like her mother in that way. Sure, her life was good in some ways, Maxine. Winning the pools, paying off that house in Sandhill Park, but she was always partying too much. She had plenty to contend with too, the wee boy being disabled, then the kids were taken away. She died awful young herself. Beautiful looking girl too, Maxi. Like a catalogue model.'

I asked William to allow us his DNA, just to rule himself, and through his familial link, rule out his brother from our enquiries too. Willie hesitated, and then he said, 'Sure, go on. Get this out of the way.'

I gloved up and took a swab from inside his mouth.

Chapter 29

I called Janet and told her that we had got speaking to William Samuel. 'He said that he used to babysit with you.'

'He might have sat with me; he didn't do any of the work,' said Janet.

'He thought you two were romantically involved back then.'

'We might have had a little kiss, that's all.'

'He also said he had no recollection of Karen.'

'Karen might have fancied him. Most of the girls did. He was a very good-looking boy.'

'He said.'

'And he was. He looked not unlike George Best.'

'Were you two an item for long?' I chanced.

'We weren't an item, we might have had a half-baked flirtation that lasted a couple of weeks, but that would be all. I wasn't keeping anything back from you when you mentioned him before. I'd honestly forgotten about him. It was his brother who you'd have to watch.'

'He has since died.'

'Oh, I didn't know. How did Arthur die, do you know?'

'He took his life.'

'Oh ....'

'We have DNA from William, and if it has a link to either brother, we'll know.'

'That's something good. Thanks for telling me.'

'No problem,' I said. 'Janet, did you babysit the Halls?'

'I practically babysat every child in the area.'

'Do you recall the Halls?'

'Yes! Wee Kenny, bless.'

'He had a sister.'

'Anita. They had things hard.'

'How so?'

'The little boy poured antifreeze into his diluting juice.'

'How on earth did he manage to drink that?'

'It was sweet then,' said Janet. 'So they say, not that I ever tasted it myself. It damaged his kidneys and brain. He was severely brain damaged as a result.'

'When did this happen?'

'No long after Karen was killed. I wasn't babysitting anyone then. Kwong gave me more hours behind the counter, and people didn't ask me to mind their kids after Karen died. I just remember thinking how I was so grateful Kenny's accident hadn't happened on my watch. I wonder where they are now.'

Janet hadn't been calling in on the Halls like she had with Barney Orr. That was something, at least.

My phone dinged. A text. *Wait till I see you in person.*

'I'll talk to you later,' I told Janet.

It had to be Jason leaving messages now, for the first time in a long time leaving evidence.

He had to know what I said about him at the engagement party. Now gone was the name-calling; he had jumped right to threats. I might have blocked his number, but he just kept using other ones. But why should I have to change my number again? I had changed my life entirely already, and it wasn't enough.

Any calmness from talking to Martin Walsh was gone.

*

That Monday afternoon, I tried to chase up Larne on the DNA from Flynn, the groundsman's nephew, but to no avail. DI Posner was on annual leave, and no one else seemed to know what I was talking about. So I read all the diaries again, photocopied and underlined. I noticed that Karen had never called Willie her boyfriend, so perhaps it was just a crush. Or maybe she was trying to wind Janet up by making out like there was something between them in case Janet invaded her privacy and worked out the code.

Arthur Amuel kied me and I ran away.

Had he? Just because his brother said Arthur didn't have relationships didn't mean that was true. Maybe he had kissed Karen.

I understood what Willie was saying; Arthur did not settle down or want a relationship.

However, there seemed to be more to this. Perhaps Arthur did not know the subtleties because of his past experiences, and he forced a kiss on Karen, in the process scaring her. It could be that that was all there was to it. Or perhaps he had pushed it more. That, too, was not beyond the realms of possibility. Even though I hated to think about it, the victim often becomes the perpetrator. I've seen it time and again.

Chapter 30

'Has Larne got back to us yet?' Chief Dunne asked during Tuesday morning's briefing.

'Not yet, sir. We got talking with William Samuel yesterday and got a sample of his DNA.'

Fleur Hewitt asked after his brother, 'He has a criminal past.'

'Robbery,' I said, having a new understanding of Arthur. 'He was hurt in his past.'

'And hurt people hurt people,' Hewitt said.

'I suppose you're right, ma'am, but Arthur was more about thieving than hurting people.'

'So, if I stole from you, you wouldn't be hurt?' asked Chief Dunne.

'I'm not saying that,' I said delicately, feeling attacked. I could say that Arthur was sexually abused, but I didn't, mainly because they wouldn't give a shit. 'Sir, I want to speak to Anita Hall some more. She is the sister of Kenneth, our young eyewitnesses,' I added.

'I believe he withdrew his statement,' said the chief.

'I don't know if it was that clear cut.'

'You have all Napier's notes to go by.'

'We do, yes, Chief, but Anita told me that soon after, Kenneth drank antifreeze and was brain-damaged. He lives in a care facility now. And his sister, well, I think she knows more than she let on.'

'She admitted to the murder herself back in the day,' said Fleur Hewitt.

'What?' I asked. This was news to me.

The chief perked up at this.

'She gave a few statements.' Hewitt lifted them up.

'Where did you get those?'

'I did some plundering in those boxes.'

'There was another one?' asked Higgins, exasperated.

'No, these were in one labelled *1978, Hall*. A different case. I can only imagine our man Mack put it in the wrong box.'

'What age would Anita have been in 1978?' asked Dunne.

'Fifteen, sir,' I said.

'Could she have done it?' he asked.

'She and Karen would likely have been the same height. It's not unthinkable.'

'Don't underestimate the female of the species,' said Higgins. I wouldn't; I'd done that before, to my peril.

'Why didn't Napier charge Anita?' I asked Hewitt.

'Because,' she said, 'Anita also gave a statement to say it was Wayne Simpson.'

'Mack had his mind made up.'

'Is that everything?' asked Chief Dunne, reminding me of a worker at a fast-food drive-thru, rushing us to be done, handing us our order while we were still driving.

'No, Chief,' said Hewitt, 'Anita also gave a statement that she suspected Karen's boyfriend, but she never gave a name, and we know now that it was unlikely she had a boyfriend.'

'Napier probably saw her as a nuisance,' said Higgins.

'What about Willie Samuel? Was he not Karen's boyfriend?' asked Dunne.

'Just a crush, it seems,' I said, 'he had a brief teenage fling, if you could even call it that, with Janet.'

Greg Dunne coughed. 'Okay, so moving on,' he said, 'Sloane, speak to Anita Hall and find out who this boyfriend of Karen's was. Get DNA for her too, to be on the safe side.'

Hewitt leafed through her papers. 'Napier wrote that, in a suicide note, Anita said she knew who *did it* – he presumed she was talking about Karen's murder – her mother gave the note to police.'

'A suicide attempt?' said Higgins.

'Obviously, she survived it,' said Hewitt.

*

After our meeting, Hewitt showed me the newly-found paperwork, which contained Mack's thoughts and three statements from Anita Hall. *Elder sister of the eyewitness, the little boy, Kenneth Hall*, Napier had written on the top.

In one statement was an admission; Anita claimed she had killed Karen; in the next, she blamed Karen's boyfriend, who Anita did not name, like Hewitt had said; in the last one, Anita accused Wayne Simpson, who would have been arrested at the time.

'She told me she got in trouble for wasting police time,' I told Hewitt. 'Why was her admission ignored in the first place?'

'Like you already said, Napier had his man,' said Hewitt.

'But it's unlike a man to suffocate a woman,' said Higgins.

'It's also the sign of someone who knew the victim,' I said, 'someone who thought it tamer than a more violent attack.'

'Someone who did not want to damage her face,' said Hewitt, 'it seems very much like encounter that just escalated.'

In his notes, Mack indicated that during each statement, Anita was incoherent and unreliable. He was only interested in Anita because of her suicide attempt, which he had taken as a sign of either guilt or knowing something that would incriminate someone else.

The note she left for her mother, Maxine, had been given to Mack Napier. But we scoured those boxes, all of them from 1978 or filed under the name Hall, including the box in which Fleur had found these other statements, we looked in between each sheet for hours and could not see the note or what it said, and then Kate Stile called me and said, 'Harry, are you sitting down?'

Chapter 31

'The hair sample found in Karen Ward's hand is not a match for Wayne Simpson. Instead, it bears the DNA of another person.'

'And let me guess,' I said, 'they aren't in the system?'

'You're getting good at this,' Kate Stile replied.

*

Higgins and I went to Clarawood House. We stood in Simpson's flat, right next door to the one Karen and Janet would have lived in. A little girl, a granddaughter about seven years old, sat looking at her iPad.

'Could we speak to you privately?' I asked.

'I'm an open book,' he said, 'go ahead.'

The little granddaughter never looked up.

'Wayne,' I said, 'there was DNA left at the site of Karen's .... It has been tested, compared to a sample that you let us take. It is not a match for the DNA.'

'So that's it?' he asked, beaming.

'You have been eliminated from the investigation.'

Wayne whooped; he ran over and picked up his granddaughter, and swung her around. She looked bemused. He set her on the seat again and shook his fists like his favourite team had just scored a goal.

He'd had this hanging over him practically forever, but I had never seen someone act so inappropriately after being eliminated.

Weepy, maybe. Happy, yes. Solemn and thoughtful, usually. His absolution meant that the person who killed Karen was *out there*. And out there was the worst place for them.

In his flat, Wayne Simpson continued to celebrate, shouting, 'Get in!'

I thought of my father that January in court. The judge gave a compassionate speech, proffering sympathy to my father. No one was whooping then. My brothers stayed away. My sisters left separately. I stayed with Father, brought him to my house and made him his dinner. No one spoke.

Uncomfortable with Wayne's display, we left him to celebrate. This news would be a blow to Janet, even if she wanted to be open-minded. She had thought for so long that it was her next-door neighbour in the flats.

I called her from the service car, giving her the heads-up before the media got wind.

'I hated him,' Janet said, 'he carried Karen's coffin. He was always around, and my mum hated him.'

'You didn't say, Janet.'

'I wanted new eyes, fresh eyes on the case. I wouldn't help by telling you I loathe this man and had to move away to not be near him because he wouldn't move. He just refused to, and you know, plenty of people tried to make him go. If it wasn't a block of flats, he'd have been burnt out. And it wasn't him all along,' she levelled with me. I heard fury in Janet. It would be hard for her to unhate Wayne Simpson, to unpick what she had thought she had known.

I was impressed by her strength. By her ability to seem as impartial as she could manage, and to swallow all that hurt. I also felt a little fooled by her, again.

I had not come across any statement of where Janet actually was on the evening of her sister's death. But I daren't have asked her then.

Chapter 32

By lunchtime, just as the sun was peeking through the clouds, we arrived at the supported living bungalow where Kenneth lived. We needed to talk to the social worker first, and luckily Carmel was there doing paperwork in the office-cum-staff-bedroom, where she brought us while support workers stayed with the residents.

'I have to lock the door,' Carmel said. 'Otherwise, we might have a visitor.'

'A visitor would be fine,' I said. I did not fancy being locked in any room.

Carmel insisted and locked the door regardless of my weak protestations, and I soon saw why she insisted when Trevor – the other man she was supporting, and Kenneth's housemate – tried to open the door. He pushed and pulled, making grunting sounds.

Carmel waited it out. 'I'll see you in a minute, Trevor,' she said.

'I see? I see police?' he asked.

'I'll see you soon,' she said.

We must have spoken too loudly at the door alerting Trevor to the fact there were two police officers in his home. After five minutes of the support workers trying to ease him away, Carmel left for a while, asking us to lock the door to keep Trevor out. She left Higgins and me with Kenneth's files to peruse: personal history, care plans. The reports went right back to Kenneth's birth.

She denied that there were police in the house.

'I'm doing paperwork, Trevor. First, you help tidy your room and next, I'll see you.' Then bribery. 'Then, we'll go get an ice cream.'

From his personal file, I read that Kenneth's mother, Maxine Hall, was fifteen when she had an unplanned pregnancy with Anita's father, an unnamed, married man who did not want another baby in his life. Anita had five siblings on her father's side. By the time of the report, 1978, she had never met them, and they did not know she existed, Maxine confided.

Kenneth has a different father, some social worker had written at the time. I quailed at all this confidential information being here for new staff to acquaint themselves with. Judging a young girl who was likely exploited by a much older man.

Carmel knocked quietly on the door, and Higgins let her back in. She went through the files.

'Here you see normal things, vaccinations and dates. Falls. Then social worker reports of Maxine leaving Kenneth in Anita's care when he was two, and she was only eight. A neighbour had reported this.'

Carmel flipped forward through things she deemed irrelevant. Incidents, (minor) accidents, near misses. She turned to the middle of November 1978, straight after Karen Ward was killed.

The following reports were in connection to Kenneth's brain injury. His social worker's sequential record-keeping was refreshing, compared to Mack Napier's haphazard stash of pages.

I read about the accident in which Kenneth drunk antifreeze. I read about his mother, Maxine, having been neglectful. How she preferred partying, especially after winning the pools. In the following report, I read that his sister Anita had attempted suicide.

Each report I passed on to Higgins after I read it.

'Kenneth's injury happened very soon after the murder we are investigating,' I explained to Carmel.

'When his mother poisoned him,' said Carmel.

'Are you sure of that?' I asked.

'It's common knowledge.'

'But she wasn't convicted. Says here it was most likely an accident.'

'Really? Where?' Carmel looked again. 'It's widely believed his mother did it. She seemed like she wanted to be a single girl.'

'Wanted to be a *single girl* enough to poison her son?'

Carmel looked at me without reply.

'But not enough to poison her daughter?' I wondered aloud.

Munchausen syndrome by proxy interested me, though I didn't want it to be the case here. I thought it unlikely. From what I had known of the condition, those mothers wanted sympathy. They thrived on it and stuck around to be hailed as an angel for looking after a sick kid. There was usually a long-lasting drip effect there. This, conversely, seemed like a genuine accident. And if I was wrong, then someone wanted the boy dead.

'What else have you heard about his mother?' I asked Carmel.

___

166

'Maxine stopped coming to the hospital to see them.'

'Them?'

'Kenneth and Anita.'

'When Anita tried to harm herself?'

'Long before my time, but it could be.'

'Anita tried to kill herself around that time,' I said.

'These notes are person-centred around Kenneth, apart from the family history section.'

'So, I see that Maxine lost custody. Did Kenneth come to live here then?' asked Higgins.

'The children's version of our service,' said Carmel.

'There was no other family to take them in?'

'There was a grandmother, but you could see where Maxine got her ways from.'

'Meaning?'

'She was quite a self-centred woman.'

'Visited, did she?'

'She died a long time ago now; she never visited. She didn't want the kids when they were taken into care.' Carmel flicked through the pages and showed us Kenneth's admission papers into children's services. It mentioned a stepfather, Geoff McDonald.

'Who is he?' I asked.

'I never met him either, and I've worked here for twenty-five years. From talking to Anita, I garner he was her mother's boyfriend. It says stepfather, but they weren't married. At one stage,' said Carmel, 'Anita mentioned to me that she had wanted to live with Geoff in the past, but it's not in Kenneth's notes, obviously.'

'I wonder if he is still alive,' I said.

167

'Anita hasn't mentioned him in so long.'

I read on. Geoff had no fixed abode and couldn't manage Kenneth's treatment, but the report stated that he offered to look after Anita.

'He reneged on that offer,' said Carmel, 'or the courts didn't see fit to give custody of a teenage girl to a man who wasn't her biological dad.'

'That makes sense,' I said. 'So what happened to the house, was it paid off, with Maxine winning all that money?'

'That should have been left to the kids. Maxine's mother crawled out from under a house, sold it and kept the money after Maxine died. At least Kenneth has us. But I always feel for Anita.'

'Why is that?' asked Higgins.

'She fell through the cracks. She was in her early thirties when I first met her. She's still a lost wee soul.'

Chapter 33

After getting an address for Anita from Carmel, we drove two minutes away to her home on Cliftonville Road. 'Anita, we want to talk to you some more about the statements you gave to the police following the murder of Karen Ward.'

'Oh, okay, go on ahead,' she said, sitting on an old armchair in her sparsely decorated living room.

'You gave three statements, do you remember?'

'Three statements,' said Anita.

'In one, you said that you killed Karen.'

Her eye began to twitch. 'Am I in trouble?' she asked.

'We just want to find out the truth,' said Higgins.

'The night of Karen's death, what do you remember?'

'I don't know.' She fidgeted with the hem of her cardigan.

'What age were you at the time?' I asked.

'Thirteen,' said Anita.

'And Kenneth was … what age?'

'About four.'

'He was nine,' said Higgins impatiently. 'Quite a difference between four and nine.'

'A big difference,' Anita said, nodding.

'And you were fifteen,' I said.

'Okay.'

'Tell us about Karen Ward, what you remember about her?'

'She had brown hair.'

'What else do you remember about her?'

'She loved David Cassidy. She fancied Willie Samuel because he looked like him.'

'Did she go out with Willie Samuel? I mean, on dates,' I asked her.

'Don't be silly. Willie was Janet's boy.'

'Did Willie ever come babysitting?' I asked.

'Only with Janet. She was the blond one, right?'

'Maybe she was blond then.'

I had forgotten again to ask Janet about that. I took out my phone and zoomed in on the smiling photo of Karen from the leaflet to clear up any confusion. 'This is Karen.'

'She was killed,' said Anita.

'Do you remember when it happened?'

Anita's eye was doing that twitchy thing again. I wondered if it was worse when she was stressed.

'Kenneth saw something that night,' I pressed. 'Do you remember he went to a payphone and phoned the police with a description?'

'I know,' said Anita, 'I was with him.'

'With him when he saw something or ....'

'I helped him use the phone.'

'What did he see?' asked Higgins.

'Someone dragging Karen into the bushes.'

'Can you remember more about what he saw? I would like to ask Kenneth more, but I don't think he'd understand me now.'

'He saw Karen ... shouting, crying for help.'

'Anything else?'

'Them strangling her.'

170

'She wasn't strangled,' said Higgins, a bit too quickly.

'What happened to her again?' asked Anita.

'She was suffocated,' I said.

'That must have been what Kenny saw. I forgot.'

'Where did Kenny see this from?' I asked.

'His bedroom window, must have been.'

'But *you* didn't see it?'

'I didn't see it.'

We needed to go to that house in Sandhill Park and work out if it was possible to see the trees from the Halls' old house and the boy's bedroom in particular.

'Where was Kenneth's bedroom? Front of the house? Back of the house?'

'Back … I think.'

'What number was your house?' asked Higgins as he jotted down some notes.

'Forty-three.'

'Thank you, Anita.'

'You're welcome.'

Higgins put his pen in his pocket.

'You must have been close to Karen if she was babysitting you for years,' I said.

'Not that much; sometimes it was Geoff.'

'Who's Geoff?' I wanted to hear it from her.

'My stepdad.'

'When was the last time you saw Geoff?'

'Mum had left, we had to go to court, and I asked him to take us and look after Kenneth. That was the last time.'

'So you haven't seen him in decades.'

'A very long time.'

'What happened in court? Did he want custody of you?'

'People say he changed his mind about having us.'

'Did he live with you before?'

'Sometimes he did. Sometimes Maxine kicked him out.'

'Your mother, Maxine?'

Anita laughed. 'Yes.'

'When you were removed from Maxine, your mother's care, did you want to stay with Geoff?'

'I did, but she wouldn't let me. She still had a say, even though she poisoned Kenneth.'

'Do you think she did it?'

Anita shrugged her shoulders. Her eye began to twitch like a wing.

'Where did Geoff work?' asked Higgins.

'Nowhere.'

'He didn't work?'

'He didn't work.'

'Did your mum work?'

'Nope.'

I remembered that Maxine Hall had won the pools. She must have lived on the winnings, paid teenage neighbours to look after children so she could go out and socialise. Children she could have just left on their own. Anita was old enough.

'Geoff minded you too, sometimes? Or did he go out with Maxine?'

'Sometimes.'

'He lived at your house?'

'Most of the time, he lived with us or in his car.'

'For how long? Months? Years?'

'He was there for my birthday when I was six, but he wasn't always there. Then he came back.'

I wondered if his return coincided with Maxine's win.

'What did you think of Geoff? He was good to you?'

'Yes, the only holidays I ever had were with him.'

'How is Kenneth, do you think?' I asked.

'He's happy in himself; that's what people say. He doesn't know any better. He doesn't know how sad it is, how he used to be. He used to be smart. He won prizes in school.'

'What about your statements, Anita? I have to go back to them. I know you were going through a lot, personally, with your brother being ill and what happened to Karen, but you did claim to have this information.'

'I don't know. I don't remember any of what I said. My memory is shit.'

'At one stage, you said you killed Karen.'

Anita laughed. 'That's mad!'

'Is it?'

'I was a wee pet then. People say I was soft.'

'I'd like you to come to the station and give us more information, Anita. How about now?'

'I'd have to ask.'

'Who do you have to ask?'

She didn't reply.

'Time has gone on. It's difficult to find anyone who knew the Ward girls like you did. I bet you have lots you can tell us. It would be a great help.'

'Do I have to?'

'We want to understand why you would have implicated yourself.'

'But I don't remember.' She became tearful. 'Can I come in tomorrow? I've someone coming soon.'

I looked at Higgins. What was another day after forty-one years? I gave Anita my card and asked her to come to the station at ten a.m. the following day.

'I'll see if I can get a lift,' she said, and we left. Anita did not walk us to the door.

We sat behind the rose bushes in the street, and I called Sarge Fergus Simon.

'I want you to go to this address,' I said, looking at Higgins' notebook, 'forty-three Sandhill Park. Go and see if, from any of the bedrooms or any rooms in the house, you can see the park, especially the area where Karen's body was found.'

'Not a chance you'd see anything,' he said.

'No?'

'Not a chance, Harry.'

'Not even from a back bedroom?'

'I'll go and see, but I'll tell you now, no one would have been able to see that area, not from that far up the street.'

'Anita said Kenneth saw her being dragged into the bushes.'

'I can go and check. But a child is even smaller.'

A prim young woman aged about nineteen or twenty came along the street, she was wearing a checked dress and patent shoes. She walked up Anita's path. Anita opened the door for her.

'Listen till ya hear,' the words bounced from her. 'The police were here asking if I killed Karen Ward.'

'What did you tell them?' the girl said, sounding tense.

'I told them I didn't.'

Then, the girl laughed awkwardly. 'Don't open the door to them if they come again, okay? Phone one of us. Don't speak to them alone.'

'If you say so.'

'I'll put on the kettle.'

'Does it fit ya?' Anita shouted after her.

I looked through the rose bushes, lowered Higgins' window and craned my neck. The girl went indoors, but the door did not close after her. Anita came out into the garden; she had no idea we were still there.

'Did I kill her?' Anita said to herself, pulling old dead branches off the rose bush and making it spasm. 'Yes, I killed Karen. What are you going to do about it, Detective bitch?'

Chapter 34

'Hear that?' I whispered.

'She confessed,' said Higgins. He was out of the car like lightning, and I was behind him.

'Anita?' he called her. She looked around, dropped her branches, then ran inside and slammed the door. We went and knocked on the door, the young woman came to the door. Anita was cowering behind her.

'Hello, what's going on?' the woman asked.

'Anita Hall,' I said, 'I am arresting you for the murder of Karen Ward. You do not have to say anything. But, it may harm your defence if you do not mention when questioned something which you later rely on in court. Anything you do say may be given in evidence. Do you have any questions?'

Tough if you do, I thought, they are never answered at this point.

'What did you hear?' Anita cried as I got her in handcuffs.

'I think we'll talk about that at the station,' said Higgins.

'Where are you going? Where are you taking her?' the young woman shouted after us.

*

I took DNA from Anita and fingerprints, got her into the system.

She was checked in by the desk serge who asked her if she knew why she was there.

'No,' she said, 'I don't.'

'Murder,' Higgins reiterated.

'Murder,' Anita repeated.

We brought her through to the interrogation room and let her waffle, then we introduced the signed statement she had given in the past: *I, Anita Hall, killed Karen Ward.*

I read it out. On hearing the old statement, Anita looked surprised. 'Really, I said that?' she asked.

'You said that,' I said. 'It's written here.'

'That doesn't look like my handwriting.'

'That was probably written by a police officer and then you'd have signed it. Is that your signature?'

'Yes. It is,' she said, with a hangdog look on her face.

'Then you blamed a boyfriend of Karen's after that, who you didn't name. Then you blamed it on Wayne Simpson.'

'It *was* Wayne Simpson, everybody said.'

'Wayne Simpson has been eliminated from our enquiry.'

'You don't think he did it?' Anita asked.

She hadn't heard the news? It had been on the TV, on the radio too, and online.

'You know it wasn't him, Anita,' I said. 'You were lucky you didn't get done for perverting the course of justice back then.'

'Perverting the course of justice?' Anita half-laughed.

'Before her death, when was the last time you would have seen Karen Ward?' asked Higgins.

Anita shrugged.

'Did you see her on the day she died?'

'Yes.'

'Good,' I said, 'Anita, tell us about that day.'

'What date was it?'

'6 November.'

'Before Christmas.'

'What do you remember about that day? Were you doing anything special?'

'Shopping for Christmas?' asked Higgins.

'I was in town buying presents.'

'Who were you with?'

'I was with Kenneth.'

'You would have gone into town on your own, the two of you?'

'We used to do that before his accident,' she said.

'You two were alone?'

'We were alone.'

'And after shopping … you went back home?' asked Higgins.

'Yes, we went back home.'

'And what happened next? Did you see Karen?'

'Yes, I saw Karen.'

'What was she doing?'

'Deliveries for the Chinese.' We knew that was true. 'Kenneth saw her too.'

'Did he see Karen talking to a man?'

'He did see Karen talking to a man.'

'Did you see this?'

'No. Definitely not.' It was different to see her so adamant and animated.

'Go on,' I told Anita. 'Tell us what Kenneth told you. What else was he intending on telling the police?'

'He spoke to her.'

'What did he say?'

'Hello.'

'So, explain, to me, how it went from Kenneth saying hello, to Karen being killed.'

'What do you want me to say?' Anita burst into tears.

'What Kenneth told you.'

'But he didn't tell me anything. I told you I can't remember,' she shouted aggressively.

'We're just trying to help Janet by finding out who killed her sister.'

'Then tell her it was me.'

Higgins' jaw dropped.

'What was you, Anita?'

'I did it. I killed her.'

I sat back, kind of frozen. I was speechless.

'Now can I go?' asked Anita.

'How did it happen?'

'I got her and … ' Anita mimed pulling an invisible person.

'You need to speak,' I said, 'did you drag Karen?'

Anita nodded.

'For the purposes of the tape, could you speak up?'

'What do you want me to say?'

'You nodded when I asked if you dragged Karen.'

'I dragged Karen through the park. Is that better?'

'Did she fight against you?'

'Not really.'

'Do you think Karen was surprised?'

I remembered that there had been kick marks on the ground, but I didn't doubt that Anita would have been able to overpower her. Karen had been slight and Anita stocky and robust.

'She was surprised.'

'She didn't try to fight against you?'

I thought about the clump of hair we had. Higgins gave me a look, like, she's already confessed, why do this? But there was one main question I wanted to get to.

'And so what did you do to Karen?' I led up to it.

'I pushed her down.'

'Yes, and … '

'I str-, I mean, *suffocated* her.'

'What with?'

Anita looked around. 'I just … ' She mimed placing her hands over an invisible person's face. 'Did like that,' she said.

'You put your hands on her.'

'Yes.'

'And you did that for how long?'

'Until she died,' said Karen. 'Is that okay?'

'Do you think it's okay?'

'I'm glad I could remember,' she said.

I shook my head at one of the most unusual interviews of my entire career. I could see now why Willie Samuel had called Anita mad.

'Why did you do it?' I asked.

It was at that point her solicitor sat forward and said, 'Let's take a break. I want to speak with my client.'

'Okay, let's reconvene in a short while,' I said.

'Great, cheers,' said Anita standing up.

I had learnt my lesson about keeping victim's families out of the loop. With colossal relief, I went and called Janet. She didn't answer her phone, but I couldn't hang up without saying something. I didn't want her to hear it over the media first.

I left a short message. 'I'll give you a call later,' I said, 'but we have someone in custody, and it is looking promising.'

Chapter 35

'We got her,' I told Fergus Simon. 'The girl who lived in forty-three Sandhill Park.'

'Great, nice work,' he said. 'But I took the liberty of looking up the census. The Halls actually lived in eighty-three. Which backed on perfectly to where Karen was found.'

'She told me forty-three,' I said. 'So Kenneth *did* see what happened from a bedroom window.'

'He could have. Do you want me to go and look now?'

'Please, Sarge. Now.'

This was worse. I pictured Anita's little brother seeing her and going to a payphone to call us to incriminate her. They probably could afford a phone in the house, but he needed to do this in private. I envisaged Anita realising what he was going to do and threatening him, possibly bribing him to corroborate the man in brown suspect who was being identified by Wayne Simpson and Michelle Brown.

Then the chain of events that came after. Kenneth being poisoned, his mother being blamed, a family torn apart. Little Kenneth left fighting for his life. Anita trying to commit suicide. She had tried to silence her little brother by poisoning him. Anita had felt so guilty she attempted to end her life. There had been no remorse, no care for what she had done.

'I have been talking to Janet Ward,' I told Anita after a break.

'Have you told her what I said?'

I gave the question short shrift. 'How do you think she'll feel about you?' I asked.

'Janet always liked me.' Anita seemed sure of herself.

'That's likely to change now, don't you think?'

She shrugged. 'I don't think so.'

'What makes you think she likes you so much?'

'She came fishing with us a few times.'

'Janet?'

'And Karen.'

'With who? You and … ?'

'Kenneth.'

'Just the four of you?'

'No. We needed a driver then.'

'This was before either of the girls could drive?'

'This was before either of the girls could drive.'

'Who drove you?'

'Geoff.'

'Geoff McDonald?' asked Higgins, 'your mum's boyfriend?'

'At the time,' said Anita.

'And Geoff took you fishing?'

'He loved fishing. Trout. Fly fishing.'

'Where is Geoff now?'

'I have no idea.'

My phone pinged. Kate Stile had news for me. 'We'll take a break here,' I said.

Chapter 36

'There's no familial DNA link to the hair in Karen's hand for either of the Samuel brothers,' said Stile.

So that was that. They were eliminated too.

'Long hair,' I said. 'Kate, can you tell if the hair is from a female?'

'There is very little root pulp, but thankfully some, as it was pulled out of the head. Cut hair we would have no chance with. It's hard to determine gender via a microscope, but there are extra tests we can do, staining of sex chromatin in the cells. Or, we can attempt to. I can't promise anything.'

'I'll get a swab from her; it might be enough. Plus, we have a confession.'

Next, I wanted a photo of younger Anita. She did not have the bulbous nose and small eyes of the artists' impressions, but she might have been mistaken for a man in a badly lit November evening. She must have been – as she still was – broad but flat-chested, boyish in her gait. Long brown hair in a middle parting.

I was thinking about all of this when Higgins came and got me. A woman was sounding off in the reception. She was with the young woman in the checked dress who had been at Anita's house.

The woman was demanding to speak to the arresting officers. I didn't like her tone.

'Yes, that's me, DI Harriet Sloane,' I said.

'Nadine Lark, principal social worker at Homes 4 All.'

'You're here about Kenneth Hall?' I asked.

'I sincerely hope you haven't spoken to Anita yet?' she said.

'What has this got to do with you?' I asked her.

The young woman beside her glared at me.

'Is there anywhere we can talk in private?' Nadine said, aware of a growing crowd.

I brought her into the reception room nearest the front door. 'Sergeant Higgins,' I said, 'join us.'

He followed the women in, and I motioned for them to sit.

'You arrested Anita Hall, I hear,' said Nadine.

'That's right,' I said.

'You shouldn't have.'

'I think I very much should have.' I stifled a laugh.

'You're Coral's sister, right?'

My eldest sister was a social worker, too, but Coral had nothing to do with this case.

'What do you want?' I asked her.

'Your sister wouldn't like to hear that you arrested a vulnerable person in such a brutal fashion.'

'Brutal!' I laughed, then stared at the young woman who had obviously described the arrest as such. 'What is your name?' I asked her.

'Imogen Barnes,' she said, looking nervous.

'Tell me how we were brutal, Imogen, and you,' I turned to Nadine, 'mention my sister one more time, and you are out of here.'

Higgins turned to look at me. Nadine gulped. I'd been through enough. I was not listening to her aggressive shit, this incredibly petty; *I'll tell your big sister on you.*

185

'Get to the point, Nadine,' I said.

'Oh, erm … ' She flapped around a bit. 'Anita Hall lives in supported living, she has the IQ of a child, and if you are going to speak with her, she needs an appropriate adult.'

Anita was forgetful, strange in a way, but I was floored by this revelation.

'I knew she was preoccupied, but she was asked by the custody sarge when she was booked if she had learning difficulties,' I declared.

'And Anita said no,' Higgins added.

'Anita doesn't know that she has learning difficulties,' said Nadine.

Shit. It explained a lot.

'She, like her brother, both have similar issues. I know you went out to see him too.'

'Kenneth? Yes, we did because he potentially holds important information.'

'Carmel is only a support worker, not a social worker. She shouldn't have been holding meetings with you.'

'And why not? She's known Kenneth for twenty-five years.' She had known him the longest out of everyone. Social workers never stuck around in one workplace for long.

'When Carmel started with Homes 4 All, she signed a contract that she wouldn't speak to the media.'

'She probably can't recall that by now, and we aren't the media.'

Nadine ignored that. 'Kenneth has profound brain damage.'

'Which I didn't know until I visited him. Carmel hasn't done anything out of place.'

'We'll decide that. It isn't your command. Kenneth lives in the residential part of the supported living project,' added Nadine, softer.

'We didn't know that Anita had a low IQ,' said Higgins, stepping in, knowing I was about to blow my top.

'Anita needs help,' said Nadine, looking at him, sideways glancing at me, 'help with money. She's like an eight-year-old, intellectually.'

'But she agreed with us on certain things,' I said.

'She agrees with everything anyone says. She likes to please people. Anita looks *normal*, if you will, but she is very ill-equipped. She can't shower herself and needs someone else to cook for her.'

I didn't like Nadine's tone; it was creeping up again and sounded like she was talking to me like a child. Is this how she spoke to adults who had the IQ of a child?

I took a deep breath. I was proud that for the first time since Jason, someone was coming at me, and I didn't want to flee. But I couldn't kick her out. I could accept that I'd made a mistake, but her lack of respect was something else.

'We've had Anita here for hours,' I said. 'Why didn't you get here sooner if you are so concerned?'

'I was actually in meetings back-to-back all day over another emergency. Is that okay with you?' Nadine attempted to stare me out. Imogen looked aghast.

'Don't start with that tone again,' I said.

187

'When did Anita come to live at Homes … ?' asked Higgins, desperately trying to stick a pin in the atmosphere.

'Homes 4 All?' asked Imogen. 'Not until she was thirty-one.'

'What is your job description?' I asked.

'Support worker,' she said, glancing at Nadine.

'Is she allowed to speak with us? Is that okay by you?' I asked Nadine.

'That was 1995. Seventeen years after Karen's death,' said Higgins.

'What was Anita doing all that time before?' I asked.

'Living alone,' Nadine said.

'Getting into trouble,' said Imogen, clearly not caring to be silenced. 'Shoplifting, trying to survive without the skills to do it.'

I smiled at her. 'Thank you.'

'Then she got an IQ test in prison, didn't she?' blurted Imogen.

'Anita was in prison?' I asked.

Nadine screwed up her face. She gave up.

'The doctor noticed signs,' said Imogen, 'the prisons are full of people with mild learning difficulties or disorders like ADHD, Anita's IQ was very low, she joined our supported living service after her release.'

'We're all very fond and protective over Anita,' said Nadine.

'I appreciate that,' I said, still unappreciative of how they had barged in, and the implication that Higgins and I had somehow been rough.

Though I liked it, in hindsight, that Anita had people in her corner. And I liked that Nadine had nothing to say. Anita had spent time in jail, and there was Nadine running in as if we had pulled Mother Theresa in off the street.

'Imogen, we'll get Anita an appropriate adult,' I said.

When they left, I put my head on the table and felt like banging it against the surface.

'We have to scrap that interview,' said Higgins, 'they'll say we asked leading questions.'

He had, but I didn't want to fight with him too.

'We're going to have to start all over again,' I said.

Chapter 37

'Her social worker said Anita and Kenneth have similar problems,' I told Fleur Hewitt. 'Brain damage. Anita stated she had kidney problems when being checked in.'

'She and her brother were both poisoned?' asked Hewitt. 'I wonder if it occurred at the same time .... '

'I don't know. We need her records. But then, why wasn't she as ill? Really ill like Kenneth?' I pondered.

'Taller, older,' said Hewitt, 'probably didn't take as much. Hard to poison yourself fully.'

'You think this was how she tried to suicide, downing antifreeze?'

'Could be,' she said. 'Or maybe it was the mum.'

'A mother's place is in the wrong,' I echoed my old partner.

'From what I read, she seemed the sort. Two bumped off kids would have given her her freedom back.'

'That's a shitty thing to say.'

'Don't be touchy; I'm just surmising here.'

'But Napier never specified how Anita tried to end her life. Antifreeze could have been the method she chose.'

'The little brother saw Anita kill Karen,' said Fleur, 'so she tried to kill him and then herself, but was more cautious with herself. Any way to check the dates on that?'

'I can try. Or … there was this stepdad, Fleur. He lived in Sandhill some of the time. When the mum died he wouldn't take them.'

'No, hen,' said Hewitt. 'Women poison.'

'I'm not getting into men do this and women do that anymore,' I stated. I'd learnt that lesson too.

∗

That night Drew texted me to say he couldn't stop thinking about me. But that wasn't the plan. There had been no plan. Maybe if he was someone with a good job, any job, and I'd have thought he'd have been there for my kids as he was for his own, I'd have red-carded Paul and moved Drew in instead. But we were just worlds apart.

We can't do this and you know that, I texted him back.

∗

By nine p.m. Sarge Simon came back from Sandhill. 'From either of the back bedroom windows, the boy would have been able to see the area at the back of the flats,' he said, 'but he couldn't have seen where the body was left from any window.'

'Good to know, thanks for checking that. So you talked to the new people?' I asked.

'I did. The people aren't so new; they've lived there all this time from when the Halls left. But, Harry, one thing.'

'Uh-huh?'

'There used to just be a shed.'

'Okay. No wall? No fence?'

'There's a wall now; they put it up. Wasn't always there.'

'So Anita could have snuck out.'

'She could have.'

'Is the original shed still there?'

'No, this one is new.'

'I wonder if the old one had a window at the back of it. Kenny could have watched from there.'

'It was dark. Maybe the perp just didn't see him. At the side of the shed were some breeze blocks stacked up like steps that would have brought them out to the park. They are still there.'

'So access was really effortless,' I said. 'And Kenny, very likely did see something.'

'Too bad he can't tell us what he saw,' said Simon.

Chapter 38

The following day Hewitt took a call from the Crown Prosecutor, who said we couldn't charge Anita and had to let her go. Hewitt stood listening to the call, giving me her knowing look. 'Even if Anita Hall was charged,' Hewitt said after she'd ended the call, 'she would only be bailed, hen, being neither at high risk of repeat offending or of absconding.'

Now I had unearthed a 'healthy' rap sheet for Anita Hall, I had concluded she *was* at risk of repeat offending. It was not without precedent. I objected to the notion that Anita was some angel. Her record didn't stop growing once she went into supported living. Anita had attacked one of her support staff. Against instructions from Homes 4 All, that staff member had brought it to the attention of the police. She stated that many staff members had been grabbed by the neck by Anita during incidents where she had been unhappy about completing chores or making choices. I understood Anita had been institutionalised and that choice-making, therefore, became very difficult, and I felt for her. But I could not let go the fact that she had twice said she had killed Karen Ward. And hitting people is one thing, but grabbing them by the throat is a bright red waving flag. Anyone with a history of committing non-fatal strangulation is more likely to resort to more severe violence or murder. But I had to let Anita go.

Once she was released, I called Larne PSNI again. DI Posner was back on duty and had located that DNA sample from the nephew of the groundsman at Carnfunnock. He told me that he had left the results with someone.

'I called,' I said, 'you were on leave, and nobody seemed to know what I was talking about. So, can I have the results?'

'There was no familial link between the DNA found on the body of Rhonda Orr and Nick Flynn's nephew.'

'Thanks for trying, anyway,' I said, drained of energy.

'They might be unlinked murders,' said Posner.

'Can you call Rhonda's brother Barney and let him know, or do you want me to do that?' I asked.

'I'll make sure it happens within the hour, how's that?' he said.

'It's something,' I replied.

*

All morning it was dull and cold, drizzling on and off. Janet was shivering in her damp coat when she arrived at the station. 'I only just got your message. I've had a hectic day; I got here as soon as I could.'

'I'm afraid I called you too soon,' I told her.

'You have someone?'

'I apologise, Janet. It was Anita Ward, but we couldn't charge her.'

'But everyone said it was a man,' she said, frowning.

'We want to know that we have the right person this time.'

And I wasn't so sure Anita was that, not when I listened back to our interview with her.

'I just need a new name since Wayne has been exonerated,' said Janet.

Was he exonerated? The hair in Karen's hand wasn't his, that was all. The semen on Rhonda Orr's body was not Nick Flynn's. I could not give her a name.

'I want to let you know, Harriet, I'm going home. My daughter isn't due her baby for three weeks, but they're bringing her in early. Another reason why I wanted to see you in person.'

'I hope everything is okay.'

'Oh, thank you, that's sweet, and thank you for everything you've done. I appreciate it.' She sounded final, but first, I had a question for her.

'Janet, I have all this paperwork, but there is no statement from you. From that night.'

'I gave one.'

'Did you?'

'I spoke to someone and they were writing it all down.'

'Did they get you to sign anything?'

'I can't remember; my sister had just been found murdered.'

'Where were you that night? You said Karen was standing in for you, in work.'

'I was out.'

'Where?'

'The pictures.'

'Who with?'

'A boy.'

'His name?'

'Vern Brown.'

'*Vernon* Brown?'

'Yes. Stupid of me, I know.'

'Because he was older and married?'

'Oh no. The son. He was my age.'

'He's the brother of Tucker Brown?'

'Vern's a different kettle of fish. He was lovely.'

'Then why did you say it was stupid of you?'

'Because we lived so close together. It was always awkward seeing him after.'

'After what?'

'That date.'

'One date?'

'A one-off. I'm sure I said this when it all happened. I'm not keeping anything from anyone, except maybe Karen. I was going to keep it from her. I told her I was going out with a female friend.'

'Why did you lie to her?'

'I didn't think I was lying … It's just that she always fancied whoever I fancied. Got little fascinations about them. Like she did with Willie Samuel. I wanted to keep Vern a secret until maybe we got steady. We never did. It was one date, and then an awful thing happened that night. I know it sounds ridiculous, but I was raised in a very superstitious home. You saw a magpie, and you waved; you didn't walk under a ladder. Silly now, I know. I felt responsible, going on a date, sneaking around on Karen. I thought it was bad luck and my fault that she died. I came in from that date all blissed out, while my little sister was lying in the park.'

Chapter 39

A year before, I had seen Janet walking down the street crying after Fleur Hewitt rejected Janet's plea to reopen her sister's case. She wanted answers, but I suspected Janet hated facing the past; by now, I could sense when someone had little trust in the police.

I could understand: some days I had little or no faith in us either.

We knew that Karen had talked to a man, she had been seen doing it, and shortly after that, she was killed. A clump of someone's long brown hair was in a bag. We were too close to end this now. If we did, it would plague me. I could become like Mack Napier. Never knowing. I couldn't let that happen.

*

'I bumped you up the queue,' Kate Stile said in her lab. 'The DNA from the hair is no match for Anita Hall. She's in the system for a little light shoplifting.'

'And a few assaults too,' I said. 'But it's good news it's not her.'

'Is it?' asked Stile.

'I don't know,' I admitted. What was good was having answers. And eliminations. Personally, I liked Anita and was glad she was back at home and not sitting in a cell.

I sat with my head in my hands for about ten minutes.

The office was as dark as a January day. I was depressed. I lifted Janet's triumvirate of diaries, set them in front of me. She had lost her faith in us, in me. When the trust was gone, it was gone. I looked again at the sellotaped pages asking myself why I had allowed her that privacy. I began to pick with my thumbnail.

'What are you doing?' asked Higgins.

'I want to see what she doesn't want us to see.'

'We can steam it open or peel it off.'

'But that will be obvious,' I said.

'I agree we should read the closed pages. I mean, why has she done that?' Higgins pulled his seat beside mine.

'I haven't a baldy.'

'We can open it. If Janet complains we can blame it on a newbie.'

Fifteen minutes later, we had scraped the Sellotape from a sealed section of the 1977 diary. Date: Wednesday 6 April. It said:

Gonna go on a trip for Easter, think Karen might come too, trying to talk her out of it. Gonna tell Mum I'm staying at someone's house. Not like anything will happen.

Monday 11 April:

Nothing happened. A little bit of messing around. He lifted a patch of grass and put it down my jeans in front of the kids, in front of Karen, who ended up coming along. We were only allowed to go if we were going together. We pitched it as being a reward for all our babysitting, and plus, the kids were there, so Mum was okay with it.

———

198

Don't do it back to me, he said when I got a patch of grass in my hand. I did. I felt his underwear lift.

Later, we were camping, he got my hand and rubbed it on his crotch. His thingy was standing up. You did that, he said.

I went to the next sellotaped part. Monday 16 May.

We went fishing again. This time something happened.

I went to the laundry room at the campsite with Kenneth, next time I had Anita with me. I could tell by the look in his eyes he wanted me there alone. So I went, pretending I'd left my towel. He followed me. He had hidden my towel inside his jacket. I was standing at the sink when he came in and felt my bum. Then he kissed my neck. Then he pulled my jeans and pants down and asked me to bend over. I was worried it would hurt but I felt nothing. I think he couldn't get it up. He got frustrated and asked me to kiss him down there. I didn't want to get on my knees, the ground was dirty. Don't worry about that, he told me. But kissing wasn't enough, he wanted me to put it in my mouth. I told him I didn't want to. So he said, Get up, and he kissed me instead and wrapped my hand around it until it was nearly ready. We tried again, but it stayed limp.

He was annoyed, even though I told him I was sorry. Bet he never has this trouble for Maxine. She's sexy. Even I can see that. Next time I'm going to do it. I'm sixteen, sure. Some girls my age are already mums. Already married. He might be older but I want to give him this. I don't want him to go off me. I can't think of anything else.

Chapter 40

I called Janet. 'Look,' I said, 'this name cropped up when I was talking to Anita. Her stepfather, Geoff McDonald.'

'Yes,' Janet said. There was a tannoy in the background, and after a while, she said, 'give me a moment while I find a quieter spot.'

I wondered what was going through her head.

'I've heard that name a few times,' I said.

'I do remember Geoff McDonald.'

'Tell me about him.'

'He was a drifter, I suppose.'

'Did he work?'

'Geoff was like an odd job man or a fisherman. He didn't have a regular job.'

'He lived with the Halls?'

'He and Maxine, Anita's mum, were on and off more times than not. He lived there like a glorified babysitter, then she would throw him out and he would sleep in his car and then I would babysit.'

'What did you make of him?'

The tannoy went again.

'He was … I don't know. Funny, he was likeable.'

'Did you know him well?'

'No, not really.'

'Not really?'

'I had a few conversations with him.'

'I want to speak with him,' I said. 'See if we can locate him. Was he around at the time of Karen's death?'

'Erm … I can't think.' The tannoy went again. 'I'm in the airport,' she explained, 'going home.'

'Lastly,' I said, 'what age was he?'

'Probably late twenties. Maybe thirty-ish.'

I left her to ponder him. To remember laundry rooms and whatever went on with Geoff McDonald there. At sixteen, she would have been a year off the then age of consent. Sexual activity with a boy of her own age, like Michelle and Vernon Brown's son Vern, would have seemed normal. But McDonald could have been almost twice her age. He sounded like a creep to me. I wondered if Janet looked back and decided that McDonald had been grooming her. It is a symptom of grooming that sometimes victims start to believe they are in love with their abuser.

I told Constable Dylan West to look up any internal record for every Geoff McDonald in the UK.

'You know how to use the internal system?' I asked him.

'Of course I do,' he said, practically puffing out his chest.

After I wrote *DNA mismatching* under Anita's photo, I devoured the diaries all afternoon.

*

I needed a photo of Geoff McDonald to hold it against the artist impressions staring at me.

'Do you think Karen knew what happened between her sister and Geoff, that that was the conversation beside the van?' I asked myself.

'I wonder if he knew Rhonda Orr,' said Higgins.

'We need to find that out too.'

'From Janet's diary, we know he had a problem getting aroused. Maybe he tried with Karen too, and that's why she wasn't raped.'

'You could be right, Carl,' I said. 'Or he could only get aroused if he knew it was non-consensual.'

'If it was the same person, possibly McDonald, who killed Rhonda, by then he'd have gained confidence.'

'The motive for Karen's killing was sexual anyway,' I said, 'the removal of clothes and binning them.'

'Ma'am?' said Constable West in a green voice. Kalnino stood behind him, looking guilty as fuck too.

'Yes?' I asked West.

'Something's not working.'

Higgins looked up from a diary.

'Go help him, Carl,' I said.

He left for about ten minutes then, he came back and lifted his phone. 'He's right,' Higgins said. 'The internal computer system's not working.'

'What do you mean *not working*?'

'I don't know what he did, but the whole screen has been wiped.'

'Shit!'

'Never seen that before,' said Supt. Hewitt. 'What did you do?' she asked a red-faced Dylan West.

'I don't know,' he replied.

'Have you ever used the RMS system before?'

'Yeah,' West said, but his face said no.

'We need an IT person here right away.'

'Could it be a virus?' asked Kalnino.

I tried accessing the system on my computer, but whatever it was had run through my PC too.

'For fuck sake,' said Hewitt, 'nobody touches it until we work out the problem.'

Chapter 41

It stayed like that all day, in limbo, time wasting well into the evening. The IT guys were in accord: West had corrupted data, and it could possibly take weeks to fix.

Then Janet phoned me from her home in London. 'I spent all that flight thinking about Geoff,' she said.

'Yes?' I was short with her, frustrated. Surely getting handy with the Sellotape had made her think of him before.

'There's something I didn't tell you, because … well ….'

'What's that?' I asked.

'I'm tired.' Me too, I thought. 'I'm going to move on to a new part of my life. I'm going to be a granny. I don't want that to be marred by this. I had expected … hoped … that this would take a couple of weeks. It's so unrealistic, I know. And then I hoped the baby would be here afterwards, and everything would be over. Now I think it's time I gave up.'

'Why would you say that?' I asked.

'Because I found a lump in my breast last night.'

I didn't know what to say.

'It's probably nothing.'

'Hopefully,' I said.

'But it might not be. I've had breast cancer before,' Janet said. 'It's what took my mother's life. She was only forty-one.'

'I'm sorry to hear that. All of that.'

'Thank you, Harriet. It took up all my energy before. And I need my energy to help my daughter and to make sure I'm okay. To be around for this grandbaby.'

'I understand. But we don't have to stop anything. Just leave this to us. Concentrate on yourself and your daughter,' I told Janet.

'Thanks,' she said, 'that's very kind, but I don't want to waste any more of your time. I want you to close the case.'

I didn't say anything. I stared at the window as the rain thrashed it.

*

I suspected that Janet had shied away from the case because Geoff had been brought to the forefront, but no one would have opened this case if it were not for her wanting it open. Now it got personal, for Janet; threatened to show something of her, and publicly, she did not want it. Perhaps what she said was true. She had lived with not knowing, so she knew she could continue to. Unless she did know. But then why bother? Something was not right.

Janet talking about her mother's death got me thinking about my mother's death. I never liked to think about it. The last years of her life were too sad, I thought it was wrong of me to feel grief when I knew she was better off gone.

I had brought the boys to see her at the nursing home and Mother had stared straight through them.

I begrudged how she had been with her eldest grandchild, Gus. Doting and loving and energetic. That evening I was in the office alone when I needed someone to talk to. I could not burden my siblings; they had their own grief. I was always thought to be strong. Every one of them had their soft sides, and I, the baby, had the strength they all lacked.

When I got shot, no one called me. When I disclosed my rape and attack at Father's engagement party, I was not bombarded with calls asking me when it happened, offering belated support. Only Coral had sent a couple of texts telling me to call her whenever I was ready.

'I'm pulling an all-nighter,' I said on the phone.

'David's here,' Paul replied.

'I better not be on speakerphone!' I said.

He did not understand the need to forewarn, the need for privacy. He had done that to me a lot.

It reminded me of when Jason would tell his friends things I had said, always the most embarrassing things.

David, my twin sister's husband, would know about my behaviour at the engagement party. Had he been there? I couldn't even remember.

'You're not on speakerphone, and I'm going into another room,' said Paul.

'I can go now, mate,' I heard David say.

'You never told me what happened at the party.'

'What did happen?' I was fuzzy, and also, I wanted someone else to say it: you were raped, you were held hostage.

'You accused Jason of … some terrifying things.'

'You know we ended badly, that he was stalking me.'

'He sent you a few messages that I knew of.'

Paul was only concerned for himself, that I would one day accuse him. I wanted to say, Paul, you are markedly more likely to be raped, as a man, than falsely accused of it.

I saw it all the time. Since the Me Too movement, you had to take a close look at men who said shit like: Can't even look at a woman now!

Was my Paul as stupid as those men? Dr Coulter. Was he that thick?

'Jason did a lot fucken more than a few messages,' I screamed down the phone, and that seemed to do it.

Paul had seen me stressed. He'd definitely seen me at my worst. I had been at my worst since Jason. I couldn't remember being at my best, and that was the most significant loss. The old Harriet.

'You could have told me,' he said. Paul sounded on the verge of tears, like I had never heard him either.

'I called you and asked that you keep the boys safe.'

'I didn't know why.'

In our two and a half years, there was still a lot to learn. I didn't know him at all. But I did know that when he spoke to our pretty young babysitter, Lola, he would flirt outrageously. And with my twin, who is prettier than I. And I would often feel a flare of envy that would almost make me consider fucking him.

Now, I had a horrible vision of Paul trying to fuck Lola, though she was an adult, and had images of him perving over my pretty young nieces.

I hardly knew him or if I trusted him, and yet he was at home with my children.

I cried on the phone for ten minutes straight. Every now and then, I heard Paul mumble, 'You're okay. Harry, I love you. You're going to be okay.'

But I did not believe he loved me.

He was trying to end the call, to close down my feelings, wind them up and pack them away for me. I should have left him when he betrayed my father. I decided I was done with him. Well, as done as I could be with a man I could not leave.

Chapter 42

I left my car so I wouldn't be tempted to do something daft. Well, dafter; like drink drive. On the way to the hotel, I got the taxi driver to stop at the off-license. I started drinking in the room and kept it dark, just one light on by the bathroom. By the time Drew got there, I was already drunk. We didn't say a word at first. He came over to me and we kissed, and soon we were in bed. After we fucked he said, 'That was better than in a car, more room to manoeuvre.'

He wanted to cuddle but I didn't, so I poured myself another drink and climbed back into bed with it.

'Are you okay? I didn't hurt you, did I?' he asked with an odd amount of concern.

'Hurt me?' I laughed. He was athletic enough, but I was practically anesthetised with drink. I laughed harder. Is this what all men wanted, to hurt you?

'I just mean because ... you look like you've been crying.'

'Give me a break. Yes, your massive cock brought tears to my eyes.'

'Your bedside manner's shocking,' said Drew.

I didn't want to think about how I had been drinking and crying in the dark. I tried to kiss him, and he held me away. I stared at his perfect face.

He was so bleakly lovely, though it could never be a real thing between us.

'I haven't had a good day,' I said.

'I don't know how you do it,' Drew said. 'I've never told you before, but I do appreciate it's a shit job.'

'Somebody's got to do it, right?'

'You're only human, like the rest of us. I know that now.' How he had once hated me!

We interview paramilitaries, exert our stop and search powers, say: 'Turn out your pockets,' and yet once it had been the plan with community policing, to have them work with us, not against us. Some would say that conflict of interests means that we don't put them through the wringer enough. It was our unspoken thing and why we worried for our loved ones.

People like Drew had us where they wanted us. They ran the show.

'What's wrong?' he said, 'I knew there was something, you're crying.'

'Don't worry yourself,' I said.

'You're my girl. I'm going to worry about you, so don't tell me not to.'

'I'm not your girl.' I laughed.

'I was inside you a minute ago. My DNA is inside you now. If those things don't make you my girl, then nothing does.'

Then nothing does, I decided. I thought of the body of Rhonda Orr. Who told themselves she was their girl?

This possessive statement waved a red flag; Drew knew I had a family. And would it be such a loss to lose Paul? I figured he probably wouldn't care if Drew showed up at home and blew my cover. Just like I used to dream of doing to Greg.

I would imagine myself going to his house, and telling his wife, Jocelyn, that he was not to be trusted. That we were together. Then I got over that infatuation, that distraction away from thinking about Jason.

I was trying to fill a void with Greg like Drew was doing with me. But what if he was right, and I was his now? Was that so bad?

I had worked so hard for everything, and he was all kinds of wrong. I needed to end this shit and fast. I cried more and drunk more wine.

'I'm not bullshitting,' Drew said, 'when I say I want to know what's going on with you.'

So I told him, without once looking him in the eye, all about Jason, everything he had put me through: those days, beatings, my escape, my termination, then I stopped because I couldn't believe that I had said it, and so easily.

'What is his name?' asked Drew.

'Oh, no, you don't,' I said to stop this madness in its tracks. I was grateful he had not asked me why I didn't report it or any of the usual stuff. Drew Taylor, without hesitation, believed me.

He coolly asked me for a name again.

'Why do you want a name?' I asked.

'I'll let the boys have a word with him.' He laughed gently so I would know he was joking.

'No, Drew!' I said.

'Harry,' he said, 'you know everything about me and my life. Couldn't have a shit a while back without you there, breathing down my neck ….'

'Not quite,' I checked him.

'I just want to be here for you. You can talk to me about anything.' Drew wound his fingers around mine. 'What does he work as?'

'He's an architect,' I said.

'He would be,' Drew said with a smirk. I didn't know what he meant by that remark. Maybe he had a chip on his shoulder, a distrust of anyone with an education. He wasn't wrong about Jason, however. I recalled the enormous pride he got from telling people his profession. He was conceited and entitled.

Bolstered by Drew's immediate dislike for my ex, I told him how Jason and his brother owned a practice. I left out names. And it felt good to tell him, to tell someone who listened and didn't seem to judge – didn't seem to judge me, at least.

'Lately, my father got engaged to his mother, and then my ex started his shit again,' I said.

'I like how you say *father* and *mother*.' Drew smiled.

'My ex used to stalk me, you see.'

'Intimidation.'

'Yes, intimidation.'

'It's over, if you want it to be.'

'What does that mean?' I asked. 'If I *want* it to be?'

'You could royally fuck him over. If you wanted.'

'Do you think I don't *want* it to be over?' I cried.

'Confront him, then.'

I laughed. 'That easy!'

'It's that fucken easy,' said Drew.

What did he know about this? Jason wasn't selling drugs on my patch.

I'd lost my home. I'd been degraded as far as someone could be, though the transitory drunken idea that all I had to do was confront Jason made me feel good. Drew's confidence in me made mine multiply as I held his face and kissed him.

Chapter 43

I spent most of the night awake, listening to the rain. I must have slept a bit because I woke and cringed at the sight of Drew Taylor lying next to me. More than that, I cringed that I had opened up to him my biggest secrets and fears. I had taken this jump at Drew, connecting and not meaning to connect.

Drew ordered us room service and attempted to have breakfast with me. I necked a coffee and took a shower, trying to eek it out until he would get the hint and leave. But he slipped into the shower with me, and what can I say? I'm a weak woman.

After, I said, 'That was a crazy night.'

'Intense,' he said, staring at me as I dressed.

'How embarrassing,' I said. 'I don't know why I was so emotional.'

Drew frowned. 'I mean the sex,' he said, 'we have some mad chemistry, don't we? It's like nothing I ever had before.'

I turned on the hairdryer and looked in the mirror, where I met his gaze. His eyes recorded me, and I became self-conscious. I turned the hairdryer off.

'I mean, I said things I shouldn't have, Drew. It wasn't … ' I was about to say 'professional of me', but I remembered I wasn't at work.

'You want to keep this casual,' he said.

'Yes,' I almost cried, 'yes. We have to.'

'Who wrote the rules?'

I almost laughed. The thought of a DI with a paramilitary! Though he had come up clean in recent investigations and was trying to be better for Roxanne's sake and for their kids, I also knew his background too well. Despite his few pleasant characteristics and how attractive he looked, how good he smelled, and the alchemy there had proven to be in the sack – he wasn't wrong there – there were more important things than fucking.

I looked at the time; Paul would be leaving my boys to the nursery. I wondered if they asked for me that morning.

'It has to stay like this,' I told Drew as he lay on the bed vaping. I surprised myself. I had planned to say *it has to stop*. But I couldn't. I did need this. After everything, I deserved *this*. 'Like this. Nothing deeper, nothing permanent, Drew. Just sex.'

*

With the system down, I good-old-fashioned Googled Geoff McDonald and found a few locals with the same name. None of them his age. Then we called out with Vernon Brown. Vernon was surprised to see me back. 'Do you remember a Geoff McDonald?' I asked him.

'Refresh my memory,' he said.

'Geoff lived with Maxine Hall in Sandhill Park.'

'Maxine. Now she was one sexy woman.'

'Really?' I asked.

'Sexy Maxi. She had it off with plenty of fellas.'

'Really?' I repeated, unimpressed.

215

'Tragic what happened to the lad, like.'

'Kenneth?'

'Aye.'

'Da,' came a voice from the door. 'Peelers are outside; what's Tucker been up till now?' In walked his other son. It had to be. He looked just like Tucker but taller and more drawn out. 'Shit, sorry!' He smiled. 'I was only joking there.'

Vernon laughed to himself.

'It's not about your brother, for once. It's about that wee girl Karen Ward from yesteryear.'

'Yeah?' The man sat down clutching a bag of Space Raiders.

'He's the good son,' explained Vernon, 'that's our Wee Vernon.'

'Wee Vernon.' The man scoffed good-naturedly. 'Six foot four and coming sixty, but I'm still *wee Vernon.*'

'Is Tucker not the good son, then?' asked Higgins, going with the jovial mood of the room.

'Oh no,' said Vernon Senior. He took in a sharp breath and smiled again. 'I know he's ours .... '

'He's not mine,' interrupted his son.

'You know what I mean. I haven't disowned him.'

'Not yet,' said the son.

'I can't say nothing bad about him, is what it is. Except, I will say – and I've said it to Tucker's face – you know I have, Vern, he's not a worker, like, is he?' Vernon, the father, looked at me. 'Not like this one; Wee Vernon's got a great job.'

'It's been many moons since Karen Ward was killed,' his son changed the subject.

'Did you know her? May I call you Vernon?' I asked.

'Sure. Don't call me Wee Vernon, though. Aye, I knew Karen. Knew her to see, we played out there swinging around lampposts and the like when we were wee tots, didn't we, Da?'

'That you did.'

'But we grew up and I moved, see, to Bangor.'

'He has a lovely house in a nice area.'

'Didn't to begin with, Da. I was living in a one-bedroom flat in Sufferin Avenue. It was dire. But who wants to hear about that,' he said. 'I saw on the news that you were reopening investigations. I hope you get him this time, but I can't say I hold out much hope. And that's not to offend you; it's just been so bloody long.'

'Your man Simpson didn't do it. Remember everyone thought he did?' said the father.

'Aye, I heard that,' said the son.

'So, you knew Janet better than you knew Karen?' I ventured.

'Oh, lovely wee Janet,' said Vernon Senior. 'He fancied her something shocking.'

'Da!' Vernon Junior laughed. 'When I was seventeen!'

'Did you ever go on a date with her?'

'Once. To the pictures.'

'I didn't know that,' said his father.

'Why would I tell you, big mouth,' his tone grew grave, 'it was the night her sister was killed, actually.'

'Janet said. That night you didn't see anything suspicious?' I asked.

'Nope. I'd had a wee kiss in the back row. I was only seeing stars.'

'He's an aul romantic,' said Vernon Senior.

'Michelle, your mother, Vernon, gave a statement and a description of the man she saw talking to Karen, and it was strikingly similar to one by another witness.'

'Don't I know? Mum lost her life for it.'

'She didn't,' his father interjected. 'That was ... '

'Who? A friend of Tucker's?' asked Vernon Junior.

'I don't know about that.'

'Who's to say that one isn't the other?'

'Do you think your mother was targeted because she gave a statement to the police?' Higgins asked.

'It was that or someone trying to get Tucker. He often drove her car. Like he lived here and had everything handed to him.'

'Vernon, sure you know why that was,' said his father wearily.

'Yes, Da, I do, because you two were heart-scared of him.'

'Heart-scared!' His father tutted. 'He was my son. *Is* my son.'

'Chance after chance, sure, I just get on with my life.'

'Wee Vernon has a brilliant job.'

'Ach, stop going on about that. You'd think I'm the foreign secretary or something. I work as a cashier in a bloody bank.'

'You won an award and all.'

'Team leader of the year. I'm not solving murders.'

'We're not solving any murders right now either,' I said, 'but we want to. We weren't here back then.'

'No, you probably weren't even alive.'

'Not long after.'

'I still had a decade to go,' said Higgins, flouting his youth in my face.

'I was telling your father that your mother gave the RUC a description. She said that the person she saw talking to Karen Ward had long hair, dark hair. I'm wondering if it might have been a man who lived in the area then. He was called Geoff McDonald.'

'Never heard tell of him,' said Vernon Senior.

Vernon Junior's face creased, then lit up. 'Yes, yes, you have. He's *your man*.' He backhanded his father on the arm.

'Who's *your man* now, when you're writing home?' asked his father, startled, as if waking up.

'I just explained to your father,' I said. 'Geoff was the partner of Maxine Hall.'

The son stared at his father. 'Geoff. Your man in Sandhill who slept in his car. You know him.'

Vernon Senior laughed, then screwed up his eyes. 'Was he a hippy-looking lad? Liked his fishing?'

'Did he?' asked the son. 'I don't know, but he was a bit of a hippy, surely.'

'I remember his missus, Sexy Maxi.'

Vernon Junior tutted. 'Sexy Maxi,' he repeated, 'Maxine would kick Geoff out quare and frequent; she was always throwing his clothes into the garden, out the window.'

Vernon Senior laughed again. 'The things you think are important when you're young!'

'He was a nice enough guy,' said the son, 'she was a crazy one. Sure she poisoned the kids.'

'Did you ever think there was anything concerning about him?' I asked.

'No,' said Vernon Junior. 'Not saying I knew him well, only had a couple of pints with Geoff.'

'You'd have been too young to drink back then.'

'Hate to disappoint you, Da. He can't ground me now, can he?' He laughed. 'I'm nearly sixty.'

'Stop ageing yourself, son; you've a couple of years yet.'

He was the age Karen would have been had she been alive. I wanted to rid the joviality from the air, but this was their weekly visit, and they didn't want to spend the time being depressed. There was enough of that about. Having a laugh didn't help Janet or me.

'Could you describe Geoff to me?' I asked.

'He was tall, with long hair.'

'His face, any distinguishing features?'

'How do you mean?'

'Birthmarks?'

'Not that I noticed.'

'Scars? Tattoos?'

'I can't remember. His eyes, though.'

'Yes?'

'They were sort of smallish.'

'Nose?

'He had one.' He laughed at himself. 'It was sorta,' he bobbed his head in thought, 'a biggish nose.'

'Did your mother know him?'

'Oh no. Doubt it. Different circles. She didn't drink in bars. She wouldn't have known them.'

'Kept herself for her church friends,' said Vernon Senior.

I found the artist impressions on my phone. 'Who does this look like to you, any neighbour, anyone from that time?'

Vernon Senior lifted his glasses from the arm of his chair and looked at the impressions as I moved between them, then he said, 'No. That face is not ringing any bells for me, dearie.'

'Da, give me your glasses.'

'They're not prescription, only out of Poundland.'

'That's okay, give them here.'

Vernon Junior looked at the images, sizing them up. 'This could be Geoff,' he said.

Chapter 44

Father and I went fishing together years ago. It used to be our thing. I imagined two young girls from working-class East Belfast thinking it a tedious pursuit, though respite from their everyday lives of caring for their mother.

It was also when Geoff would groom Janet. With this in mind, I phoned her at noon.

'Have you thought any more about Geoff McDonald?' I asked. I decided I would not tell her that I had read her diary.

'Geoff,' she hummed and hawed. 'Och, kind of.'

'He would take Anita and Kenneth fishing,' I said.

'I don't think he did. Only when I was there.'

'So you went on one of the trips, Janet?'

'I went on a few, as I recall. I was there to mind the children. Geoff was getting them out of their mother's hair, but he wasn't an angel.'

'Wasn't he?'

'People think other people do good things to be good; you might think it's unkind of me, but I tend to ask myself what's in it for them.'

'What *was* in it for him?'

'He liked to keep Maxine happy when he could. She was good to him in return. You see, Maxine had money.'

'Tell me more about that,' I said.

'People talked about Geoff as if he was a saint, but Geoff didn't have to work. With Maxine, he had a roof over his head. Yes, he did mind her kids when, in that day and age, everyone thought a mother's place was at home. They would say that he was *mad to take up with her*. But, believe me, Geoff was indubitably the lucky one.'

'Why is that?'

'Oh, Harriet, Maxine was drop-dead beautiful, and she gave him security. She'd won a large amount of money. Not only that, when I was babysitting, she would make dinner for the kids before she went out.'

'Yes, Maxine liked to party, I heard.' I was sick of hearing it, but it felt remiss to leave it out just because I felt judged by the comments.

'She was just a sociable girl, you know. Friendly and funny as anything. Maxine was a young girl still herself; fifteen when she had Anita, and everyone around her wanted her to have this monotonous life. Maxine had no one and nothing, and then, these two children. They were gorgeous, yes, but a handful, too. And she had to do it all on her own. So I do think she deserved a night out a couple of times a week. It was what the other girls who weren't married were doing. Plus, can you imagine being a mother at fifteen?'

'No,' I said. One of my nieces was that age, Charly's eldest girl, Elle. The thought of her as a parent terrified me.

'Maxine did a great job,' said Janet. 'Those children were clean and looked after, she did homework with them, but nobody else saw it like that.'

'Why was that?'

'I suppose they weren't in her house like I was. They just wanted to focus on how she liked a night out. Say things about her. The kids were in bed sleeping by then, anyway. At least, Kenny was. He wasn't missing her.'

'Thank you for that,' I said.

'I know the stories you'll be getting told by people who never darkened Maxine's door.' Janet stopped and then added, 'Do you remember what I said about closing the case?'

'I'm afraid that's not an option now,' I told her.

'I understand. But can I ask that you leave me out of every detail?'

'If I have questions, I might need to contact you. There was no one closer to Karen than you.'

Janet sighed long and hard. 'I will help,' she said, 'but I'm not strong enough to go through this again. Which probably sounds awful to you when you are doing so much, and I'm the one who asked you to.'

'It does not sound awful,' I tried to reassure her.

'I thought I'd just find the strength. I could have pushed for this … thirty-odd years ago, but my daughter was my focus. I didn't want to make her childhood about this awful thing. Then twenty years ago, I thought about it, but she was having a bit of a crisis. Turned out to be nothing too dreadful.' Janet sighed. 'Forgive me, Harriet, but I found that there was never going to be a good time, and now, it's maybe the worst of all …. I'm about to be a granny any day. I don't want that little one's life blighted by what happened in the past.'

'Janet, I get that. I won't get in touch unless I have to.'

'Okay. Thank you.'

'But can you spare ten minutes now?'

Too polite to gripe, she took her time, then said, 'I can.'

'Tell me everything you know about Geoff McDonald, and please, Janet, don't leave anything out.'

Chapter 45

'I can't remember what he even looked like,' she said.

Did she forget conveniently? Was Janet saying all these nice things about Maxine out of guilt of being with her man? For now, I would let her keep her secret. I'd been allowed a few of my own over the years. If I got suspicious that she was bullshitting me, I might need to wheel Geoff out and their dalliance in the campsite laundry room, and what we knew. Though she had not named Geoff in her diary, that person she wrote about had to be him.

'Where was he after Karen was killed?'

'You seem to think it was him,' she said, somewhat surprised.

'We don't know. We're testing all avenues. Where was he after Karen was killed?'

'No one else ever mentioned him before.'

'Janet, where was he?'

'He came to mine one night and said he was sorry to hear about Karen. He sat with Mum.'

'Did he say anything to you alone?'

'He might have, I can't recall.'

'Try.'

There was no response.

'Were you friendly with Geoff?'

'No.'

'What did he say when he came to your place?'

'He was asking what people saw that night. He was being helpful.'

That was a bad sign, of course, being interested, watching the fallout of the crime, being around, getting off on it, trying to act natural.

'He was like that,' said Janet, 'but a lot of folks were. Then, soon after that, we all believed Wayne Simpson had something to do with it. He was way worse than anyone for asking questions and being around. It was Wayne and only Wayne for a long, long time.'

'But Geoff McDonald,' I said, 'did you get a feeling about him?'

'A bad feeling?'

'Just like something was not right with him?'

She didn't answer.

'Janet, can I ask you to tell me anything you remember about him now or later when you've had a chance to think about him more?'

Perhaps now she realised she'd been abused by a predator. In England, sex at sixteen was legal, but not here, not then. Janet was entrusted to him by her parent, who must have liked him to have allowed it.

Or perhaps Karen was their little chaperone, and the thought that he possibly did the same thing to her little sister after Janet's introduction was too much to bear for Janet. She was in denial, I concluded.

'What did your mother think of Geoff?' I asked.

'Most people liked him. He was sincere.'

*

That Wednesday afternoon, since I couldn't look up the corrupt files, I called the supported living setting where Kenneth lived. 'Does Kenneth have any more fishing trip photos?' I asked Carmel.

I didn't want to ask Anita. I'd leave her be for now.

'I'll check and get in touch,' Carmel said. 'I can do that, can't I?'

'If you would, I'd be very grateful.' I gave her my work mobile number.

'I got a right ticking off from the very top for talking to you,' she said.

'That's not good, Carmel.'

'I don't care. I'm about to leave soon anyway; I'm going to work for my daughter, so they can shove any bad reference where the sun doesn't shine.'

'Where are you going to be working?' I asked.

'My daughter has opened a beautiful little florist's in East Belfast. Violet's, it's called.'

'Nice. Good luck to you.'

'Thank you, Detective.'

'Are you sure you don't mind helping us?' I asked her.

'I'm helping the police. How can that ever be wrong?'

'I don't want to put you in an awkward position.'

'You're not,' Carmel said.

Within half an hour, she called me back and said, 'I looked in Kenny's photo albums; there are some photos.'

'Fishing?' I asked.

'Yes.'

'Do any of them feature a man?'

'Yes. They feature a lot of people.'
'Can I come out and take a look?'

∗

I was out with her in no time.

'Where's Kenneth?' I asked.

'My colleague took him and Trevor out for a drive. They are going for ice cream. Do you think you'll be long?' asked Carmel, losing her nerve.

'Shouldn't be,' I said.

I looked through the photos; there were photos of an attractive woman.

'That's their mum,' she said. 'And that is young Anita.'

She had lank brown hair, but she and her brother were dressed nicely. They looked happy; Kenneth had his characteristic big smile plastered over his face. I understood what Janet was saying, they looked like a happy family, but then again, families could be deceiving. They could pull it together for a photo.

'Does he only have photos from this time?'

'No. One box of more from when he was a baby. There are some in it from when he was starting school.' There was a well-worn album, too. His favourite photos compiled by staff. On his bedroom wall, there were photos of him by the water.

'Fishing with his stepfather?' I asked.

'I believe so.'

'Any photos of the stepfather?'

Carmel flipped through the album. 'Here.'

229

There was a photo of a man with long brown hair. He was dressed in seventies gear. There were two girls. One standing at each side of him, kissing each of his cheeks. I looked closer. One blond, one dark-haired. Those girls were the Ward sisters, I was nearly sure, though the photo was very blurred. One of the Hall kids had taken it, or it was on a timer. The man was sitting down, so it was impossible to see his height. He was smiling, and his eyes were scrunched up. I took a photo on my phone.

'Does he ever get in touch?'

'No, but Kenneth hasn't forgotten him. He points at the photo and tells you the names.'

'Can he show me when he comes back?'

She frowned. 'Maybe, and we can get Trevor to stay in the car. He doesn't react kindly to strangers being in his home, and it is his home.'

Carmel might have held minimal respect for the regulations of her employer, but she respected the rules of the house and the people she supported.

'Please,' I said, 'if it isn't too much trouble.'

She sent a text to the support worker in the car, and hot on the heels of that, Kenneth came in and saw me standing in his room.

'This nice lady wants to see your photos, Kenny. Will you show her?'

'Photo,' he said and ambled toward me.

He attempted to hug me when Carmel intercepted, got him firmly but gently by the arm and steered him away.

'I'd love to see your photos, Kenny. Is that okay with you if I take a look?' I asked.

230

'Photo,' he repeated.

'Discretion about what your name and profession is, okay?' said Carmel.

'Noted,' I said. 'Do you like fishing, Kenny?' I asked.

'Fish,' he said, closing his eyes and almost losing his balance. Then blinking like Anita did.

'I love these photos of you fishing. I used to go fishing with my daddy when I was a little girl.'

'Girl,' Kenneth said, taking every last word from each sentence. I wasn't sure if he understood anything, but I needed to know what he remembered.

I looked at the photos. 'What is this?' I asked him.

'Kenny, is this a lake?' asked Carmel.

'Lake,' he said in a deep blink. Then he opened his eyes, honed in on my handbag and started to rifle through it.

'Oh, no,' I said, 'you can't.' I took it from him, thinking of my pill, my breath freshener, headache tablets and three packets of polo mints.

'Kenny, look. Who is this?' Carmel distracted him with a photo of himself as a boy.

'Me,' he said enthusiastically, pointing.

'Great man, and who is this?' She pointed at the photo of the man.

'Geoff.'

'Who is Geoff?' I asked.

'Geoff,' Kenny repeatedly, blinking.

I felt very depressed. He looked happy, but Kenny Hall seemed to lack the understanding that he had lost such valuable things: his potential, independence and adulthood, half of his childhood.

I was furious toward whoever did this to him. His sister, his mother, or this Geoff character.

'Who are these girls?' I asked about the two girls kissing Geoff.

'Nita,' Kenny said.

'I don't think that's Nita,' said Carmel. She looked at the next page, and there was Anita, unmistakable with her long dark hair. 'Who are these girls?' she asked again, flipping back.

He tried for my handbag again, found a packet of polos.

'Kenny, not a choice,' Carmel told him.

He was losing interest in answering me.

'Kenny,' I said, 'is this Karen?'

He didn't look.

'Or Janet?' I asked him and his eyes lit up. I was clutching the polo mints in my hand. 'Can he?' I asked Carmel.

'No, they run right through him.'

'Jan-ah,' he said slowly, sweetly. While he blinked, Carmel mimed for me to get rid of the polos; I put the mints in my back pocket and put my bag over my arm. Out of sight, hopefully, out of mind.

'Oh, I think Kenny likes Janet,' said Carmel, trying to distract him.

'Do you like Janet?' I asked him.

'Jan-ah,' he repeated, all smiles.

He flipped a few pages forward, and there she was, in another photo. Geoff too, standing side-on, watching her, and smiling.

'She went fishing with you when you were young, didn't she? Did she babysit you?'

'Short sentences, keywords,' said Carmel.

'Janet fishing?' I asked.

He thought. 'Yah,' he said.

'Karen?' I asked. 'Karen fishing?' I flipped back and pointed at the other girl. 'Janet's sister.'

He smiled and nodded. 'Janet.' Blink. 'Sissy,' he said.

'Can I borrow these?' I asked. He pulled them towards him.

'Distraction,' said Carmel, her phone beeped. She glanced at it. 'Trevor is coming back. Kenny, help make dinner.'

'Help,' he said and took her hand.

She looked back as they left the room. 'Confiscate a few images, restore later, okay?' A code.

'Okay,' I said.

'Be discrete?'

'I will.'

They walked on.

'I'll let myself out,' I said.

'Thank you,' she called.

'Lady?' asked Kenneth.

'Yes, lady. Bye, lady,' said Carmel.

In a moment, I had left with the photos in my bag. I waved in the window. 'Bye, Kenny.'

'Bye,' he said, then remembering, 'pol-ah mint?'

Their service car returned, so I quickly got into my own before it precipitated issues with Trevor.

Poor Kenneth. I almost didn't want to leave him, but I was glad that I could.

———

Chapter 46

By four p.m., we arrived to speak to digital forensics specialist Ashley Stinnett. I laid the photos out of Geoff McDonald, and the copies Higgins had made of the artist impressions. 'Any chance it could be the same person?' I asked.

'The sketches have that rounded nose and small eyes you were telling me about on the phone,' Stinnett said. 'The photos, although they are not great quality, I see a likeness.'

'What about the side-on photo?' asked Higgins.

'That one is harder to tell, all that hair covering the side of his face. This one is clearer.' Stinnett meant the one where the girls were kissing him. 'His mouth looks wide, his nose more bulbous at the end.' She ran a lidded pen around his nose. 'Let me check.'

'Will this take long?'

'You can go and get a coffee if you like. Come back in half an hour.'

We did just that. When we returned, Stinnett had the image almost restored on her computer monitor with a grid over his face.

'I did some ratios,' she said, 'eyebrow to forehead. Eyes to chin. The images still aren't wonderful but when you use the maths, and then measure these.' Stinnett tapped the artist impressions. 'It's as good as we're going to get.'

'And, how does it match up?'

'It matches very well.'

*

As Higgins drove, I did a simple Google search of Geoff McDonald. I left off the search terms *Belfast*, or *Northern Ireland*, like I had Googled before, and this time I looked under the News category.

'Here is a Geoff McDonald in Birmingham. With photo.'

'Does it look like him?' asked Higgins.

'I don't know. This Geoff McDonald is totally bald and looks to be in his early fifties. Hold on … he was the stepfather of Kira Tooth.'

'Who is that? Rings a bell.'

I looked into the case. Just as I had suspected, Kira was a missing girl who turned into a murdered girl.

'She had gone out to meet her boyfriend and never came home. Kira's body was found dumped in a derelict house a few days later. She had been bludgeoned to death. This was in 2001.'

I scrolled back to the photo of Geoff McDonald. In the photo, he was standing beside his partner, Nanette. They were offering a one hundred-grand reward for any information that would lead to an arrest. They looked forlorn. They also looked like an odd couple. Nanette was obese; this Geoff was a streak of piss. He older, her much younger.

'That was almost twenty years ago. The age is right,' said Higgins as he drove through the Holywood Arches.

When we got to Strandtown, I ran to my desk and searched more on the net about the Kira Tooth case.

'A thousand men in the area had their DNA tested, hundreds of statements were taken,' I told Higgins. 'Guess what? No conviction.'

I looked for more photos of him and of Nanette Tooth, Kira's mother. There was nothing that wasn't related to the case. That petered out, as they do. This Geoff McDonald wore glasses and was gaunt. I could not tell if it was the same guy from the lake with the long brown hair. His features were different. The glasses perhaps magnified his eyes, offset a large nose. The likelihood was that it was not him. Still, I saved the image and emailed it to Ashley Stinnett.

Chapter 47

Stinnett replied quickly, saying, 'From the sketch, it's hard to tell, but it could be him. From the old photo, the one of him standing side-on, the pose is not unlike the one at the lake. The neck measurements are the same. And the nose, and given how he would have aged since then, show a strong possibility that it's the same person.'

Most recent records said that Nanette Tooth was living alone in Birmingham. I got a number for her and phoned at six p.m.. I explained that I needed to talk to Geoff to eliminate him from enquiries for a historical case.

'He doesn't live here anymore. We split up in 2003,' she said.

Two years after Kira was killed.

'I read about your daughter, Kira. I'm sorry you went through that.'

'Not more than I am, bab,' said Nanette.

'Of course,' I said. 'I'm working on a case of another young girl who was murdered forty years ago in Belfast.'

'Well, I know how that mummy feels.'

'Pardon?'

'We are part of a special club no one ever wants to join.'

'Unfortunately, her mother died a long time ago. She died not long after her daughter.'

'I had a heart attack not long after Kira was found. A broken heart. And Geoff, he was my backbone throughout it, and him poorly himself.'

'Poorly?' I asked.

'Going through cancer. A few times it returned. I thought I'd lose him too, and then I did.'

'Have you kept in contact or heard how he is now?'

'We kept in contact for a while, then he left me completely. I hope he's doing okay.'

'Was he originally from Northern Ireland?' I asked.

'He was a Belfast boy. Yes, he was.'

'What did he work at when you lived together?'

'He didn't,' Nanette told me, 'early retirement on medical grounds.'

'Oh yes,' I said. 'Before retirement?'

'He was a civil engineer.' The Geoff I wanted to get my hands on didn't work. I supposed it was possible, if it was him, he could have trained, had a career, then lost it again all within the last forty-one years.

'Do you know where he lives now?'

'I don't.'

*

He had to be in England. I contacted an ex-colleague who now worked at the London Met. and asked him to run a search for me. I named him as Kira Tooth's stepfather. And he had been Anita's and Kenneth's. I wondered how many stepchildren Geoff McDonald had accrued over the years.

How many had met a devastating fate? I had to come clean that that was what I was thinking to the officer on the phone.

'Age?' he said.

'About seventy by now.'

'Previous address?'

I gave him the Birmingham address where he had lived with Nanette Tooth.

'Could he be Geoffrey? Or spelt with a J?'

'No, Nanette Tooth told me it was Geoff. G.'

'That narrows it down. There is one, a Geoff McDonald on the UK census.'

'About seventy?'

'Age 55-60.'

'Too young.'

'This was from eight years ago. He was registered as living with Kathleen Gilmour, age 50-55, and Eloise Gilmour, age 10-15.'

'Where do they live?'

'Watford, London. Green Road.'

*

'I want to go to London,' I told Fleur Hewitt. 'Geoff possibly killed his stepdaughter, Kira. He possibly tried to kill Anita and Kenneth, and with Karen, he succeeded. Now he is with another woman who has a young daughter.'

'Don't you think it's gone on a little long? It's time to get back to your real work.'

'What is my real work if not this?'

'It's heating up here with the drugs gang.'

It was always the same; they dropped breadcrumbs, we weren't allowed to touch them.

'Let me finish this.'

'Are you sure?' she asked. 'This is juicy.'

I wanted a professional distance from all of that. I wanted to immerse myself in this old case and stay clear of Drew and his mates.

Chief Dunne came over then. I explained to him about my findings. Hewitt, knowing bitch that she is, and his niece, lifted the updated picture of the twins on their second birthday and showed it to Greg.

'Did you see this?' she asked him. 'Dotes, right?'

He looked at the photo; he couldn't help it. She had it right in front of his face. I looked away.

'Very nice,' he said. 'I think you should go to London, Sloane. I'll sanction it.'

I was pissed off with Fleur. As good a friend she had turned out to be, and as much as I enjoyed her private jokes, these were my kids, and Greg did not deserve to see them.

Albeit he had almost bought his way to them, I was thankful he had no interest in being a dad all over again.

Greg walked off.

'Higgins isn't going,' Hewitt said.

'But he's been with me every step of the way,' I said.

'Harry, has he done anything stupendous?'

'No, but nor have I.'

'Where is he?' she asked.

'He finished at his normal time.'

'Your idea to track McDonald.'

'It is.'

'I trust your instincts.'

'Thank you.'

'I'll clear our jolly with Uncle Buck.' She nodded towards Greg as his office door closed behind him. I had to snicker at this nickname she had for him.

'I've already cleared it,' I said, staring at the twins' photo. 'Dunne said he'd sanction it.'

'I mean for me to join you,' Hewitt said.

*

I brought a late dinner home for Paul and me. Indian takeout, his favourite. I planned to give my bad news after a lovely meal. 'I have to go away with work,' I said as we washed the dishes.

I could tell he was annoyed, but he just said okay. Maybe I was fooling myself that my leaving for a while would annoy him. He probably wanted the break.

When I packed my bags, he called his mum to rope her in to help with the boys. I set my phone on the bed and called Coral on speakerphone. I skimmed over her asking if I needed to talk about what I disclosed at the party. She agreed to make herself available if Paul got stuck and needed support.

Chapter 48

The next morning, I visited my eldest brother, Brooks. After four months inside, he was out of jail now, in his own place, a flat off the Ballysillan Road. As soon as I clapped my eyes on him, I knew Brooks was using again. After gaining weight, he looked so skinny again. He was anxious and scratching at his head.

'It's a lovely day, clear and blue, and you're cooped up in this flat,' I said before noticing his friend sitting on the sofa.

'Is she the girl who's bringing the buds?' asked a friend wearing glasses that sat on the dip at the end of his nose.

'That's my sister,' said Brooks.

'Which one are you?' asked the man. 'The nice one or the bitch.'

'Bit of both, actually,' I said.

'Bet you're the cop.'

'How's the kids?' Brooks asked me rolling a cigarette on the arm of his chair.

I stopped myself saying, how are yours? His boy and his girl, they were in their late teens and early twenties. Their birthdays sat in the deep recesses of my mind. Brooks' kids Ethan and Roni were living in a tower block in Walthamstow with his ex-wife Lydia. They hadn't seen him in forever.

'The boys are good,' I said. 'How are you? On gear again, I see.'

'It's all I know,' he said.

Forget the private school and skiing trips, and the brilliant creative brain he had; Brooks couldn't remember life before his first fix.

There was a time when our mother had just died, and he was arrested for armed robbery, when I found myself frustrated and angry with him. Now I had my old feelings towards him, sympathy and love. I always had a soft protective spot for the big lump. Big skinny lump he was now, compared to in jail when he was fattening out, eating. Off the gear. Until he got prescribed Pregabalin in prison.

'Can I talk to you in the kitchen?' I asked him.

He got up from his seat and followed me in. There was a tourniquet on the plastic table. Drugs paraphernalia on the kitchen counter.

'Daddy's engaged,' I said, and he laughed. 'To Jason's mum.'

'Your Jason?'

'Not *my* Jason. But, that one …. '

Brooks regarded me attentively.

'I wouldn't mind anyone else. I would be happy for him. It's just … Jason …. '

'Was an asshole,' said Brooks.

'You think so?'

'You told me about him.'

'I didn't tell you much.'

'I can tell he was a fucken fake. Just incredibly materialistic and had to have everyone like him.'

'He was,' I said. 'He really was like that.'

243

'It's okay,' Brooks said. 'Charles will probably kill Yvonne too.'

'You don't agree with what he did to Mummy?'

'Harriet, he could have gone to Switzerland with her. Done it right.'

Brooks was one to talk, with his ill-gotten drugs.

'How would he have gotten her there?' I asked. 'She would have had to agree, and she was beyond that, Brooks. It's easy to be idealistic now.'

'She was still my mother.'

He couldn't accept Mother's illness. Not that her condition could be blamed for how he was; Brooks always had a substrate breakability. He was her firstborn; she was off work when she had him. Brooks had probably had the best of her. His view of our father's actions was utterly different to mine.

Mother could not tell us what she wanted, but there was the chance that she could have told us in the early days. She could have said, put me out of my misery if it drags on and on. But she had not. Not to my knowledge.

At least Father hadn't revealed this in court. But that was his arrogance showing. He didn't reveal much at all. And it worked for him.

'I'm sorry, Brooks,' I said.

'Not your fault. Don't fret, my wee pet. It won't last with Yvonne Lucie.'

'He lasted fifty years with Mummy.'

'That's what people did then. So, he has started again?'

'Who? Daddy?'

'I'm talking about Jason. Remember he used to send you those crazy messages.' Brooks remembered when I was pregnant with the boys and Jason was harassing me. I'd told my brother dribs and drabs.

'He's started again,' I said, 'I think it's because of this engagement.'

'Tell your dad what he did, and he'll drop her.'

'I did and he hasn't.'

'Fuck, I don't know then. If your right arm's causing you pain .... '

I frowned at him.

'Cut it off, Harry.'

'Got a machete I could borrow?' I joked.

'For your arm?'

'No. Jason's fucken head.'

Brooks laughed. 'It can be arranged.'

'You know I'm joking, right?'

'I know, kiddo. Just hold tight. One day at a time.'

'Have you turned into Addam? You sound like you've found God.'

'Oh, I have. She's swimming through my veins as we speak.'

Chapter 49

I collected the twins early from the nursery to spend some time with them before I left. Ate with Paul, then I drove to work. I opened the drawer where I placed the boys' photo face down and locked it every night. Today it was face up; a money wrap sat on top of it. Greg must have been looking at the photo, killed with curiosity since Fleur's little prank.

She marched in with her overnight bag.

'This is probably too big for hand luggage,' she said. I closed and locked the drawer again.

'Is Higgins okay with you going?' I asked.

'What do you think?'

'No?'

'He's chuffed,' said Hewitt. 'He's going to propose to his girl this weekend, so I didn't think it nice to scupper young love.'

'Is he really?'

'He didn't tell you?'

'Of course he did. I just forgot for a second,' I lied. He normal bent my ear a lot, but I hadn't realised he was bending Hewitt's ear too or that he had decided to propose.

'I've contacted Hertfordshire Constabulary to let them know we're coming. They'll be there to chat to us on the other side,' said Hewitt.

We drove to the Airport and got our flight. Being a nervous flier, I ordered a drink on the flight. Then another.

When we arrived, Hewitt decided we'd get started the next day. It turned out it was the only time DI Strickland offered up to meet with us. That evening we got freshened up in our rooms then met for a bite to eat. I ordered a bottle of Merlot.

'Go easy, hen,' Fleur said as the night went on.

'Thought we were on our jollies?' I joked.

'Not really,' she said, considering me, her thin lips crimping into a smile, 'stop at that one, alright.'

I went to the bar and paid for all the drinks separately, so she could put the meal on the company card.

'Heading to bed,' I shouted over. Hewitt looked around at the people sitting near us as if they were looking. That pissed me off. I went to bed, almost missing my step, and Hewitt met me outside my bedroom. Her room was next door to mine.

'Are you okay, Harry?' she asked me.

'Totally,' I said.

I was nothing if not professional. If I thought I'd be hungover, impeded from doing my job in any way, I wouldn't have drunk or ordered another bottle for the room.

Chapter 50

On Friday morning, we went to Shady Lane and Watford police station, where a young man with an upturned nose and heavily gelled hair met us. 'DI Strickland,' he introduced himself before he walked fast ahead of us into a quiet office. Fleur had already spoken to him on the phone, filled him in on the whole backstory. He pulled up a seat and sat facing us. Fleur perched herself on a desk and tried to flatten her unruly brown hair.

'I know your hopes are high,' Strickland said, but he looked like his were not at all.

'I don't know where they are at this point,' said Hewitt.

'My hopes are the highest they've been yet about this case,' I said.

'Geoff McDonald has no previous,' Strickland said, looking at me. 'He's not on the system.'

'We have an address for him,' I said, 'and we want to go and talk to him.'

'We need your assistance,' said Hewitt, 'in case things get ugly.'

'We'll send one of ours, is that alright?'

'That's very alright,' said Hewitt.

'Green Road,' I said.

Strickland whistled. 'Some nice houses out that way. Nice for some, not on our police salaries, I'm sure. Unless the PSNI gets better wages than we do.'

'I doubt that,' said Hewitt.

*

We went to the address with Sarge Pete Alison driving us there. I sat in the backseat like a kid or a crim while Sarge Alison talked football all the way there. He and Hewitt chatting about Watford FC and league tables and cups while I zoned out and pictured the photos of the Geoff McDonald who was the stepfather of Kira Tooth.

I imagined who would answer the door and if it was him or a completely different man. I imagined a man answering the door and seeing us, knowing justice was finally meeting up with him, regardless of how he had managed to evade getting a criminal record. If he was the same Geoff.

We pulled up to a substantial Neo-Georgian property, pretty and homely, the facade covered with ivy. It was completely private with a mature, well-kept garden. There was a new, black BMW in the driveway. How could evil live here? Surely a lovely couple, ageing, kind and with a love for nature, would keep a home like this. The home would not have looked out of place on the Malone Road, a more modern version than the home I grew up in, only at London prices. It would have cost a fortune. A lovely, ageing, kind and *loaded* couple lived here, that was for sure. Maybe it wasn't our Geoff McDonald at all.

Hewitt and I went to the door while Sarge Alison hung back in the car.

No one answered when we rapped the knocker and buzzed the doorbell. Some of the curtains at the house were closed. It was ten a.m., and I supposed they could have been sleeping.

When we were checking out if there was anyone in the back garden, Sarge Alison got out of the service car. After seeing no one in the garden, I came back to the front and saw him put something through the letterbox. He was putting his pad in his back pocket.

'What was that?' I asked him.

'A note, asking Geoff to call us when he gets in.'

Fleur visibly gasped. 'We're not DHL, buddy,' she said.

'We'll come back later, see if he calls.'

'Would you call the police if they left you one of those?'

'I wouldn't be hiding anything,' Alison said.

'And if he is?'

I looked in the letterbox to see if I could reach it. It was a no go.

'We can wait and see.'

I was afraid to deploy my thoughts.

We sat back and waited for a couple of hours. I read more articles about Kira Tooth and found that there were accounts during that time and after of girls walking to school in groups who claimed to have seen a man wearing a baseball hat lurking in garden sheds. And not just the one shed, but multiple, and the man always wore a baseball hat. It could be no coincidence.

If this was Geoff, he would not be the type to call us back. The damage was done.

Regardless, we went back to Green Road and that lovely house. This time a woman opened the door to us. She was in tartan pyjamas and fluffy slippers. Her short grey hair was unkempt.

I asked for Geoff, and she started to cry this awful noisy cry. Hewitt and I exchanged a glance.

'Are you Kathleen Gilmour?'

'I am. Come in,' the woman said. She walked away with a bowlegged deportment. The house was huge inside and classically decorated. In the room she brought us into, a young woman lounged on the sofa. 'Eloise,' Kathleen spoke to the younger woman, 'the police are here.'

Eloise was beautiful. She wore her platinum hair in an ultra-modern pageboy. She, too, was in her pyjamas. Funky ones. Leopard print. The top had the words *I Hate Everybody* emblazoned on it. They must have been still in bed when we called earlier. Our note sat on the coffee table in the middle of the room.

'You called earlier,' Kathleen asked.

'We did,' I said, 'is Geoff at home?' I wondered what the tears were for. If she knew why we were there. If he had confessed.

'You've missed him,' Eloise said. The one and only thing she did tell us that day.

'Do you know when he'll be back?' I asked. 'We need to speak to him about a historical case in Belfast.'

'He won't be coming back,' said Kathleen, 'he's passed away.'

Chapter 51

'When did that happen?' asked Hewitt.

'Monday. A week ago,' said Kathleen.

The day we reopened Karen's case. The bitter irony!

'You were Geoff's wife?' I asked Kathleen.

'I was.'

'I'm sorry to hear about his passing,' I said. 'Geoff was a person of interest for us, and I'd still like to eliminate him from our enquiries.'

'That's so upsetting,' Kathleen said, finding a tissue in her pocket and pressing an edge of it against her tear duct.

'I know it must be. Can you tell us about Geoff? How did he die?'

'Cancer, my love.'

'That's bloody tragic,' said Hewitt, shaking her head, doing her fake sincere act. 'He died in hospice, did he, hen?'

'No, not in hospice. He'd gone to get treatment and died … ' Kathleen picked at her tissue ' … over there.'

'Where? Where is "over there"?' Hewitt looked directly at me as if I was the one she was asking. I even shrugged.

'Spain, Granada,' said Kathleen. 'There is this centre that Geoff goes to, and they've helped him in the past. All holistic. Far better than what you get on the NHS.'

Eloise sighed. She pulled her feet up under her bum.

'But it was too late, this time,' said Kathleen.

'Okay,' said Hewitt. 'Geoff knew a girl back in Belfast forty-odd years ago.'

'That's where he was born.'

'Yes, that's definitely the same person, then.'

'How did you trace him here?' asked Kathleen.

'We have our means,' I said.

'But, I just mean, he has no ties over there, so I'm curious who told you.'

'Geoff spoke to you about Belfast?' I asked.

'Recently, yes.'

'What did he say?'

'He didn't say any certain thing. He had no family over there. It was our wedding, and he had no family left to invite.'

'You only got married recently?' I asked.

'Last month.'

Christ! Kathleen was only a newlywed.

'How long had you known him?' I asked.

'Eight years. Together eight years.'

I knew that from the census.

'Together quite a while before you decided to tie the knot,' I said.

Fleur looked at me, so did Eloise.

'I had no interest in marrying again,' said Kathleen. 'But he suddenly wanted to.'

I guessed that Geoff knew he was dying, that that was the rush to wed. I looked around the fancy room at the rather lovely piano, the marble fireplace, the chandelier.

'Do you play the piano?' I asked.

'Eloise used to, for a short while.'

'What do you work as, Kathleen?' I asked.

'I am the deputy manager at the local cinema.' Small wage, didn't fit. 'How is this relevant?'

'We like to understand what we're looking at.'

'What are you looking at?' she asked.

'This is a beautiful house, and from my understanding, Geoff didn't work.'

'Oh, he did. Was a civil engineer until his health started to decline.'

'Where did he work when you met him?'

'He'd retired on medical grounds already. You want to know where the money comes from,' said Kathleen. She didn't seem offended. 'My aunt and uncle lived here. This place was in their will, the piano, the chandeliers. I was their only relative, so when my uncle died ten years ago, I moved in. The mortgage was paid off, and I didn't hate the decor. I mean, I can't lie, the heating bill is a bugger in winter, but we manage.'

Manage? A house like this in London, who was she kidding! It had to be worth two million. Geoff liked new money; he liked women who would keep him. He stayed until there were fumes left.

'Have you had a funeral?' asked Hewitt.

'We had it. Small and … sad.' Again Kathleen pushed her tissue to her tear duct. Eloise stared at her mother.

'To eliminate Geoff from this case, so we can move on, would we be able to have his DNA? Do you have his toothbrush?' I asked.

'No.'

'Hairbrush?'

'He was bald. Plus, his toothbrush is in Spain. It obviously wasn't returned.'

'Didn't he have a spare?' asked Hewitt.

'No. He didn't.'

Kathleen fetched a clean tissue. Her hands shook as she blew her nose.

After the balls-up with Sarge Alison, we had been given a service car. Fleur drove. She is a control freak like that. Hates me driving, and maybe my blood alcohol content made it a good idea that I just let her do her thing. As she drove, my work mobile phone began to ring. I didn't recognise the number. I waited to see if it would leave a message. Then it started again. It could be Paul's mother. When you have kids, there is no luxury to screen calls, so I answered.

'Harriet,' said Jason, 'you're fucked. You're dead next time I see you.'

Knocked bandy, I hung up on him.

'Okay?' asked Fleur.

'Fucken PPI,' I said.

I went quickly in and blocked this number, not before taking a screen snap of it. I was ready to fight back. But he wasn't playing clean. Sure, he never did.

Because I had kids, I didn't have the luxury to play dirty; there wasn't just myself to worry about anymore. I rued that I hadn't sorted him out years before.

But if I knew him, and I didn't know that I ever did, he would start off nasty, and then it would turn into, please don't tell anyone about me, but with an edge of intimidation. Today a death threat. My phone pinged.

'You're popular today,' said Hewitt.

I read it. It was from another new number: *Heard about your outburst and I WILL kill you, you bitch.*

This was bad; now he was back to leaving actual receipts. I let that settle. Rationality told me he would not kill me. Jason had had days to try. Unless he had only just been told about what I had said …. Then I remembered how he almost killed me before. Then I remembered he was very capable. I'd seen so many murder cases where people were in utter shock that the perpetrator was capable. But I know we all are.

'Pull over,' I said to Fleur.

'No, it's a sweater, but thanks for noticing.'

'Is that a line from *Dumb and Dumber*?' I asked her, trying to seem upbeat and not panic.

'Is that where that's from? Just came to me.'

'Seriously, though, Fleur. Pull over.'

I got out on the roadside and phoned Father. He answered with hesitation and that edge in his voice he had always warded over me.

'What is it?' he asked.

'What is it?' I replied. 'Who are you giving my number to?'

'No one,' he said coldly. 'Anyway, good thing you called, I want to talk to you. I was not impressed by your outburst at the party, not one bit.'

'Outburst?' I asked. 'Jason used the same word when he texted me just now. When he sent me a message that he is going to kill me.'

He considered this. 'It's quite the allegation you made.'

'And what, it's not true?'

Father said nothing.

'Have you ever known me to lie?'

'On occasion.'

'What occasion?'

He had not. The only thing I could think of was my omission of who the twins' biological father was; that was the height of it. Apart from that, I told Father everything. I told him too much, too much about work, too much about specific cases. I could have blown up, but I couldn't with him. He was an old bastard, but bastard or not, he was my father, and I needed him to understand.

'What are the lies I've told?' I asked.

'I'm tired of this nonsense with you,' he said.

'Alright,' I said. 'Be tired. It's Greg Dunne.'

'What is Greg Dunne?'

'I had an affair with him for a while, after Jason, after I escaped after days at gunpoint. Jason was having a breakdown. I don't know how I'm still going, Daddy. I'm not well since. He ruined my life.'

'You're a DI, Harry, for fuck sake. You could have gone to a police station.'

'I might be a DI now, but I wasn't then. And my job title is nothing to do with it. Do you think that only women in minimum wage jobs get raped?' I asked.

'Don't forget who you're talking to, and don't ever put words in my mouth again.'

'You don't understand,' I said.

'No. I don't.'

'He stalked me for years after.'

'If that's true, then why didn't you say?' Father asked.

From the tone of his voice, he had moved his life onto Yvonne and a new start with a woman he could mansplain to, who wouldn't challenge him, who he could feel big beside. Even if he did believe me, which he did, I *knew* he did. This was easier, to cut me off.

Hewitt was frowning at me through the window. I turned my back on her.

'Daddy,' I said. 'Is he there?'

'Who?'

'Jason.'

'No, he's not here.'

'Is Yvonne?'

'Absolutely. Of course, she is.'

'Please go into another room, okay?' He was moving. 'Daddy?'

'What?'

'That's my one omission to you, that I was seeing Greg to get over all that. Maybe so he would protect me. It was a bad decision, but I don't regret it. I have my beautiful sons now.'

I had a feeling that my sons were less-real people than his. When I had gone into labour, Father showed up at the hospital as I battled pains. Days after the twins were born, Paul told me that Father had said,

'Harriet thinks these babies will be born today; she hasn't a clue.'

I asked Paul why Father had said that. The twins had to come out. I was in active labour. They were born just before midnight by an emergency section.

It was not pleasant.

And not nice on top of it to know that my father was implying *what*? That my very real, very immediate, and ultimately distressing pregnancy was a phantom? A lie in itself?

Everything, thinking back, was illogical to him. Everything to do with me was papery. How little he had thought of me when I had always idolised the man. Until now, I had never seen what an asshole he was.

'I thought you didn't want children. You said yourself it would hold you back career-wise,' he said now down the line.

How had I not realised? He wanted me to be the first female Chief Constable, take over his old job. Keep it in the family.

'I'm a disappointment to you,' I said, thinking of my beautiful family, my home. I seemed to many to have everything; people would tell me that. But not Father.

He had counted on me to make up for the rest: Charly, the housewife; Addam, the minister; Coral, the soft social worker; and Brooks, the junkie.

I saw it now, on the side of the road in Watford. It was only because he believed in me most, and that had been our thing, playing us kids off against each other.

Charly had opted out and focused on her family. They had all opted out.

I was only competing against myself, to be his favourite, and he couldn't be proud that I had been through so much and was still hanging in there.

He also didn't say, 'but Greg's married' because Father didn't care. This man killed his wife, and I was looking for his approval.

This man killed his wife, and I wanted him to care that my ex-husband was abusive. Christ, I'd been stupid!

Charles Sloane didn't give a fuck; we kids were all a disappointment to him now he had this new family, the Lucies: Jason and his fiancée (pity for her); Jason's brother Alex and Verity. All accomplished in their architecture business, and all *seemingly* normal, and they always had and still did have, time for him. He was tired of all the drama that the Sloanes had proven to be. And he didn't correct me or say that I wasn't a disappointment. He supplied, instead, 'You go about things arse-about-face, don't you?'

I needed a drink. I needed to feel numb again.

'I learnt from the best,' I said, having never spoken to him like that in my life. 'Now, just tell Jason this … I'll kill *him*. I'll get my gun, and I'll rape him, repeatedly. I'll rape him with the gun.'

I started to shake. A sensation came back to me that I had buried deepest. The cold metal in my vagina.

I caught myself on the corner of that memory.

'I'll smack him in the face. I'll scream in his face. I'll split his head open, but I won't stalk him, no, I'll fucken finish the job like he wasn't man enough to.'

I realised the tone was dead. I had no idea how much of my rant Father had heard or chosen to take on board.

Chapter 52

'We should go home,' said Hewitt.

'Why?' I asked. 'We still haven't eliminated Geoff?'

She cast her eyes over me. 'You look much calmer now.'

'I didn't look calm?'

'You didn't before you took that call. Can I ask who it was?'

'My ex.'

'Greg?'

'Ex before that.'

'Oh, the husband. Wasn't that years ago you finished up? What's he want with you now?'

'Just to kill me,' I said.

Fuck. This was easier than I'd ever thought. Just say it sober, just get it out there.

She laughed. 'I'd like to see the bastard try.'

I remembered his face the time he did try.

'Harry!' Fleur nearly shouted. 'Are you joking?'

'Nope, he threatens my life regularly, has done for years.'

'What does the sad bastard do? He in the service?'

'No, he's not in the service. He's an architect.'

'Oh, excuse me. You like them fancy, alright.'

'Dead fancy,' I said.

She regarded me. 'What's he going to do, kill you with a blueprint? Give you a papercut?'

'He's a psycho. But probably nothing.'

'I had a friend back in Glasgow who was killed by her ex.'

'Ah, Fleur, did you?'

'We were twenty. Thing about it was, when we went out of an evening, they were never apart. I'd be saying to her, "Girl, I want what you have." You know, he loved her. Obsessed, like.' She fell silent for a while. 'Anyway, Harry, they had this argument once, and she was in a towel, just came out of the bath. The argument was over nothing. He locked her outside, nearly naked, just to humiliate her. Plus, he'd been beating her. She never let on about that.' Hewitt tongued her cheek. 'Then I woke up one Monday morning, about to go to work, and I got a call from her ma.'

I looked away.

'She's been killed, then he turned the knife on himself. So, I fucken know, Harry, you never take a threat at face value. Cos you never know when they'll do it for real.'

'Let's stay,' I said. 'See what else we can find out. I think we owe it to Karen Ward.'

I was slightly ashamed. This was more than me. It was bigger than me. Anxiety welled inside. I was about to drown. When we got back to the hotel, Fleur went to her room, and I went straight to the bar.

*

That night, Fleur did not join me at the bar. 'See you in the morning,' she said as she went to meet a friend, and I stayed alone and drank.

It was a Friday night, after all. That's a laugh! I didn't discriminate one day from the other.

Then I went to my hotel room, played the music channel on the TV, and I drank. When I was pretty much drunk, Drew Taylor texted to tell me he thought he was in love with me. I thought I was seeing things. I sat up and squinted at my phone, then laughed my head off. *Thought* he was 'in love' with me was my favourite. Boy, did I laugh at the 'thought' part. Though it was kinder than the last text I had received, that wanted me dead. As much as I found Drew's half-assed declaration funny, I was flattered, and it took my mind from stewing about Jason Lucie for a while. *Thought* he was 'in love with me' was non-committal. Easily got out of. It could flip, do a one-eighty to 'I never liked you anyway', if I didn't return the sentiment. I wouldn't return it. I did not love Drew. I didn't know love. I loved wine, and was downing the stuff like there was no tomorrow. Because maybe there wasn't. For me anyway.

Get back with Roxy, I texted Drew back.

She doesn't want me, he replied.

Apologise to her.

I want you. What r u wearing?

Ha!

Are you okay?

Nope.

Then, he called me, and we spoke. He said he did; he really loved me. I reminded him it was only supposed to be sex. As Drew spoke, I set my alarm for the next morning, nice and loud. We ended our call.

That was the last thing I remembered. I sat on, drank on, stewing more over Jason. Shaking my head and muttering to myself about Drew. I must have ordered drink to the room and kept going until I blacked out.

I woke to that horrendous alarm. I was still wearing my clothes from the day before. Already I had the dreads as I grabbed my phone, worried I had called Jason back or called Father to give it to him again or to cry. Thankfully there were no such calls. Drew and I had spoken again, two long calls. And I had a text from Paul saying: *I will in the morning. Are you working this late?* followed by a suspect emoji holding its chin. Before it, I had sent him a text I could not remember sending: *Kiss the kiss for me and kiss yourself.*

Kiss the kiss? Drunken typo! What was I doing telling him to kiss himself? His emoji back meant he knew I was drunk and wasn't surprised. I worried now. Worried that I needed Paul to be a more vital ally. Especially now Jason was calling my work line. I needed Paul on side.

Fleur could appreciate that Jason was a bastard, as could Brooks, and Paul was a good guy. He surely could be a support. But was I asking too much? He was already supporting me a lot.

I necked two coffees and stepped tentatively into the shower, still a bit wobbly.

I decided my relationship at home wasn't as one-sided as I often liked to think. Paul was living in a house he loved; the postcode alone almost gave him a hard-on. He hadn't been born to money like I had, now he had the life, the cute kids.

———

He helped me, sure, but I had unselfishly shared this with him.

I smirked at the thought.

Chapter 53

I mixed two sachets of Dioralyte into a glass of water – my best hangover cure – popped a couple of Pro Plus, got handy with perfume, body spray and breath spray, then I made my way to the foyer where I had a double espresso in the lobby. While I waited for Fleur to finish her breakfast, I mentally punished myself for going at the drink so hard.

When Fleur was done, she sat down beside me.

'How was your night?' I asked her.

'Had one drink and was back early. Slept well, actually. Yourself?'

'Had an early night too.'

'Thought I heard you talking quite late.'

'I called Paul about the kids.'

'Aren't you eating?'

'I did. Earlier.' The thought of food made my tummy turn.

'Well, I have news for you, Harry. Just heard from Kate Stile. DNA found on Rhonda Orr in Carnfunnock matches the hair that was in Karen Ward's hand.'

'Oh, that's good,' I said, sounding far from enthused.

Hewitt drove along the A414 to Hatfield, all of half an hour away to where Janet lived in a little cottage off the quaint old town. Her place was every bit as stylish as she was, all pastel shades and soft metallics.

She offered us coffee, and I didn't say no.

'Janet,' Fleur started, and I happily let her have the reins. An hour or two and I would be back to brand new, but I was still under the Merlot cloud for now.

'Yes?' Janet sat forward hopefully.

'We have good news and bad, if I can put it like that,' said Fleur. The good news, she proceeded to inform Janet, was that the crimes matched. Rhonda and Karen were murdered by the same man.

'We know that much, so if we catch one, we've caught both.'

Janet clutched her necklace. I sipped my coffee. She said nothing, I kept waiting for her to, but she was literally speechless.

'We didn't come all this way to tell you that. We came to England to interview Geoff McDonald and hear his side, but we can't. Unfortunately, he's dead.'

'Really?' Janet broke her silence. 'It's a lot to digest.'

'I know, sorry about that, hen.'

'Don't be sorry. It's moving forward. Thank you.' She smiled lightly. 'When did he die?'

'Very recently,' I said.

'Geoff was ill for a long time,' said Hewitt.

'He must have lived locally if you are here.'

'Half an hour away.'

Janet looked shocked. 'He lived and died not far from here?'

'Well,' said Hewitt, 'he actually died in Spain. His wife says he'd been there seeking cancer treatment.'

She frowned. 'Where?'

'Granada.'

'Granada,' Janet said thoughtfully.

'It's someplace you can go to get treatment.'

'It's usually the USA people talk about when they want treatment,' said Janet, 'when they want to be sponsored. I've seen Just Giving pages. Not Granada. That's good to know that there are closer places people can go to.'

'Exactly,' I said. I wondered if she had the results from the lump she found.

'He wouldn't need sponsored. I don't think money was a problem,' Hewitt said.

'No?' asked Janet.

'He landed on his feet. Again,' I explained. 'Like he did with Maxine winning the pools.'

'Family inheritance this time round,' said Hewitt.

I wondered if Nanette Tooth was wealthy. She didn't look it from the photos. Geoff liked new money, and new money shows their wealth, wears brands. I remembered that there was a hefty reward on offer for information.

'We'll see if he had any biological family, and if there is any way to eliminate him through DNA. But that's not looking promising so far, according to his wife. I mean, widow.'

'If it was him,' said Janet, 'he killed Rhonda Orr too.'

'We won't leave this, Janet. Geoff McDonald remains a suspect. It might be a struggle now to get his DNA.'

We chatted for a while, a sense of despair in the air.

'Has your daughter had her baby?' I asked.

'They have her in hospital now, they've been trying to hold off, but she'll be induced tomorrow if nothing happens.'

'Good luck with it.'

'This is it then,' Janet said. 'The end.'

'No, not necessarily,' I said.

'It's been nice getting to know you,' Hewitt said and shook her hand.

At the doorway, I got Janet alone. 'Have you been to the doctor for yourself?'

'He wants to run tests because of my history. But he's not concerned.'

'That's a relief,' I said, pulling back, paranoid of wine breath.

'I'm almost sad that I won't see you again,' said Janet, 'I feel a connection with you. Maybe it was because I saw you with your babies on that flight.'

'Struggling,' I said.

'It's easy to see women like you as superhuman.'

'*Women* like me?'

'You have a perfect little family, handsome husband, and a brilliant career. That's probably my working-class showing. I shouldn't be like that. I have my daughter.'

'My life is not perfect,' I said, 'far from it.' If you only knew, I thought.

'I think it could be if you let go of the stuff that doesn't matter,' said Janet. 'Not *you* you. All of us. I wish I had not let Karen's death rob me of happiness for so long.'

There was nothing to say. Yes, she made sense. But she had to go through the grief, in my opinion. It's human nature. You can't just wake up, especially in those early days, and say, right, that's enough sadness, I'm going to be happy from now on.

'Thanks for everything.' Janet hugged me like she was holding me up. This job, her sister's case, was the only thing holding me together, and we were too late.

'I'm not happy,' I said to Hewitt as we drove back to Watford.

'No? I was just thinking that you've been a barrel of laughs this holiday,' she replied.

'I'm not happy to leave it like this. To leave Janet.'

'We don't win them all, you know that. We can probably say it was Geoff. In the meantime, we can hope he has some random, distant nephew like Nick Flynn did. Only with better results.'

'I'm not happy, Fleur.' I sighed.

*

When we got back to Watford, I called Paul. 'I'm coming home soon,' I told him.

'Any luck?' he asked.

'Some. The main suspect died in one of these Spanish cancer places.'

'A Spanish cancer place,' mused Paul, 'what are you on about?'

'He was at this place in Granada.'

Paul had cancer as a child, which was a very long time ago, but he was a doctor, so cancer interested him personally and professionally.

'The guy's widow,' I said, 'says he'd been a few times over the years.'

'There is no place in Spain that cures cancer, or everyone would be going. Think straight, Harry.'

'Treatment,' I said. 'I didn't say it cured cancer, fuck sake, Paul.'

'There is a university I know of that does oncological research. Pfizer-University. Jared, give that toy back to your brother. No. He had it first. Give it …. Googling it now on the iPad, Harriet. So there are cancer foundations and oncology departments in the local hospitals, but there is no treatment centre. Do you have a name for it?'

'No,' I said, feeling stupid that I hadn't thought to ask.

'I know someone,' said Paul. 'Aimee Main.'

'Your ex?'

'She had a doctor friend living somewhere near Granada. I think she worked in the cancer field. Do you want me to ask her if she could shed some light?'

'Your ex?'

'No, Aimee's friend.'

'How would you get in touch? Through your ex?' I asked, feeling jealous and knowing I had no right.

'I don't have to contact Aimee. If you'd prefer that. Everyone in the world, except for you, is linked up on Facebook. Found her already. Federica Salas. Do you want her number?'

'She has it on Facebook?'

'No, I'm Googling her. She has a website and a contact form.'

'That was quick.'

'Don't worry, I'm not after your job. Now, do you want this number?'

271

'Go on, forward it to me,' I said.

I phoned Federica within minutes and explained our link and the case I was working on.

'There is a treatment centre in Granada that our prime suspect has been going to for years,' I said.

'Is it part of a hospital?' she asked.

'No, it's a specialist, holistic place.'

'There is no such place,' said Federica. 'That is simply a lie someone has told you.'

Chapter 54

I looked up *Granada Cancer treatment* and *treatment centre Granada Spain*, then translated the words into Spanish and tried again using every variable I could think of. Everything Paul had said was right: I could see the website for Pfizer-University, cancer foundations and regular hospitals that treated cancer. Then I Googled *Geoff McDonald cancer treatment*. There it was in the Birmingham Mail, a tiny little snippet that had not appeared before in any of my searches. It mentioned that men in the area were all DNA tested, and there was a quote from Geoff saying that he had just got back from having treatment abroad. Even back in 2001, he was talking about this place.

'Could it be some weird big house?' said Fleur. 'Somewhere you would never find through a web search?'

'Like underground cancer treatment?' I asked.

'Some funky experimental shit going down?'

'Kathleen said holistic.'

'You see, that sounds hippy-dippy to me.'

'Funny he was getting treatment when local men were all being tested for their DNA,' I said. It was out before I processed it. Hewitt hit me with her elbow.

'Holy good God!' she exclaimed. 'No one questions the dying man. He did it. He did all three, the lying bastard.'

Kira, Rhonda, Karen.

'We can ask his GP. Find out if Geoff ever had cancer. Maybe he did himself in.'

'It's a Saturday.'

'Shit, you're right. Out of hours?'

Hewitt took the laptop off me and typed *Geoff McDonald death*. Nothing. Next *Watford death notices*. She scrolled back two weeks. Nothing.

'Hold the phone!' she said.

'No mention of his death?'

'What the hell is going on?' Frantically she did more searches.

'Local registry office?' I asked.

'It's closed today too … oh, except in emergencies.'

'I'd say this is an emergency. Flash the badge.'

So that's what she did. A well-upholstered official with a high pitched voice met us there and went through the recent death certificates. There was none for Geoff McDonald. I asked her to have a look at wedding certificates. There was one, from 16th May at Watford Register Office for Geoff McDonald and Kathleen Gilmour. That, at least, was true.

*

Around three p.m., we went back to Green Road and watched their home from an unmarked vehicle.

'I can't believe that nice wee woman lied,' I said.

'Don't be surprised when a liar lies to you,' said Fleur, 'it's what they do.'

My phone pinged, and my heart leapt. It was a text from Drew that said: *Hell never harm u again.*

Hell? I thought. *He'll!* Who was *he*?

'Well, looky here at that brazen bastard,' said Fleur.

I almost gave myself whiplash looking up from my phone. I saw a man. That face. I had studied it well. Kira Tooth's stepfather. He had a newspaper under his arm.

'Bald,' Fleur said in a low voice, 'bloody tan as fuck. Back from the dead.'

The man cut down Kathleen's drive. He took a key out of his pocket and let himself into the house. Hewitt went to grab her car door handle.

'Wait,' I said, 'please.'

I typed in *Jason Lucie* on my 4G. Nothing. I typed in *Belfast architect* and looked under Google news. There it was, *Belfast architect killed in a hit and run*.

'Wait,' I said again.

'What?' said Hewitt impatiently.

'I need to make a call,' I said.

Hewitt looked like she was about to thump me. I looked out of the window and watched the house.

'He's oblivious,' I said as I phoned Charly.

Charly answered with a 'yup?'

'Is Jason dead?' I asked her, getting to the point.

'Is he? I don't know.'

'Look up the news,' I said. 'Tell me, is Jason dead?'

'Hold on, hold on.' She looked it up and said. 'There's a photo of his office. Hit and run!'

I felt queasy.

'This can't be right,' I said. 'Is there a name?'

——

275

Hewitt threw her hands in the air. The man was leaving the house again. On foot again. He looked relaxed. I was sure he had not clocked us.

Hold on, I mouthed to Hewitt.

'If what you said is true, then why would you care?' said Charly.

'*If* what I said … ?' I stopped there.

'I don't mean it like that.'

I hung up the phone and threw it in the footwell.

'Who? What?' asked Hewitt.

'My ex-husband, I was just telling you about yesterday.'

'Is he dead?'

'Dead. Hit and run.'

'Remind me to never fall out with you.'

'What?'

'Nothing. He's away.' Fleur looked at the man ambling down the street.

'But he'll be back,' I said, dazed. 'He didn't see us.'

'He bloody better be. That's some voodoo shit you put on the ex, Harry. Just saying.'

Chapter 55

I went back to the hotel room and phoned Drew. 'What were you thinking?' I asked him.

'Chill! It was a case of this guy is going down for ten years anyway, so he was told to sort him out.'

'Told to *kill* him?'

'You don't need to know that. Best if you don't know.'

'I'm a detective,' I said. 'I need to know.'

'That's why you can't be implicated.'

'Drew, don't patronise me.'

'Not trying to, Har.'

'Who did it?'

'Nobody. Don't you worry about the details.'

'Tell me.'

'Are you sure?'

'Drew!'

'Okay. So … TB …. '

'*Tucker Brown*?'

'Listen, that doesn't matter. I just want to see you happy. I told you last night, I love you, Harriet, and I'd do anything for you.'

'You didn't tell me that. You said you thought you did.'

'At first. But we spoke about it after that. We both said a lot.'

I didn't remember. Not at all. I hung up my personal phone. Turned it off and kept it off. What had I told him? I had blacked out and couldn't recall.

During the drugs bust a few months before, they were all quick to talk about each other's misdemeanours to get off light. Tucker – if Drew had told him why he wanted Jason gone – might agree, he might even say I ordered the hit. Though I was no one to order anything. Everyone knew now what Jason had done years before, and for years since.

I was as bad as Father and worse than Brooks, potentially bringing all that scandal. Seedy Sunday rags would have a field day with photos of the hotel room where we had sex, and the car, and they would make it seedy and not how it was at all. *Leggy brunette cop in sex tryst with Casanova drug lord*, and similar. All my pain, all Yvonne's, and this fiancée of Jason's, whoever she was, would be scarred by media sleaziness.

'Can we let them think it's over?' I said to Hewitt, 'and go back tomorrow.'

'I suppose,' she said. 'I am made of time. Take some personal time. Your head must be fucked. But back at it tomorrow, hen, alright?'

'Yes, Fleur.'

She lingered, hesitated and then said, 'Come here, you. Get an early night, okay?'

She gave me a hug. I excused myself to go to the toilet while she went out to visit Load of Hay, a gay bar she had pointed out when we first arrived in the area. 'Had a good night there before,' she'd joked. 'Pulled the best looking bird I've ever seen.'

It could have been a laugh to go together, but I had something I needed to do.

———

278

I ordered a bottle of wine and got a table. The barman came over and said, 'I'd like to give you a glass, not a bottle.'

'What?' I asked.

'You went from zero to one hundred last night. You almost blacked out. I helped you to your room.'

'No, you didn't.'

'Yes. I did.'

I was so mortified I called him back and told him to forget the drink. I went out to a wine lodge, got a couple of bottles and had them in my room. A bottle in, I had a flashback of calling Drew upset the night before and crying. I couldn't remember if I had asked him to help me. I couldn't be sure I hadn't said I was going to kill Jason or if I even asked Drew to help me do it. Even if I didn't say I wanted it done, there was an inner yes. I had wanted Jason dead.

Chapter 56

I kept my phone off on Sunday morning. I was sticky. The sky was cloudy, and the air hot as I stood outside. I imagined Jason was everywhere. Everyone. Driving cars that drove past the hotel, walking in the street, even on the way back to Green Road.

'I think we need to speak to his doctor and find out more about his diagnosis,' said Hewitt.

'I think we don't,' I said. 'It's clear to me he's been lying.'

'BMW's not there,' said Hewitt. 'Fuck it.'

Eloise was there alone. She was wearing white trainers and ripped jeans that showed an oval of pink skin and the face of a roaring lion tattoo.

'Where is Geoff buried?' I asked her.

'Um ....' She just stared at me.

'We know he's not dead.'

She panicked. 'Don't take him away from Mum. He's all she has.'

'You're telling me your mum was lying.'

'She didn't want to. It wasn't her idea,' Eloise said, she clicked her fingernails off each other nervously.

'It was his idea?'

'We've been through an awful time as a family. Mum hasn't been herself.'

'Was Geoff *ever* sick?'

'Yes.'

'Did you ever go to an appointment with him?'

'No,' Eloise admitted.

'Did your mother?'

'She doesn't drive. Neither do I.'

'That's a strange thing to say,' said Hewitt.

'He went alone. Always.'

'Did he even go to Spain?' I asked.

'I don't know. Geoff said his cancer was back once before, and then he went away.'

'Alone?'

'He insisted on going alone. Said it wasn't nice to see.'

'Do you think he really went?'

'He'd come back with a tan, and a completely bald head but stubbly. He left some of it on the sofa.'

'Left some … hair?' I asked.

'No. The tan.'

'It was out of a bottle,' said Hewitt.

'I was suspicious,' said Eloise, 'I'm not gonna even lie, how can you be in hospital and get a tan, even if you are in Spain? It certainly wouldn't make a stain. What do you think he did?'

'Eloise,' said Hewitt, 'we're here investigating the cold case of a teenage girl who was murdered in Belfast back when he lived there.'

'The murders of two teenage girls,' I corrected Hewitt. Maybe Kira Tooth was a third.

'You think he did it?' Eloise asked in disbelief.

'I think *you* think he did it,' said Hewitt. 'You said, "Don't take him away from my mum." Now, why would we do that if he's done nothing wrong? And why hide from us, if that is the case, too? And lie?'

'I didn't lie. I didn't say anything.'

'You didn't correct your mother, and that is essentially harbouring an offender. Why, if he's innocent, would he need to hide and lie to this extent?'

Eloise stared open-eyed and open-mouthed; she went to speak and stuttered.

'So, tell me honestly, where is he now?' I asked.

'In bed,' she said, her eyes flitted to the ceiling.

Chapter 57

The back door banged, and I gave chase after him through the residential area, but he was a lithe thing, and I lost him. I had no idea where he went, and I hardly knew the site, so I called for backup.

'You alright?' Hewitt asked as I walked back to her. 'Eloise says her mother is at work. Where is the car, Eloise?'

'They went out for dinner last night and left it in town. Got an Uber home. Or walked. I don't know.'

'Funny that,' I said, trying to get my breath back, 'pretend you're dead and then don't even keep your head down.'

'He thought we'd pissed off back home,' said Hewitt.

I hoped it was the last supper of freedom for Geoff McDonald.

'Call your mum, and put her on speakerphone for me,' Hewitt told Eloise.

She did as she was told. The line was dead.

'Phone's turned off,' I said. 'Call the cinema she works at.'

Eloise started; she said hello.

'Speakerphone,' I reiterated.

'It's Eloise. Is my mum there?' She held the phone out and let us listen.

'She just left,' came the response.

'He has her,' said Hewitt. 'Hang up.'

Eloise did as Fleur said. I wondered if Kathleen was in danger, but then again, did I care? She had lied for him.

'What is Geoff's registration?' I asked.

Eloise told me, and Fleur got back on to Hertfordshire Constabulary to tell them to check the ANPR videos recording footage on the motorways in and out of London. She also told them that Geoff had left his car at a nearby restaurant the night before.

'You said that two teenage girls were killed,' said Eloise, 'and I know about Kira. But Geoff didn't kill her.'

'How do you know that?' asked Hewitt. 'Look at how he is evading us, the lengths he is going to. Faking his death.'

'They took his DNA at the time, and it proved he didn't kill her.'

'No,' I said, 'I don't think they did. That was another time he claimed to be in Spain getting treatment at a place that doesn't exist.'

Eloise looked genuinely shocked.

DI Strickland rocked up in a service car. 'Has Geoff got a mobile phone?' he asked.

'No,' replied Eloise.

'Did you get my message about his car?' Hewitt asked.

'We just passed the restaurant,' said Strickland, 'no black BMW.'

'Check the main roads around the area,' she said.

'They're on it,' said Strickland. 'Thank you for your help, Superintendent Hewitt, DI Sloane, but we'll take it from here.'

'Strickland,' said Hewitt, 'can I speak to you over there?'

They walked off together. Of course, it wasn't our area, but it was our case, and we couldn't let it go. *Fight for us, fight for the victims*, I thought as I watched Fleur talk to Strickland on the driveway.

Meanwhile, I asked Eloise for permission to look through Geoff's stuff, and she granted it. I asked her to accompany me back inside the home; I did not want to let her out of my sight should she call Geoff. I mean, I found it hard to believe he did not have a phone. Who does not have a phone? Even a basic one?

Inside, upstairs, Geoff's chest of drawers in his room sat askew. His bed was unmade from when he'd jumped out of it. He had heard us downstairs and changed quickly into day clothes. Now, his PJs and slippers lay disarranged on the floor.

'Can you call your mum again?'

Eloise took her phone from her pocket and dialled.

'Speakerphone,' I said. The call went to voicemail. Maybe they knew that if Kathleen turned off her mobile phone, we could not track them.

Beside the bed, there was a photo of a little boy with Eloise. Beside that photo, a framed wedding photo of Geoff and Kathleen. Kathleen was kissing him on the cheek. I scrolled through my phone's camera roll and found the old artist impressions given from Michelle Brown and Wayne Simpson. I held them beside this photo. I wasn't sure until I found the old photo of him, Karen, and Janet, both of them kissing him on his cheeks.

In both photos, the man had the exact same scrunched up expression on his face. I almost dropped my phone when I saw the likeness.

I stopped and held my breath, stared hard at Eloise.

My eye was drawn to the open drawer, and inside it, a mahogany box. The lid was half-covering it. He needed something from this box before he left.

I gloved up and lifted it. Eloise watched as I did.

'That's his memory box,' she said.

Inside was a feather, a molar, a scarf, a baby's dummy, a little diamond stud earring, a silver locket, and, underneath them, more. The sight of all made me a mixture of sickened and excited. The earring fitted the same description of the one that had gone missing from Rhonda's dead body.

I turned the locket over. It had a heart engraved on it in a curving, twisting style. Just like Karen Ward's. Just like the one Janet had shown us and sometimes wore. I opened the locket to find a small brown pill inside.

I took my phone from my pocket and took photos of everything from the box, then put everything back and wondered why he left them exposed like that when he could have easily lifted the box and dumped it as he and Kathleen ran.

Chapter 58

By lunch, I turned my phone back on, there was only one message. From Coral:

Dad says the wedding's off. Yvonne told him she can't do it. She's bereft, as we all would be. He was her little boy, after all. Killed like that. Sad, really. Call me when you can xxx

Little boy! And sad? How was it sad? I couldn't call her. Instead, I called Paul.

'How are the babies?' I asked him.

'Fine. But I thought you'd phone sooner.'

'I would have, I wanted to, but it's been hectic. We have a runner. Looks like we have our man, but he has disappeared. Couldn't credit it! I have you to thank; there was no place in Spain.' All the while I was talking, I was reminded and thinking, shit, shit, Jason. Dead at my request? Possibly.

'Glad I helped in some way.' Paul didn't sound glad. 'Have you not heard?'

'Heard what?' I played dumb.

'There was a hit and run.'

'Where? Our street?'

'At your ex's architecture office.'

'Anyone hurt?'

'You haven't seen the news?'

'No, I haven't seen it. What happened?'

'Jason's brother, Alex, he was driven at, pinned against the wall and then dragged. He died in hospital from his injuries.'

'Alex?' I said, my throat constricted. The skin contracted on my cheeks.

Alex, lovely Alex. Poor, poor Verity and their boys, they were only eight and ten. 'Oh my god!' I cried; my reaction was honest after I had been planning to act, rehearsing it silently in my hotel room.

'Must have made an enemy somewhere,' said Paul. 'It sounds brutal. Perhaps you should call your dad, and we'll send flowers. I know his brother was a bastard, but he can't be judged by that,' Paul paused, 'I know what he did to you, Harry. I can't believe you have been going through this alone.'

It meant something to finally be believed. It had sunk in with Paul. He'd talked to someone, perhaps, researched why victims don't talk about their experiences. It seemed like he understood; it was a pinhole light in all of this.

'Can you arrange the flowers?' I asked him. 'We have a manhunt to deal with here.'

'Yes, sure. Be safe.'

'There's a nice florist's in East Belfast. Violet's, it's called.'

'I'm sure there is one closer ....'

'Use Violet's. I know the owner's mother. She's a good egg.'

'Okay, I'll arrange that.'

'And Paul, I'm not calling that man again. He's out of my life.'

'Who? Your dad? Really?'

'Really.'

I couldn't call him; blood was no longer thicker than water. I had done so much to appease that man, now I wouldn't. I was worried that straight away he'd put it to me that I was somehow involved in the brutal murder of an innocent man. And I couldn't talk about it. I hadn't wrapped my head around it or what I would say, to him, Drew or anyone. Innocent Alex Lucie was dead, and the blood was on my hands.

Chapter 59

On Eloise's arm was a tattoo of the dates 2014 – 2017.

'What's this?' I asked. She pulled her sleeve up to show a tattoo of the name, *Albie*, with angel wings around it. Eloise looked down at her arm.

'My tribute to my angel,' she said.

'Was he the child in the photo beside your mother's bed?' I asked. Eloise nodded.

'Och, no. Is that your wee baby?' Hewitt asked, looking at the tattoo. 'What happened there?'

'He had an accident.' Eloise stared at me.

I remembered the tokens Geoff had kept in that creepy mahogany box, and the soother for a baby that had turned my guts the moment I saw it. A baby. Fuck sake.

'Tell us how he died, hen?' asked Hewitt.

'He was accidentally poisoned,' Eloise said, and she looked even more perplexed. We must have not registered this usually-shocking news. 'How come you don't look surprised? Why are you asking about it? Have you already read about it? Is that what it is?'

I said nothing.

'Was it in the papers?' asked Hewitt.

'It was in the local papers. We begged them to not name us. Geoff didn't want a media circus.'

'It was mainly Geoff who wanted to keep your son's death out of the papers?' I asked.

'Yes. After what he saw happen when Kira was killed.'

'What was that?'

'Media hounding them non-stop for quotes. He didn't want Mum to blame herself. She was minding Albie while I went out on a date.'

I let that soak in.

'That's just awful, about wee Albie,' said Hewitt.

'It must have been very hard on you and the child's father,' I said.

'Albie had no father,' she said.

'You live here, don't you?' asked Hewitt.

'Yes,' said Eloise.

'Good. At least,' said Hewitt, 'you had your mum and Geoff to help you get through it.'

'Where is Geoff now?' I asked. 'If you know, Eloise, then please, please say, it's so important that we speak to him.'

'He likes to surprise Mum sometimes,' Eloise said, 'pack a bag, take her away for the weekend.' She eyed us suspiciously.

'Go where?' asked Hewitt

'Fishing,' Eloise and I said at the same time.

Chapter 60

We checked the closet, and the fishing gear was gone. I had an awful sense that we were being played, with the car being left somewhere else, the boot packed already with fishing gear, should they need a getaway.

Strickland told us there was no sighting of Geoff's registration plate yet on the ANPR.

'So they are close,' said Fleur. 'Where does Geoff go fishing, Eloise?'

'He likes Hampermill Lake.'

'Where is that?' I asked.

'On the edge of Watford.'

'How far away?'

'Ten minutes. Maybe fifteen.'

'We need to go mobile,' said Fleur.

'I'll follow,' said Strickland.

Eloise got into the back of our car and gave directions bringing us on to the A4152. I worried about what we'd find there. Geoff had been waiting forty-one years for this day. He might want to go out in a blaze of glory.

'Can we check if he has a gun licence,' I asked Strickland over the radio.

'We can,' he replied.

I had no gun in England. The constabulary isn't allowed to carry them. I was naked without and vulnerable. I just hoped Kathleen was still alive.

'A gun,' said Eloise, dumbfounded. 'What if mum is with him? I don't want her getting hurt.'

'Nobody has intentions to hurt anyone. I just want to talk to Geoff. We'll keep it very civil. Question him away from your mother, away from you. No one will get hurt, okay?'

We got to the lake, past a couple of farmhouses.

'Have you been here before?' I asked Eloise.

'I was at a swimathon once. It's private land.'

'I see that,' said Fleur, looking at the signs.

'You have to book in advance to go fishing.'

We drove around. There were only two people fishing and a burly man walking around wielding an iron bar.

'Everything okay?' he asked us as we slowed to speak with him.

'We're looking for someone. Geoff McDonald, he is one of your regulars.'

'Haven't seen him in months,' said the man, but I wouldn't have trusted him.

'What's the metal for?' I asked the man.

'This is private land.'

'Alright,' said Fleur, 'we're going to drive around and take a look. Don't get into trouble.'

'What do you want him for?' he asked.

Fleur drove off, and the man watched us go.

At the other end of the lake were a few swimmers.

'He doesn't like swimming,' said Eloise.

'He'd have known we'd come here,' Fleur said.

'He likes to trout fish, doesn't he?' I asked.

'I think so … I've never been with him.'

'But he's asked you to go with him?'

'Oh, lots. It's just not my jam.'

My personal phone was going berserk in my bag. Drew. Charly. Unknown number. Probably Jason. Could they pin it to me now? Tucker Brown and Alex Lucie, were they unlinked enough?

I remembered afresh that Jason was not the dead one, and again, I felt nauseous. But I had done nothing wrong. Nothing I could remember. And I was slightly relieved, if only for a nanosecond, that it was Alex, and there was that disconnect. But the whole thing felt like a bad dream. I did not know how I would get through it. It was now beyond me. So far beyond me, I knew I could not control it. And in some strange way, that made me feel totally in control.

'Anywhere else he goes fishing?' asked Strickland, over the radio.

'Boxmoor, sometimes,' said Eloise.

I looked it up. It was a trout fishery. 'That's the one,' I said.

'Boxmoor Fishery is in Hemel Hempstead,' Strickland said.

'Let's go,' I said.

*

Twenty minutes later, we were there. We rolled into the car park, where there were no BMWs. We drove for another minute then we saw one, in a lane off to the side. New and black. But the registration was different.

I got out of the car to check.

'He could have changed the plates to beat the cameras,' said Strickland, standing beside me.

He radioed through for the plates to be checked, and then we waited.

'Received,' Strickland said, and to me, 'The plates are fake. He's here.'

'He has planned this. All of this,' I said. 'Christ knows what he's planning to do next.'

'So we call for backup, locate them, and we wait.'

I got into the car beside Fleur and told her the plan.

'Any word on that gun permit?' she radioed Strickland, as she took off slowly.

'Not yet,' he replied, driving just behind us.

We approached from a distance and sat behind foliage. Geoff and Kathleen were sitting by the lake. Strickland came to my door, crouched down and handed me a pair of binoculars. 'Is that them?' he asked me.

'Yes,' I said.

'I can't do this to Mum,' Eloise said from the back of the car.

'I get that,' said Fleur. 'Plus, Geoff was your stepfather. You are trying to protect him.'

'He's never been my stepfather. I suppose this last month, yes. On that technicality.' She sighed. 'I'm not blindly loyal to him like that.'

'Reason why I say that word is that Geoff has been a stepfather already.'

'I know about Kira. We don't need to go there again.'

'Geoff was a stepfather to two kids in Belfast. They're older now, of course. Much older than you.'

'Are you sure about that?' Eloise asked. I could not mistake the outright innocence in her eyes.

'Eloise, were you in a relationship with Geoff?' I asked her. She looked taken aback, and then she nodded. 'And do you think Geoff might have hurt Albie?'

'Geoff wouldn't have done that to Albie. He wasn't his stepfather.'

'No, he was his grandson,' I said, and she shook her head. 'Eloise, was Geoff Albie's biological father?'

'How did you know?' she asked me angrily.

'I'm afraid Geoff has a history with younger girls.'

'What age would you have been when it started, hen?' asked Hewitt.

'Sixteen.'

'That fits,' said Hewitt.

'How did you know?'

'Eloise, you said you went out on a date, so maybe Geoff was jealous,' I explained.

'He was jealous.'

'Did the baby see something he shouldn't have?'

Eloise stayed silent and stared out of the window irately. 'You think he killed my baby on purpose?'

Geoff wanted her as a secret. A beautiful young girl who lived under his roof. For the first time, I wondered if he had been abusing Anita in the past.

'Look, I know you're worried about your mum, and we won't put her in danger,' said Hewitt.

'Mum doesn't know any of this, I promise you. She doesn't know he is bad.'

'I believe that. Geoff sounds like a manipulative man with an answer to everything.' Later we checked the Chartered Engineers Register, on which he was never listed.

'Mum doesn't know about the thing we had.'

'Has it stopped, Eloise?'

'Yes.'

'When did your relationship with Geoff stop?'

'Around May Day, when I met someone new.'

'You know that's your right? No matter how guilty he made you feel.'

'I know I'm too old to be living with Mum and Geoff. I wanted to get out and find a man of my own.'

'Are you dating now?'

'Yes.'

'Do you think that's why Geoff married your mother lately after all these years?'

'To punish me? In a way. Yes, I do.'

'He's not all that nice then, is he?'

'The baby knew. Albie saw us in bed together and almost said in front of my mum.'

I had guessed it. I exhaled silently.

'What would have happened if Albie had told your mum what he saw?' asked Hewitt.

I looked at the pair by the lake again through the binoculars. They were drinking tea now. Drinking tea like it was any other day, and they didn't have a care in the world.

'Mum would have thrown him out. She looked after him, you see.'

'Financially?'

'Yes.'

'And you, Eloise?'

'I didn't kill my son!' she shouted.

'Shush!' I looked towards Geoff again to make sure he hadn't heard. Where the fuck was our backup?

'No, I mean, she would have thrown you out too.'

'If he wanted to be with me, we could have left. He was more interested in living in that house. Can I say I'm any better? I'm worse; I betrayed my mum.'

'You were only young. He groomed you, pet,' said Hewitt.

'I wasn't a kid the whole time.'

'Don't beat yourself up about it,' I said.

'He might have done some fucked up things, but he wouldn't harm his son.'

I got my phone and flicked to the photo of the trophy box.

'Eloise, you recognise this from Geoff's bedroom, surely?'

'The memory box,' she said. 'Everything he has from people he's lost. A little piece of them. Something intimate.'

I zoomed in on the dummy. Not a generic one, but a zebra pattern on it that was worn away at one side.

'That's Albie's,' said Eloise, 'to remember him by.'

'Eloise,' I said, 'these are tokens from every murder Geoff has committed. There is the diamond earring of Rhonda Orr, who was aged eighteen when she was raped and murdered in Carnfunnock Country Park at the start of the 1980s.'

Eloise closed her eyes and rubbed her temples.

'The locket,' said Hewitt. 'Whose did he tell you it was?'

'An old girlfriend … from Belfast. She died of cancer.'

'No,' I said, 'it belonged to Karen Ward, a young girl. Forever seventeen. He used to take her and other children on fishing trips. Geoff was already in his thirties. Karen was murdered in East Belfast forty-one years ago. Her mother was the person who died of cancer around that time.'

'And what about the scarf?' she asked.

'Kira Tooth's,' said Hewitt. 'She was wearing a thin beaded scarf when she left home for the last time.'

I couldn't recall that detail from all the articles I read about Kira, but I had been certain that something in that box belonged to her. Or that maybe he forgot to take an object from her at the time of bashing her to death. Maybe he simply went to her room after and helped himself. Put it in the box brazenly in front of Nanette and told her it was a memento for his memory box. Have her feeling touched instead of horrified.

I had suspected the molar was Kira's because of the violent way in which she died. Now we knew that the molar was someone else's, another victim we would have to work out. And what about the feather? And the rest?

'Now you're going to tell me that she was murdered too, as we already know.'

'Ever notice how death follows him?' said Hewitt.

'What do you mean? Everybody dies.' The tears streamed down Eloise's face.

'Geoff poisoned the stepchildren he had in Belfast,' I told her. 'They were witnesses to Karen's murder. They were both left brain-damaged, one profoundly.'

'He has to live the rest of his days like that,' said Fleur, 'with kidney problems and no memory. The wee guy can hardly form a word.'

'I don't believe this.' Eloise wept.

'That boy was an eyewitness who saw Karen Ward, his babysitter, attacked by a man. He tried to speak to the police but then he was silenced. Just like Albie was.'

'No. No!' Eloise shouted. It was upsetting to see, but it was that moment when she finally believed what she was being told. Eloise looked embarrassed, hurt and bewildered. There was never a doubt in my mind that she was seeing him straight, at last, in the back of that cop car, through the binoculars.

'Where is this backup?' Hewitt asked.

Strickland looked stressed. Still crouched by my side, he asked Eloise to keep quiet. 'Breathe easy.' She looked utterly shipwrecked one minute, crazy the next.

'Get him before I get him,' she said, almost hysterical, trying to open the door which was thankfully locked.

I got out of the car.

'DI Sloane,' Strickland said in a strained whisper.

I decided to go a long way round and surprise Geoff before Eloise blew our cover. I walked at speed. I ignored the whispers behind me. Soon I approached the couple, my head bent. I avoided twigs I might step on. I tried to come up behind them, only Kathleen looked over her shoulder, recognised me and told him. Geoff got up then and ran in the other direction. I heard screaming. Eloise was running towards the water.

'Fuck you, murderous bastard,' she was yelling. 'Mum, he killed Albie. He fucken killed my Albie.'

Eloise fell.

I looked back and saw Hewitt running. Strickland too. Before me, Geoff was escaping. I trained my eye on him and picked up speed. Chasing him through shrubbery until we came to a wall. He tore over it with ease. I tried. Ripped my trousers on barbed wire, landed on my feet though, and started running again. Geoff didn't look back at me. He kept going.

We were out on the road now. Where did he think he was going? I wouldn't have been surprised if he jumped in another vehicle. I was glad it was nowhere near his own car. Shit, I thought, should have let the air out of his tyres.

Passing cars stopped, drivers watched him through their windows, ready to go again when next came me, following behind. He cut into a field. Sirens nearby whooped. I knew Fleur was behind me without looking. I filled my lungs.

'Stop, Geoff, you're under arrest.'

Of course he did not stop. He ran through the field. He may have been slim and old, but I was younger. I had a runner's muscle memory.

'Found all your trophies,' I shouted. 'You're done.'

Then suddenly he stopped, turned to face me. I stopped too and stared, braced myself. I was worried he would produce a gun, regardless of permits. Killers don't apply for permits.

I expected to be afraid of this moment, but I wasn't.

'Hear me, Geoff. You're a serial killing bastard, and we know it. You are never going to see the light of day again.'

'Here's your arrest,' he said in a nasal Belfast accent that sounded quite shocking. I had never thought about his voice and how it would sound. Geoff felt under the collar of his shirt, and seemed to produce something.

'Hands in the air,' I shouted at him. Hewitt was beside me now, trying to catch her breath.

'Geoff,' she said, 'do what you're told.'

Geoff slipped something into his mouth, swallowed and a second later, he was flat on the ground. Dead.

Chapter 61

'Cyanide,' Hewitt said.

'Cyanide?' repeated Janet across the café table that Monday morning. Her daughter Lynne held a tiny pink baby in the crook of her arm.

'He had it sown into his shirt collar just waiting for that moment.' I couldn't tell her about the one he kept in her sister's locket, his backup. Nor did I mention the one Kathleen held in her hand that he had told her to swallow. At least she had finally stopped listening to her husband and doing what he said.

'I wonder how long he'd lived like that,' said Lynne, 'waiting for his past to catch up with him.'

'For a very long time probably,' I said, 'he was a coward. He couldn't face the music for what he'd done.'

'I'm pleased he's gone,' said Janet. 'I know that sounds awful.'

'Not at all,' I said.

'But I'm not pleased with how he died. I'll never have a reason.'

'What reason could he give you that would make a difference?' asked Lynne.

'You're right,' said Janet.

We never told her about the other girls, but Fleur would, the next day, over the phone, the poisoning, the killing of his little son, Albie Gilmour. That was too much, and she already had so much to deal with.

Geoff McDonald was our man, and we had him, and he had died knowing we had him. I was delighted about the fact.

All those years and all those lives. Strickland was now looking into the dates when Geoff said he in Spain and was not. Seeing if those dates tallied up with other unsolved murders. We knew that sometimes he was not lying about going to Spain. It turned out he had been there just before the impromptu wedding, when Eloise got a new fella. Geoff took himself off fishing in the Rio Frio between Malaga and Granada in the foothills of Sierra de Loja. It was an excellent place for trout fishing, but one needed a permit to obtain a foreign fishing licence. First, they had to pass an exam in Spanish. Which he never bothered with. So he had been prosecuted. It wasn't the only time either.

He had also booked to go to Andalucia later in the summer for the fishing competitions. Now Strickland looked into it, he found that Geoff had attempted to attack a girl while he was there. Thankfully she managed to get away. Then he managed to get away, and come back to Watford in the clear, as he usually did.

You could see why he thought he was above the law; it had been unable to touch him.

Geoff used the excuse of treatment and illness every time he needed to hide out. That had been him hiding in different garden sheds around Birmingham at the time Kira was killed, and the time police were testing DNA of local men.

'I'll reach out to Barney,' Janet said. 'I'll call him soon.'

'That would be good, I'm sure, for both of you to chat,' said Hewitt.

'I've been afraid of Belfast, honestly and truly,' Janet said. 'I've loathed the place, and I didn't know that it had followed me here, that I was living so close to this man. Trauma follows you, literally.'

'Leaving was the best thing for you to do at the time,' Lynne said, squeezing her mother's hand.

'It was. Sometimes you need to face up to it. I kept asking for help to find Karen's killer, but part of me wanted to be turned down. The knockbacks were frustrating, but I believed they were protecting me from further hurt, picking at old wounds.'

I closed those sticky pages in her diary in my mind and let Geoff float away so I could concentrate on Janet.

'How are you feeling?' I asked her. 'It's been a long, long road for you.'

'I'm going through the motions,' she said bluntly. 'I wish I could say I'm glad, and I will be. But I can't take it in. Not completely.' Janet looked at the baby and said, 'It's sad that there are no nieces and nephews, that Karen was so callously murdered, and for nothing.'

I gave her the heart engraved locket, sans cyanide, and she took her own off and set them both on the table. Karen's was broken where it had been snapped off her neck, but apart from that, it looked perfectly new. A tear sprung to Janet's eye.

We were leaving a few hours later. I had something I wanted to close myself. Or open.

'So, are you go back to Belfast now?' asked Janet.

305

'Later today, thought I'd call in on some family I have here first.'

'That's nice. Harriet?'

'Yes?'

'My diaries ….'

'I'll have them returned to you, and Karen's one too.'

'Will you do something else instead?' asked Janet.

'What?'

'Will you destroy them?'

'You want us to shred them?'

'I do,' she said.

'Do you want me to send you a photo after, for proof?'

'No, why would I want that? I trust you implicitly. You alone did all of this.'

'Not alone,' I said, 'we're a team. You were a great help.'

'No, Harriet. You alone.' She gave me a hug. I thought of Verity, and people comforting her. Her crying over Alex. All my fault.

'Enjoy the new baby,' I said. 'She's doing well for being early. I can't believe she's out of the hospital already.'

'She's a little trouper,' said Janet, smiling proudly.

That was when I should have left, headed for Walthamstow and been none the wiser, only Lynne came over to say goodbye and thank me again. Fleur was in the car already.

'Has she got a name?' I asked.

'Still awaiting inspiration. Though Mum did try to talk me into calling her Harriet.'

'You're joking,' I said. Janet beamed back. 'I hope you're joking. Don't do that to the poor child.'

She was so tiny and perfect. I must have been looking at her all gooey when Janet asked if she was making me broody.

'Oh no,' I said. 'I'm forty now. I think I'm done.'

'Too old at forty?' said Lynne. 'Don't say that.'

'We'll be seeing you,' said Janet, hand on the pram, trying to walk away.

'I'm forty,' said her daughter, 'and I'd like to think I have time yet for another. Maybe two more.'

'But Harriet got two in one go,' said Janet. 'Got it all done in one go.'

'You're lucky,' said her daughter.

'It was my birthday two weeks ago. When were you forty, Lynne?' I asked quickly.

Janet wheeled the baby out, saying, 'Bye again.'

'Umm.' Lynne stalled, surprised at her mother's need to move away. 'It was the big one last month, but I was preggo. I have some catching up to do with a party.'

'You do indeed,' I said.

'Thanks again,' said Lynne as she left behind her mother, who was walking hurriedly up the street.

I watched her daughter follow after, tenderly, sore, tall, dark. Small eyes. Somewhat bulbous nose.

She reminded me of a certain person from all my hours poring over his younger photos from fishing trips.

'Fuck me,' I said in the car.

'What?' Fleur said, shoving a stick of gum into her mouth.

'She's McDonald's child,' I said. 'His biological daughter.'

'What?'

'It doesn't matter,' I said, realising that it really didn't. Lynne was blissfully unaware. But I was cross; her mother sat through all that, knowing. He must have known Janet was pregnant, and she must have been a couple of months along when she went on that one and only date with Vernon Brown Junior.

I imagined McDonald getting possessive that November, learning from Karen that her sister was moving on from him, going on a date with a boy. I thought of him, knowing that she was carrying his child and burning up with hatred, having a discussion with Karen that ended in rage. Hurting her to hurt her sister.

Janet had told me that first day in the canteen, 'It should have been me.'

She had to have suspected. She had wasted all this time. Decades and decades. But we got there, and maybe her daughter didn't need to know that the man who had fathered her was a serial killer. What good would that do? She deserved to just love her new little family. Janet too. None of it was her fault.

But saying that, it took me a while to see her correctly. She had not lived with an aunt and studied and had it easier. She had been a teen mother, struggling in a new city. No wonder she had so much empathy for Maxine Hall. Janet was trying to study alone, to achieve what she thought was Karen's ambition, and she succeeded. I respected Janet Ward for that.

*

After Janet left, I travelled to Walthamstow to a block of flats, not unlike Clarawood House. The last time I was here, my niece, Roni, was just born. Now she was nineteen. Her mother, Brooks' ex Lydia, was staggered to see me at the door. Roni did not remember me. Her brother was at work. They welcomed me all the same. Lydia asked me to stay for a bite to eat.

We didn't mention Brooks. I sensed Lydia still could not forgive him for choosing drugs over her and the kids. Instead, I told them about the case I was working on, which Roni thought sounded crazy. Then, I showed them pictures of the twins. Lydia cooed.

'Bring them next time you call,' she said.

I was struck by how tight they had it. I wanted to help, but I knew how proud Lydia was. When I was leaving, I asked to use the bathroom. I left a bundle of money on Lydia's dressing table. It was one of Greg's. Before I left, to my niece, I handed the gift voucher Paul had given me for my birthday and made her promise to split it with her brother, but I hoped that she wouldn't.

Chapter 62

By ten p.m., we were back to the Belfast rain.

'Well done,' said Carl Higgins, clapping as we walked into the station.

'I believe you gave Usain Bolt a run for his money.' Fergus Simon came over and gave me a hug.

'*Run*,' said Higgins, 'pun not intended.'

'You wanna seen her. Chased him down,' said Fleur, 'and it didn't take a feather out of her.'

There was a large cake that had already been tucked into.

'You got us a cake made?' asked Hewitt.

'Leftovers from Higgins' engagement party,' said Simon. 'Plus, we're celebrating; I.T. sorted the system. Lucky it didn't affect any files.'

Higgins looked uncomfortable. I pinned him down later. 'I wasn't invited?'

'You were away. Plus, Melinda limited numbers.'

'But you could have said.'

'I could, only she didn't want exes there.'

'I'm not your bloody ex!'

'We had that snog at that Christmas party.'

'You told her that!'

'I kind of was starting to see her at the time, so yeah. I felt guilty.'

'So she hates me.'

'She doesn't know you. But yeah, she hates you.'

Great, I thought. She probably *loved* our partnership.

I had to knock this picking-the-wrong-men business. I had to stop boozing.

'Congratulations, Carl,' I said. 'Treat her well.'

I cut myself a slice of cake and forced myself to eat it. To look happy and normal. But I had been weighing up what to do. Should I hand my badge in before it came out about Alex's death at Drew's say so? How could I be a police officer with that on my conscience? Then I realised I could do it the exact same way they all did; if it got out, I'd deny, deny, deny. I'd seen it work for the best and the worst of them.

And scandal, I'd known it well that last year. And I'd survive it. I'd survived worse. Right now, the boys were all I worried about, and right now, they were too young to find me an embarrassment. Right now, the only messages I was getting were from Drew. Jason had stopped. For now.

Can we talk? Drew texted from a burner phone.

He'd fucked up, and now I had my excuse to get shot of him. Now he was offering to put things right. But how would he ever be able to do that? Kill Yvonne's other son? That chance had been lost. Jason would be there to stay, and I would have to find some way to live with that. I understood Janet. I, like her, did not want the person who had ruined my life dead.

I wanted him to know I still lived well despite his best attempts to drag me down. It was too late for her little sister, but the rest of us eventually get our lives back if we are lucky.

Now there were apologetic messages from Drew. No *I love yous* anymore.

The woman he really loved was probably waiting for him to apologise and then fit securely back together. At least that is what I hoped that night when I got online at Violet's Florist's website and made a couple of orders: an engagement bouquet for Carl Higgins' house, for Melinda. Call it a peace offering. I would not quit work until I had to. Chances were Higgins would be my partner in the future. And while I was at it, I ordered three dozen red roses to be sent to Drew's ex, Roxanne, at her workplace. Along with a message:

I've been stupid. I'm sorry. You're my girl.

I signed off as Andrew, as she always called him, and went to wash my hands.

Epilogue

Once I return home from London, I spend a couple of days off with the boys, appreciating them, making picnics with Paul, bringing a frisbee to the park and a bottle of Merlot, making videos of me happy with the boys. Making memories in case it all stops here. Then I make a follow-up appointment with Martin Walsh, try to keep a low profile during Alex's funeral. I let them get the funeral over them, then I start to worry it will start again. I cancel my appointment. I start to drink. It can't go on.

I have a dream. A bad one. He is following me as I run, he chases me down a lane. His eyes are deep black wells. Then I wake up. Something snaps.

I call into work sick, bring the boys to their nursery, message Coral and ask her to collect them and mind them until either myself or Paul gets home – I don't know how long this will take, this purge – and thankfully, she can help.

I drive to my old house in Osborne Gardens, pull a picnic seat from my car boot and sit facing the front door. I stare at that door for hours.

A woman – must be Jason's fiancée – comes outside and says, 'I'm going to phone the police, you've been there for hours.'

I stare through her until I can see the back of her skull, and the door I escaped through, *crept* through, so

313

as not to waken the monster that day I got free. But I didn't get free. Today I will be, I have to be.

Jason comes home from work early and looks straight at me, and I stare through him. His fiancée reappears, and he gets her by the arm and brings her inside. I stare harder. I can't blink. I can't stop looking at him, letting him know I see him. See him. See through him.

He always smiled. That was just him. Even when he was having a breakdown and he was crying, beating me, threatening to kill me, he still had a look of a smile on his face.

Today he is not smiling.

This is his chance to kill me now, if that's what he thinks he'll do. Like he has promised me hundreds of times. *Do it*, I beg him silently. *Try your best.*

He goes inside and cannot resist, and neither can she, to look out at me through the blinds. My eyes follow every movement.

'Come on, you rapist bastard,' I whisper, hardly moving my lips. I pull a blanket over my lap when it gets cool. I am like an old man fishing. Like Geoff. Like Father. I pull my hood up and sit like that for what could be hours. Who's counting?

Old neighbours slow to pass me and give me uncertain waves. Staff from the nursing home where my mother once lived give me friendly, more confident, waves. I smile back, and then I let that smile follow them out of the road, and I smile at Jason through the window he's hiding behind.

'Come out, you cowardly fuck,' I say, louder.

He doesn't. He closes the blinds, but one of the two cannot resist peeking through them now and then to see if I'm still there. I can't see the eyes to know who it is.

Yet his eyes are nothing, not like in my dreams, not black tunnels, not hazel either, not even threatening, just eyes that don't matter. And he is just a man. And I am just a woman who has had enough and has left her gun at home.

Eventually, mentally exhausted, I decide it's enough. I put the fold-out chair in the boot of the car, and I find a bottle of Merlot. I walk to the door of my old house, and I fire a bottle of red wine at it. It smashes. Wine drips like blood down the door I escaped from. I feel powerful. Big. I get in my car and start to drive when my phone pings. I reverse back hard and hit the curb, thinking, *bastard. I'll get him to his face.*

But it's not from him, it's from Paul. A text, it says:
Nearly home? You have a visitor.

I'm relieved, for the first time, knowing that anything can end, knowing that everything will end. I know in my heart it is finally over with Jason.

*

When I get home, Paul is standing in the hallway. Greg at the playroom door. Paul turns to look at him, to instruct him. 'Would you mind locking the gate, mate?'

Greg fumbles with it. 'Didn't have these when my boys were younger,' he says.

Too late, Jared has gotten out. He pulls at Greg's leg, and Greg lifts him. They look like pieces of the same puzzle, only young and old. Then Rowan wants in on the act.

'Can I help you, sir?' I ask him. I think I am losing my mind to see him in my home. It has been a day for craziness; maybe I am hallucinating.

'I was more hoping that I can help you, Harriet,' says Greg.

I think he has come here to tell me to leave Jason alone, that someone has called him to report me. I have never dreamed he would show up like this, ever, touching my boys. Our boys. He has one in each arm now, and the twins are laughing at each other.

I feel like I need to sit down, but I have sat all day.

'Greg,' I say, 'what are you doing here?'

'Will you excuse us?' he asks Paul.

Always so polite, now Paul refuses. 'I'm here for Harry. Harry, do you want me to go into the other room?'

'Stay where you are. It's your home,' I say. I don't care if that is strong or weak, or if a difference has ever existed between the two.

'Harriet,' says Greg, holding our boys who are chatting to him. He is tempted to smile at them, but feels the gravity in the room and passes up the opportunity, keeping hold of his grim demeanour. 'You're never off work sick. Is everything okay?'

'Fine, sir. I mean, I will be. I'll be back tomorrow.'

'Good. Okay. Well, you know what happened.'

'What happened?' I ask, taking Jared from him, but Rowan refuses to let go. Clinging to the man he doesn't know is his father. Or does he know it?

'The *package* under my car,' says Greg.

'That,' I say. The bomb.

'It's made me re-evaluate what's important.'

'So, what's important?' I ask, thinking, *no drink, Harry, not tonight, not ever again, no matter what comes through your door, you just can't trust it*. I am trying not to think about Alex. Or Verity. Or their boys. Or even about Yvonne.

'People,' Greg says uncomfortably, glancing at Paul. 'Family's important, and I want to get to know my sons. If you'll let me.'

ACKNOWLEDGEMENTS

Thank you to the Arts Council of Northern Ireland for supporting recent writing projects of mine. Thank you to my writing community for their support. As ever, thank you to my wonderful family for their constant support.

KELLY CREIGHTON
THE BONES OF IT

Thrown out of university, green-tea-drinking, meditation-loving Scott McAuley has no place to go but home: County Down, Northern Ireland. The only problem is, his father is there now too.

Duke wasn't around when Scott was growing up. He was in prison for stabbing two Catholic kids in an alley. But thanks to the Good Friday Agreement, big Duke is out now, reformed, a counselor.

Squeezed together into a small house, with too little work and too much time to think about what happened to Scott's dead mother, the tension grows between these two men, who seem to have so little in common.

Penning diary entries from prison, Scott recalls what happened that year. He writes about Jasmine, his girlfriend at university. He writes about Klaudia, back home in County Down, who he and Duke both admired. He weaves a tale of lies, rage and paranoia.

Out now in paperback and ebook

KELLY CREIGHTON
THE SLEEPING SEASON

DI HARRIET SLOANE SERIES #1

Someone going missing is not an event in their life but an indicator of a problem.

Detective Inspector Harriet Sloane is plagued by nightmares while someone from her past watches from a distance. In East Belfast, local four-year-old River vanishes from his room.

Sloane must put her own demons to bed and find the boy. Before it's too late.

Out now in paperback and ebook

KELLY CREIGHTON
PROBLEMS WITH GIRLS

DI HARRIET SLOANE SERIES #2

Where are the young women here? Can you even see them?

After taking some leave, DI Harriet Sloane comes back to work at Strandtown PSNI station, East Belfast, to be faced with a murder case. A young political activist has been stabbed to death in the office of a progressive political party where she works as an intern. The killer seems to have a problem with girls, and is about to strike again.

Set in 2018, a month after the Belfast Rape Trial and the #ibelieveher rallies that took place throughout Ireland, this novel asks questions about cyberbullying, mental health and consent.

Out now in paperback and ebook

COMING SPRING 2022...

KELLY CREIGHTON
SOULS WAX FAIR

A CONTEMPORARY LITERARY THRILLER

Powerful men can get away with murder...for only so long.

After a life of hardship, Mary Jane McCord's life in Rapid City, South Dakota, finally hits a sweet spot. She finds happiness and her singing career takes off. Everything is looking up until she uncovers the dark and secret obsessions of two high-profile men.

Twenty years pass but the people closest to Mary Jane have not forgotten. Will they bring the truth out into the light?

Available now to pre-order

Printed in Great Britain
by Amazon

45276461R00185